The Things We Thought We Knew

www.penguin.co.uk

The Things We Thought We Knew

MAHSUDA SNAITH

Doubleday

LONDON · TORONTO · SYDNEY · AUCKLAND · JOHANNESBURG

TRANSWORLD PUBLISHERS
61–63 Uxbridge Road, London W5 5SA
www.penguin.co.uk

Transworld is part of the Penguin Random House group of companies
whose addresses can be found at global.penguinrandomhouse.com

First published in Great Britain in 2017 by Doubleday
an imprint of Transworld Publishers

A CIP catalogue record for this book
is available from the British Library.

ISBN 9780857524683

Typeset in 11.5/16 pt ITC Berkeley Oldstyle Std by Jouve (UK), Milton Keynes
Printed and bound in Great Britain by Clays Ltd, Bungay, Suffolk

Penguin Random House is committed to a sustainable
future for our business, our readers and our planet. This book
is made from Forest Stewardship Council® certified paper.

1 3 5 7 9 10 8 6 4 2

To everyone who made me

Life can only be understood backwards; but it must be lived forwards.

Søren Kierkegaard

A Constellation Is Born

1999

You came for me at midnight. A squishy hand tugging mine, yanking me awake. I rubbed my eyelids, asked what the heck was going on (I needed sleep. I was a growing girl). You giggled through gap teeth, passing me my robe before continuing to tug-tug as we crept from the cave of my room, past the rumbling snores of Amma's lair, down the stairs and out of the flat.

Your brother was standing outside in lightning-bolt pyjamas. The scruffy strands of his hair matched the zigzag pattern. He looked sleepy and cross at the same time.

'Marianne . . .' I said, trying to sound stern as my body yawned.

You pressed a finger to your lips then turned away, guiding us through the night. Our feet stumbled against concrete steps, hands stretching up to metal railings that made me shiver.

On the fourth floor you signalled for us to sit in our usual places. Our legs dangled through the balcony railings as you slid your body between us and linked your arms through ours. Curls of your hair brushed against my cheek.

You pointed to the sky.

'Look,' you said.

I looked. I saw. A billion stars against an indigo sky. The brightness of them. The sheer number of them.

'That,' you said, pointing straight up, 'is the Constellation of Cartwheels.'

Your head fell back, a crescent grin across your face.

I sneaked my hand into the pocket of my robe and felt the edges of the book inside.

'That,' I said, pointing to a wispy cluster, 'is the Constellation of Mini Dictionaries.'

I looked over at Jonathan, waiting for him to object.

'No,' he said, shaking his head, his glasses wobbling on the bridge of his nose. 'That is the Constellation of Thunderstorms.'

You looked at me and I at you; we were fizzing with surprise.

Our fingers rose, arms outstretched.

'The Constellation of Lemon Sherbets . . .' you said.

'The Constellation of Hurricanes . . .' your brother said.

'The Constellation of Vegetable Dhansak . . .' I said.

We continued naming the constellations all through the night until we weren't even using words but a jumble of made-up sounds. I felt your body next to mine, warming me like a blanket. When I looked at the horizon I saw a shooting star. It skimmed across the velvet night in a streaking blaze.

Or maybe I didn't see that. Maybe that's just what I wanted to see . . .

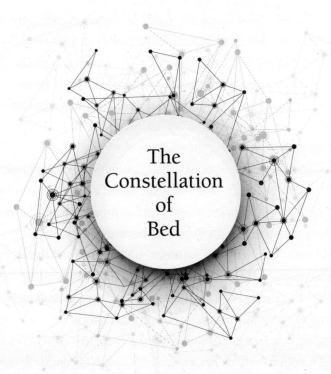

The Constellation of Bed

2010

I wake up to find my room has been entered ninja-style during the night. Streamers line the ceiling, balloons are taped to the corners in clusters and a giant holographic banner dangles crookedly on the wall. Below it a dozen photographs are tacked in a row. It's like a museum timeline done on the cheap.

> Photo 1: 1992 – Birth of Ravine (shrivelled newborn with too much hair)
>
> Photo 3: 1996 – Nativity Play (girl dressed as sheep, straw hanging from mouth)

Photo 8: 2009 – New Year's Eve (teenager lying in bed, party hat perched jauntily on head)

If there were an award for the World's Worst Listener, my mother would win hands down. Give her the simplest sentence and watch the cogs of her brain pull in the words, twist them up and spit out a new meaning. You say you want a kitten; she buys you a coat. You say you don't like cabbage; she cooks seven different cabbage recipes. You say you don't want a party and you wake up to a sight that makes you sweat so heavily your pyjamas stick to your skin and you have to check your knickers to make sure you haven't wet them.

I rub my eyes as the smell of onion bhajis floats up from the kitchen. It's mixed with the heavy scent of citrus breeze air freshener. I hope this is a nightmare. As I prop myself up, the twisting muscles along my arm confirm the truth. This is real.

'You are up!' Amma says, wobbling through the door with a cake the size of a coffee table in her arms.

She's wearing an orange sari pleated perfectly down the middle, a gallon of coconut oil combed through her hair. Leaning to the side, she kicks the stereo with her heel to 'play'. Synthesized drums erupt into the room. She stands grinning at me as though this is the finale of a great show and it's time for me to applaud.

I place my pillow upright behind me and sink back.

'Amma . . .' I say.

She shakes her head, eyes fogging over as she cocks her ear to the music. I watch her nod in time to the beat. The song continues to play, the cake begins to slide.

'*Amma*,' I say.

'Wait, wait!' she says, straightening the platter.

Cymbals crash over drums as Stevie Wonder hits the chorus.

'. . . *Happy biiiiiirthday!*'

I wait until it finishes, then watch Amma wiggle over to me before placing the chocolate gravestone across my lap.

'It took three days to make,' she says.

Covered in brown frosting and a series of plastic roses, the cake has a collection of half-used candles plotted around its perimeter. In the middle, iced in pink loopy writing, are the words 'Happy 18th Birthday Ravine Roy!!'. The letters shrink as they reach my name but somehow Amma has still managed to ice a smiley face after the exclamation marks.

My spine rolls forward like a sapling snapped in the wind. Amma interprets this as a sign of awe.

'It is not a problem!' she says, waving her hand in the air. 'Anything for my darling Ravine!'

I made it clear last week: no balloons, no cake, no party. But somehow Amma's brain has churned my words into all the balloons she can blow up, the biggest cake she can bake and as many party items as she can fill the room with.

Amma begins lighting the candles. Because there are so many this takes a good two minutes. By the time she's on the fourth match my face is clammy; the throbbing in my limbs is making my vision woozy. I suck in a huge breath, ready to blow the whole monstrosity to another building, but as soon as the last candle is lit Amma begins slapping her thigh, singing 'Happy Birthday' to me in Bengali.

Amma's been singing Bengali to me since I was in the womb, trying to trick me into learning the language. When I was a toddler she translated every nursery rhyme and changed all the animals, but 'Baa Baa, Kala Chaagal' doesn't have quite the same ring. At bedtime she sang me folk songs about boats and paddy fields until I couldn't get to sleep without them. I rebelled against her sing-song brainwashing by blocking out the meaning of all Bengali words. I can now chant the entire national anthem of Bangladesh without any idea of what I'm singing. The only Bengali I actually use is 'amma', meaning 'mother'.

With my cheeks puffed out and afraid that either I'll pass out or Amma's sari will catch fire, I blow out the candles. She stops mid-verse and looks down at the cake.

'Of course you made a wish?' she asks.

Spirals of smoke circle my body. I close my eyes and clear my throat.

'I wish for *no more celebrations*.'

I look up eagerly. Amma frowns, shaking her head as she pulls out a pillbox from the waist of her sari petticoat and places it on the bedside table.

'If you say it out loud, it will not come true,' she says. 'Everybody knows this, Ravine.'

And, of course, she is right.

Within half an hour a crowd of neighbours floods into my room. Some of them I know (Sandy Burke and her twins), some of them I recognize (Mrs Patterson and her famously large breasts) and some of them I've never seen in my life. The ones I know say hello, the ones I recognize congratulate me with forced grins that look painful. The ones I've never seen in my life stand gawping at my statue of Shiva, the pile of unread books on the floor and the out-of-date CD collection by the stereo. I hope they won't notice the museum timeline across the wall or the My Little Pony curtains, but these are the things they stare at most. I wait for Amma to click her tongue in that disapproving way of hers and make them stop. Instead, she wiggles through the crowd, placing her hands on top of each guest's hand, thanking them with little curtsies worthy of a maharaja.

I can see what she's done. Amma, cunning woman that she is, has scurried to every flat in Westhill Estate, knocking on each door and tempting residents with the promise of free cake. She's given them samples, tiny pre-cut cubes that are just enough to set their mouths watering. Then, as she dashed away, she's cried out, 'No more until the party. Make sure you are there!'

I watch as Amma makes her way to the side of my bed. I open my mouth, but before I can say a word she's spun around to face her new-formed army. She has a crazed-dictator smile as she raises her hands, clapping twice, as though doing the flamenco. Our guests lift their eyes from Bombay mix, small talk is sliced mid-sentence and Stevie Wonder is turned down in the background. The bed sinks as Sandy Burke sits on the end and works her way through a box of fun-size chocolate bars. She used to be skeleton thin, the bones of her hips jutting out from beneath her jeans like tent poles, her afro sitting like candyfloss on top of a stick. The image of Death tattooed on the side of her neck looked far healthier than she did. But now she has smooth contours of flesh on her face and neck. Her arms aren't matchsticks any more but round and shapely.

When she tilts the box towards me I shake my head.

'It is so good to see you all!' Amma says (as though it was an accident, as though she hasn't planned the whole thing).

She places her hand on my shoulder. It's my bad shoulder so she touches it gently.

'Today, my darling Ravine is eighteen years old.'

I cringe.

'This is important because it is the beginning of her life as an adult.'

I cringe again.

'Also, it is important because it is the beginning of her life outside this flat. Right, shona?'

I don't have time to cringe because she's looking down at me with round, dark eyes that could compete with a puppy dog's. They make you do things, those eyes; make you give promises. They even make you believe you can keep them.

There's a pause as everyone waits for me to speak. My muscles tense like tightropes. I lick my lips.

'That's right,' I say.

Amma pats me on the head to show this is the correct answer. She clasps her hands together.

'Now, time for cake!'

The crowd cheers as she cuts the cake into squares. From the corner of the room I catch Sandy Burke's twins staring at me. Their identical-shaped heads are tilted at identical angles, ripples of confusion etched across their foreheads and black waves of hair hanging at the sides of their faces. They are only eleven years old yet their expressions make them look like scientists trying to decide if they've discovered a new virus. I clutch the edge of the duvet, listening to Stevie Wonder's lyrics, reading the words across the banners, feeling my room fill up with smiley faces.

HAPPY BIRTHDAY!! HAPPY BIRTHDAY!!

HAPPY!! HAPPY!! HAPPY!! . . .

'I'm going to sleep now!'

The words shoot out from my throat like bullets. I sink my fingers into the covers, tugging so hard that Sandy Burke jolts up from her seat. Amma looks at me, bindi raised high on her forehead.

'But shona, it is ten-thirty in the morning.'

I shuffle down flat. 'Thanks for coming!'

The room falls silent. It's only when I begin to make snoring noises that everyone moves. They collect their pieces of cake and go down to the living room. As the last guest leaves, my body sighs. When I look over at Shiva and the My Little Ponies on the curtains, I see them sighing too.

Amma begins searching the room for painkillers before placing a bottle carefully on the bedside table.

'Happy birthday, Ravine,' she says and plants a wet kiss on my earlobe.

I keep one eye open as she leaves a piece of cake next to the bottle, watching her as she collects the rest of the food on a tray before sneaking out of the room.

I curl my knees to my chest. As the party continues downstairs I stay like this, pickling in the vinegar of my misery.

Some people have a deathbed. I have a lifebed.

It's like when you have a cold. Not a tickly *er-herm, er-herm* cold that you down a couple of painkillers for and recover from in forty-eight hours. No. This is like an All-consuming Cold. Bleary vision, clunky limbs, the feeling of your brain oozing out of your nostrils and your muscles being jumped on by panda bears.

You drag yourself to school or work or wherever you need to be that day. You're slightly productive for a few hours before the school bell rings or the clock strikes five and you get on the bus or in the car and drag yourself home. And that's when it happens. The slam of the door. The thump of your coat on the hallway floor. Heavy footsteps up the stairs.

Bed.

It's safe in bed. It's warm in bed. No one's asking you what date it is or how to solve an algorithm in bed. You sink into the mattress. You rest your head on your memory-foam pillow. Every part of you sighs – even your eyeballs and intestines. In a far-off country the doorbell rings but you don't hear it because you've already set sail. In the realm of the All-consuming Cold, this is the closest you'll feel to bliss.

Now imagine this again. Your cold is not a cold but *chronic pain*

9

syndrome. A condition that leaves the majority of your body in constant pain, the type of pain you'd feel if killer sharks were biting through your muscles. Imagine sinking into your bed every day for nearly eleven years. You wake up. You go to the toilet. You collapse back in bed and sail off. Except you don't sail anywhere because some bastard has moored you to a pole. You float in your sea of pain, hoping someone will come and hack the rope to pieces and set you free. They never do.

So yes, I have a lifebed. It probably sounds like a deathbed but it isn't. I spend my life in bed, that's why it's my lifebed.

I lie coiled up, muscles throbbing, trying not to look at the photos on the wall or the piece of cake Amma has left me. Downstairs I can hear the babble of conversation and, every few minutes, the squeal of party blowers followed by shrieks of laughter. As time ticks on, the shrieks peter out. Guests say their goodbyes until the only noise left is the hiss of citrus breeze being sprayed along the hallway. When the hissing stops, Amma appears at my door with an armful of presents.

'Didn't it go well?' she says, shrugging the load onto my bed. She drops into her seat, a grin plastered across her face. 'In fact, I'd say it went *swimmingly.*'

The presents topple to the side of my legs as I wedge the pillows behind my back. I push the hair off my face.

'I didn't want a party,' I say.

Amma flaps her hand at me. 'You're welcome.'

I sigh, looking at the repeat-print wallpaper beside me. The neck of each bird is arched back, wings cocked in the air as if ready to escape. I hated those birds when Amma covered the living room with them and hated them even more when she used the leftover rolls for my room. The sharp beaks and beady eyes give me nightmares but when I told Amma she chuckled as though I'd told her a cute joke.

'Open your presents, darling,' Amma says.

I carry on looking at the birds.

'*Ravine.*'

When Amma uses a certain voice it's best to do what she says.

I don't look up as I rip each present open: a flowery bracelet I have no use for, some glitzed-up slippers to brighten my visits to the bathroom, and a fabric-covered journal with jewel-encrusted pen.

I roll the pen between my fingers, feeling the sting of frayed nerves in my wrist. Sometimes the pain is hard and throbbing like a repeated punch, other times quick and sharp. As the light sparks against the jewels on the pen, the pain in my wrist sparks too.

'What am I supposed to write about?' I ask.

Amma nods as though this is an excellent question.

'Your pain,' she says. 'There are studies that show if you write about your physical pain it helps you heal your mental pain.'

I curl my top lip. 'That's about the stupidest thing I've ever heard,' I say.

'Also,' Amma continues, 'it will be good preparation for when you leave the flat. You will be able to record your progress.'

She taps the diary then stands up, clearing the wrapping paper from my bed as she begins humming. The pain is getting worse; the electric shocks in my wrist flash so furiously that my muscles begin to spasm. I drop the pen, trying to breathe through the pain the way my physiotherapist has taught me.

Remember to breathe, he said. *People with chronic pain tense all their muscles and forget to relax.*

I relax. The spasms ease. But there is still a trembling in my fingers, the feeling of electricity surging through my nerves.

11

'Amma,' I say, 'this talk of me leaving the flat . . .'

'Isn't it wonderful?' she says.

She carries on collecting.

I shake my head. 'It hasn't happened yet.'

Amma stands straight, holding the balled-up paper to her chest as though it's a fat, multi-coloured baby. 'But of course it will happen. You promised me,' she says.

She holds my gaze for a moment before taking the paper and stuffing it into the bin. I hear the crackle of layers crushing into each other.

'Amma,' I say. 'The pain . . .'

When she turns to look at me I can see her eyes flickering with new plans.

'We will take it slowly. Walking down and up the stairs a few steps at a time. Sitting on the balcony so you get used to the air.'

'Why would I need to—'

'Then we will walk to the park. Feed the ducks.'

'I don't like d—'

'Soon you will be able to go out on your own. See your friends. It is like the doctor says: a little exercise and a healthy social life will *lift your mood.*'

The birds begin squawking, flapping their wings as the walls collapse around me. The full force of a blazing sun hits my body, wind blowing leaves across my face before sucking me up into a hurricane that spins me to the sky.

I roll my eyes. 'My mood is just fine,' I say.

Amma lists the symptoms that indicate it isn't.

- Loss of interest in daily activities.
- Avoiding contact with other people.

- Irritability and anger.
- Reluctance to talk about feelings.

She pushes her chin deep into her neck.

'We all know about the last one, yes?'

I shuffle down flat on my back. Getting me to 'talk about my feelings' is Amma's number-one mission. She tried to get me to talk to a doctor and she tried to get me to talk to a counsellor. She tried to get me to talk in a support group and even tried to get me to talk to her. But the doctor was too clinical, the counsellor too soft, the support group made me want to jump out of the window. While speaking to Amma feels like speaking to an alien race.

The problem is simple. Nobody can understand my life because nobody else has lived it.

Except, maybe, for you.

'Make sure you write something in your Pain Diary tonight,' Amma says now.

Pain Diary. Just the name of it makes my stomach coil. I exhale slowly, waiting for my body to inhale naturally. This is a trick the physiotherapist showed me, a way of distracting my brain from the pain. When she speaks again Amma's voice is soft, hopeful.

'Will you at least try?'

My chest inflates. I breathe out.

'Sure,' I say.

I wait until I hear her feet going down the stairs then sit back up, gulp down the painkillers and gaze at the wall opposite. It still has the timeline of my life across it. The baby pictures, the teenage ones and there, smack in the middle, the picture of us on my seventh birthday. It used to be my favourite photo. Before you disappeared I kept it on my bedside table in a frame I'd made out of cereal-box cardboard and sweet wrappers. The wrappers always fell off so I had to eat more chocolates whenever I wanted to fix it.

In the photo our faces are pressed cheek to cheek as we sit in those absurd party dresses we wore whenever we could get away with it. Amma bought them in the January sales: a pair of peach-coloured garments covered with ribbons, sparkles and so many ruffles we looked as if we were made out of whipped cream. You have your tanned arms wrapped around my brown neck, and that elastic smile that stretched your face out like a rugby ball. The curly mop of your hair is flattened against my cheek as I smile my own gap-toothed grin towards the camera. As I look at the photo I remember how, after it was taken, the ribbons on our dresses were so tangled we hobbled around for the rest of the afternoon pretending we were conjoined twins.

The memory comes like an extra coin in the pocket: it has always been there but finding it again is a happy surprise. I lie on my back, rummaging through my mind for more memories. I look up at the cracked ceiling, images of our life flickering across it: you climbing down trees with twigs in your hair, us sliding down the railings to the bottom of the estate. I see flashing shots of nineties memorabilia: tie-dyed T-shirts, a *Jagged Little Pill* CD, the Commodore 64 your brother owned when really he wanted a Sega Mega Drive. Then there's the scene of when your mother decided to leave. Us sitting on the rug in front of your television, pretending to play chess (though neither of us knew how), Jonathan in the back, sulking over something or other, and your mother at the dining-room table with her head in her hands.

I sense the weight of the diary on my lap. It feels as heavy as the bricks of the walls around me. My eyes begin to sting and my throat tightens with a sharp twist as I lift my hand to hurl the book across the room.

But something, a small seed of thought, makes me stop. Streetlamps shine a honey glow, the blaze of car headlights zooms across the walls as the thought grows and blossoms. I pick up the jewel-encrusted pen from the bedside table and grip it tightly. Maybe I should write it down. All the things that happened to us the way I remember, as well as the life I have now. I could document it all and then maybe I would understand it. And you, Marianne, you would understand too.

When I have this thought, something amazing happens. You wouldn't believe it.

I smile.

And that is just at the *thought*.

The Constellation of Stinging Nettles

When the illness first came I tried not to remember anything. Memories are like stinging nettles. At first you don't realize they've stung you and by the time you do, the needles are already buried under your skin, making you itch until all you can think about is ways to get rid of the sting. I tried to get rid of you, Marianne. I hid all our toys beneath my bed, removed all the pictures from their frames yet still, even when I try to forget, you're there.

The first memory I have of you is all knickers and legs. You can't have been more than six at the time but had somehow flipped yourself into a handstand against the wall of my flat and couldn't get back down. The skirt of your dress was so long it covered not only the bottom half of your upside-down body but also your head. I remember the sight of your tanned legs against the cream of the wall, the tiny flower print on your frilly yellow knickers. Even then I was jealous of you because all my underwear was plain and white and bought from the local pound shop.

Memories are slippery. Although this image of you is clear in my mind, I can't remember what you said as I helped flip you back up. Whether you were dizzy as the blood drained from your head, whether you tried to teach me the same trick and I point-blank refused. But I do remember thinking you were someone I wanted to be friends with, even when all I could see were your knickers and legs. I had no other friends on Westhill and you fitted the bill (i.e. you were my age, you were a girl).

Amma had been worried about me at the time because I hadn't been mixing well at school. I had a habit of hiding from the other children, inventing my own games in quiet little corners and screaming at anyone who found me. At home I stayed superglued to Amma's side, asking her never-ending questions as she did the housework. After I took an interest in you she regularly pushed me out of the flat, making me knock on your door, then, when you answered, telling me not to rush home. Amma decided we were best friends before either of us did.

At school we did every project together. There was the time we tried to research a tourist brochure of our local area but the only facts we found out were how the city was (roughly) in the middle of the country, had a cheese named after it and was once home to Daniel Lambert, the fattest man in England. It took us a while to come up with a slogan. At first we thought of *Leicester: in the middle of everything*, then became more ambitious with *Leicester! Eat cheese! Get fat! Get famous!* Eventually we decided to steal Rebecca Knight's idea: *Leicester – the heart of England*. Rebecca Knight sat on the top table and was so clever she didn't have to do partner work. She was a safe bet.

When it came to the actual content of the brochure we decided to narrow our focus to facts about Westhill Estate and, more specifically, the residents of Bosworth House and their pets. Most of those people have left now. The Pattersons still live on the fourth floor (one mother, three boys, two British bulldogs) and Sandy Burke and her twins live on the first (three cats), but other people like old Mrs Simmons across the hall (two budgies and a parakeet) have gone.

People move in and out of Bosworth House all the time. In your old flat next door, a Somali family are getting ready to move after – allegedly – winning the lottery. This was controversial because the Ahmed family are Muslim and the mother had been buying lottery tickets secretly at the corner shop, even though it's against her religion to gamble. You should have heard the way they argued about it. I didn't understand what they said but it sounded bitter. Their two boys slept in the room that used to be yours and, whenever their parents argued, hid there until it blew over. Through the walls, I'd hear them debating whether it was better to do a water-bomb attack from the third- or fourth-floor balcony (third had better range, fourth had better height). But just as I got drawn into the debate they began speaking in fast beats of Somali that washed straight over me.

I miss their voices. The sound filled the emptiness the way your voice did when you spoke to me at night. It was a blessing and a curse that your bed was pushed up against the same partition wall as mine. If you spoke loudly I could hear most of what you said, but if you lowered your voice it was like listening to a radio that keeps losing its signal. If it was past nine o'clock I'd tell you to shut up because I needed to sleep. I believed in sleep then because Amma fed me the lie that without enough of it not only would I stop growing but I would *shrink*. I was too small already and wouldn't have been so rude if I wasn't afraid of disappearing. Still, you never seemed to mind, carrying on with your jibber-jabber right through the night.

'If you could have a superpower, what (*mumble, mumble*)? ... I (*mumble*) invisible. I read about this man who (*mumble, mumble*) but there was a picture of him right there so (*mumble, mumble*). Or maybe (*mumble*) was *invincible*.'

I kept my mini dictionary in my robe pocket, and wanted to check what 'invincible' meant but was scared that, if I did, the lack of sleep would make me shrivel into a speck of dust. Eventually my fear of shrinking was outweighed by my need to know and I'd end up sitting cross-legged on the bedroom floor, looking up all the unknown words you bombarded me with.

I was the queen of words back then. I'd constantly look up meanings in my mini dictionary, which you found funny and useful, and your messy-haired brother found plain irritating. He used to shove me in the shoulder when I used a word he didn't understand (which was often), making sure you were looking the other way when he did it. Sometimes he'd snatch my mini dictionary and wave it over my head until I'd have to jump up and down like a Jack Russell to retrieve it. Jonathan always knew how to rattle me. It was his one and only gift in life.

I suppose you won't remember much about Bosworth House, it's been so long. You probably remember the size of it, looming high and wide as it sits on the side of the hill, but you'll have forgotten the details. The bars they extended on the balconies so that people wouldn't throw themselves (or each other) over the side. The narrow steps with a rank stink we only found out was piss when Jonathan told us in a well-what-*else*-would-it-be tone one day. The way the council comes and repaints the outside walls each and every year but still doesn't send anyone to fix the stupid lifts. The view from the fourth floor where you can see down to the whole of Westhill Estate, white-painted blocks of flats snaking down to the main road like vertebrae. We used to sit up there on the fourth floor with our legs poking out from the gaps in the railings, swinging them in the breeze as we sucked orange-flavoured ice-lollies. We'd turn to each other and shout, 'Open wide and say *ahhrr*!' in our poshest doctor voices, then stick out tangerine tongues at each other before droning out the sound. We tried to see who could carry the note the longest. You always won.

No, when I think through the logic of it I don't believe you'd remember any of it. I don't blame you. You haven't had ten years of lying in the same bed with nothing but the same memories running through your head. That's all I've had, you see. That and Amma.

'It's my job to take care of you, shona,' she tells me on my bad days. 'I will never leave you, Ravine. You cannot be selfish when you're a mother.'

When she says this, I don't remind her about yours.

She was beautiful, your mum, or at least she had been in the photographs. She had a whole row of them lined up in silver frames on the dresser in your living room. Glossy shots of her young grinning face, ruffled blonde eighties hair, pink silky lipstick circling her mouth. When she was drunk she would tell us about when she was a beauty queen. We imagined her on stage in an evening gown, tiara perched on big pouffy hair as she rolled her hand in a royal wave. After she'd gone we found a picture under the bed of her sitting on her knees, skin tanned brown as horse hide, chin dipped down to her collarbone as her breasts lay exposed.

Your mother was always so happy in those photographs – even the nudey one. She hardly ever smiled when we were around and never at me. I had a habit of irritating her without meaning to. Every time I called her Mrs Dickerson she'd visibly flinch.

'For heaven's sake, just call me Elaine,' she'd say.

I'd nod my head. 'Yes, Mrs Dickerson.'

In fact, the only time I saw your mother use her photograph-smile was with your dad. Her eyes would light up, every tooth on display. Then, five minutes later she'd be throwing plates at his head. When she sat me, you and Jonathan down to explain he'd moved to live in 'the castle' in the middle of the city, we all believed her. It was only later that we found out this was HM Prison Leicester, which did in fact look like a giant castle, though wasn't home to any lords or ladies. You never saw him again.

On the day that would change everything, the same day we were pretend-playing chess in your living room, Mrs Dickerson only began smiling after she'd opened the letter. It had been lying there on the pile she always banned you from looking at – white envelopes with official type, brown envelopes with red writing at the edges of their plastic windows. But this letter was different. It had a loose handwritten scrawl across it, and when your mother opened it she didn't throw a mug against the wall like she did when she read the other letters, but sat upright in her seat. We were eight then and so used to her slump – lying across sofas, draped across table tops – that when she sat up straight we both looked up from the chessboard. Her pale-blue eyes were scanning the pages, dropping down to the bottom of a sheet before flicking quickly to the next. When she'd finished she simply sat, staring at the bundle of papers in her hands. Eventually she smiled. Not the same as the toothy smiles in the pictures, wide and exaggerated, but soft, slow and full of hope. It wasn't long after that she got the vodka bottle from the kitchen and pulled us into a barn dance.

Jonathan watched from the corner of the room.

'For shit's sake!' he said, as she began spinning us around.

She was whooping so loudly that she didn't hear him.

'*Ding dong, the witch is dead!*' she sang, do-si-doeing our bodies across the carpet.

Your mother's favourite film was *The Wizard of Oz* so we didn't pay much attention to the words. Her steps were so quick we almost tumbled over until she suddenly stopped. She looked at the dresser before running over to it and opening all the doors. She was in such a rush that she didn't notice how she'd upset her own pictures. The metal frames clinked against each other as she opened a small burgundy book with a gold emblem of a lion and unicorn stamped on the cover. As she examined the pages inside she didn't notice how the photographs of her former beauty – the same ones she polished each Sunday and banned you from touching – had fallen flat on their faces.

We should have known then that something was wrong.

Signs of spring: fuzzy green buds sitting on spindly branches outside the window; birds perched on said branches, twittering like maniacs; Amma telling me to stop throwing objects at said window to get rid of said birds twittering like maniacs.

I'm not always great at spotting the signs. It's easy to forget the month or day when you're in a lifebed. There's a 2010 calendar hanging on the back of my bedroom door, page turned to January, with a giant picture of kittens in a basket at the top, but Amma forgets to flip the month over because she never sees it. When she's in my room, the door stays open and the calendar is hidden away. And then when she leaves, she closes the door behind her and the calendar remains unseen. This is like life: there are things we think we've tucked away but they're still there, concealed from view.

Amma comes into my room with a tray of curried breakfast. She comes in three times a day, ambling down the hallway in her sari and socks with a tray of unsuitable food held tightly in her hands. Chapattis round and floury, steaming with heat from the pan. Soft curried potatoes, yellowed with turmeric and splattered with mustard seeds and coriander leaves, a whole green chilli angled on the side. There's no use telling Amma that chilli isn't suitable for breakfast. My mother has her own logic which bears no relation to the everyday logic the rest of us use.

Chapattis = breakfast
Rice = lunch and dinner
Curry = all the livelong day

'This is the Bengali way,' she tells me, knowing full well I don't know any better. She could tell me swimming in a bicycle helmet is a national custom in Sylhet and I'd have no way of proving otherwise.

Along with the heartburn-inducing breakfast, Amma brings me a tumbler filled to the brim with mango juice. The tumbler is decorated with red cockerels; she got it free using cereal coupons when I was four years old. Heaven, for my mother, would be a discount store and a handful of coupons.

'Good morning, my sweet eighteen-year-old!' she says as she comes in.

I wipe the sleep from my eyes.

'Morning, Amma.'

She settles the tray on my lap, places my pills in a line like soldiers preparing to march. As I shuffle up in the bed I hear the pills wobble, hard shells clinking against plastic. Amma nudges them back in line in that swift way of hers, putting things back in place before you even realize they're out.

Amma sits by the window and watches me. The folds of her sari puff out as she waits for me to have my first mouthful. Once, years ago, I tried pushing the tray away and she near forced the food down my throat, holding my head by the back of the scalp and pushing hot potato to my sucked-in lips.

'Good girl,' she says as I take my first mouthful.

Good girl, as though I'm eight and not eighteen.

I take a sip of mango juice, waiting for Amma to detail her strategy for Getting Ravine Out of the Flat. Instead, she begins her ritual with the letters. Each and every day Amma leans back in her seat, pulls out the post from the waist of her sari petticoat and begins reading me junk mail.

No, not just junk mail. Sometimes she reads me the bills.

Amma thinks that if she tells me about a new restaurant opening five streets away, or the money I could save when calling friends (which I don't have), I'll somehow gain an interest in the Big World Outside. The world that, for the last few years, I've seen only through the squares of windows. Taxi windows taking me to hospital windows, then back to taxi windows that will drive me to the same infernal bedroom window that I look out of each day.

Sometimes Amma tells me about current affairs. Troops being killed in Afghanistan, conspiracy theories about the death of Michael Jackson. When Barack Obama was elected, Amma blubbered through the whole inauguration as though the President of the United States were in fact her long-lost son. She looked over at me, baffled when I couldn't muster a tear.

'It is so *wonderful,* is it not?' she said.

I was too busy absorbing the fact that I hadn't noticed a whole presidential election had been and gone to agree.

News is seducing; like any other kind of gossip I'm always tempted to listen in. I learnt the consequences a few years back when Amma read an article to me about the bunny murders in Ruhr Valley, Germany. The report left me so disturbed I had recurring nightmares of waking up in a room full of rabbit heads. But here's what I've decided: I have no part in the world and the best thing is to keep it that way. I'm perfectly happy in the vacuum of my room where nothing ever changes. Good old Shiva watching over me from the dresser, My Little Ponies frolicking merrily on the folds of the curtains. Even the squawking birds on the wallpaper are some form of company, despite their evil eyes. Unfortunately, Amma doesn't agree. She thinks I need to know about every disaster and tragedy that pops up on the news. There is now a 'global financial crisis', she tells me. People will lose jobs, families will be on the 'breadline', our entire broken country will become a no man's land, with politicians feeding on the dead corpses of the poor and destitute (i.e. us).

'A postcard!' Amma says this morning.

I'm swallowing my pills as she says it and almost choke. When I look up at her, Amma has her reading glasses perched on the end of her nose with an oblong card held in front of her. Morning light filters through the curtains, making the postcard glow. I can see the picture of a tropical beach fringed with a luminous light as she frowns and squints, trying to decipher the words on the back. For a moment my heart holds on to its own beat, making my chest cave in, my stomach tighten.

'"Dear Mrs Roy,"' she says in her booming read-aloud voice. '"We are on the third day of our trip and are having the time of our lives! Here on Primrose Cruises not only do you get the pleasure of an all-inclusive holiday (meals included) but access to sports, bar and leisure facilities. Terms and conditions apply. Already we have been working out at the gym, drinking cocktails at the bar and pampering ourselves in the exclusive Thai spa. Why don't you come join us by following our blog on www.primrose-cruises.blogspot.com. Wish you were here! Angela and Simon."'

Amma continues to frown as she turns the card over in her hand. She peers at me over her glasses.

'Who is this Angela and Simon?'

I take a deep breath. The pain is vibrating through my nerves, pulsing louder and louder.

'It's junk mail, Amma,' I tell her, sliding my breakfast tray to the bedside table, feeling the cramping of muscles in my arm.

She sits up straight, as though I've told her a lie. She examines the postcard closely, pushing the print right up to her nose before running her finger across it. Her brows rise high, lips pouting.

'The type is just like handwriting,' she tells me.

I sigh in that way I do to stop myself from rolling my eyes. Amma hates the eye-rolling even more than the sighing and, even though I rarely show it, I love my mother. You know this and so does she, but sometimes I need to prove this to myself with these small acts of kindness.

'The wonders of a modern age,' I say, before rolling over and covering my shoulders with the duvet. The pain is throbbing now, a loud, angry pulse that pounds through the left side of my body. I wait to hear the shuffle of Amma's sari as she rises to her feet.

'We shall start our exercises later,' she says. 'I must give you time to digest your breakfast.'

'How generous,' I mumble as I concentrate on keeping my muscles relaxed.

I squeeze my eyes closed as nausea crashes through my stomach. I shudder.

'I think we shall start with something small,' she carries on. 'Perhaps getting dressed.'

The bed begins to bob from side to side like a ship lost at sea.

'I'm not getting dressed,' I say.

'Or walking outside.'

'No, thanks.'

The waves grow bigger and my bed begins to rock violently.

I open my eyes to see Amma hovering by the side of my bed. I smile at her, hoping I can hide the screaming pain. The room blurs behind her and I close my eyes.

'I will write a list of options,' she says. Through the ringing in my ears I hear the dull clatter of the tray as she collects it and moves to the end of the room. After ten years, I've learnt how to hide my symptoms from Amma, to keep her from worrying, to keep her from sitting at my bedside and mopping my brow. Just as she gets to the door, Amma pauses. I crane my neck, seeing her fuzzy shape standing at the end of the bed. The room is still swaying.

'So much like handwriting,' she says.

I imagine Amma holding up the postcard, examining the text again while shaking her head. I don't look to check in case she looks back and sees that I'd been fooled too, if only for a moment, and that in that moment, my heart missed a beat.

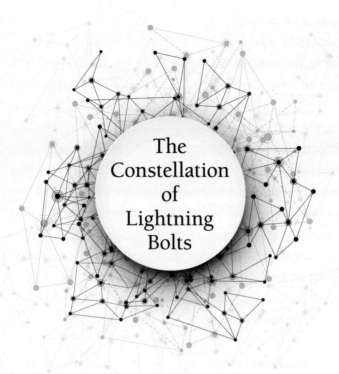

The Constellation of Lightning Bolts

I hadn't realized your mother had gone until the night I heard you crying. All Friday at school you'd seemed just fine. On the playing field you'd rolled out cartwheel after cartwheel, not caring that all the boys could see your luminous shorts flashing at them like an amber light. But when it came to the weekend I suppose the weight of her absence hit you. As I tucked myself into bed I didn't hear your usual jabbering but a quiet sobbing leaking through the walls. I asked you what was wrong but you pretended not to hear. I knew that you were pretending because your whimpers came to a sudden stop. I imagined you burying your head beneath the duvet, trying not to breathe, stifling your sniffles in the springs of your mattress.

If I'd ever seen you cry before, it was because of injury not grief. You'd perform one of your ridiculous stunts, pretending to tightrope walk on a wall or racing Jonathan up a tree, and end up with jagged red scrapes down your knees and elbows. You never cried for long, holding on to the sting with one hand as you wiped away snot and tears with the other, hobbling to the nearest adult with hiccuping gulps.

'I shall chop it off with a knife,' Amma said to you once.

She performed a chopping action as she spoke, banging the edge of one hand against the other like a cleaver against a board. She then giggled in that 'tee hee' fashion you always found so hilarious. You spluttered with laughter while I stood frozen with the image of cleavers in my mind.

You won't know this but the night I heard you crying, I crept down the stairs, out of the flat and to your front door. I'd like to say this was pure selflessness on my part, that the sound of your pain caused me so much worry that I couldn't rest without coming to soothe you. That would be a lie and the last thing I want to do is to lie to you.

The truth is I came that night because I was so used to your prattling at bedtime I found it hard to fall asleep without it. As the silence soaked the walls, I stared blankly at the ceiling, thinking about how much my body would have shrunk by morning.

It was Jonathan who answered the door. He had on his thick-framed glasses that covered half his face and thunderstorm pyjamas with lightning bolts shooting out of grey clouds. I used to call him Jonathan-Weatherboy. He hated it, even though he loved the weather, randomly announcing make-believe forecasts that no one had asked for. He sat so close to the television – watching those weather reports, memorizing the language and imitating the gestures of his idols – that we were convinced he would one day fall through the screen. Once, he ordered us to paint him a map of the British Isles so he had something to practise his reports on. He got all flustered when he stuck it to the wall and found Scotland was ten times too big, looking like an infected head, bloated and lopsided upon the dwarf body of England. When we told him the cross in the middle was to mark our location (*Leicester – the heart of England*) he ripped the map in two.

'What do you want?' Jonathan asked that night.

'Marianne,' I said.

He sighed a dramatic sigh, legs bending and head rolling back as his jaw gaped open. 'For shit's sake, Ravine,' he said, smacking his hand across his face.

I gasped. 'She's crying,' I told him. 'And don't swear.'

Jonathan looked at me through his glasses as though I were an idiot. 'No, she isn't.'

I rolled my eyes. 'I heard her through the wall. I heard her *weeping* and *sobbing*.'

Jonathan, ignoring my great use of synonyms, screwed up his lips. 'Bollocks.'

I gasped and he smiled, smug that he'd got me twice. I stared at your brother through narrowed eyes, ready to punch him in the nose. To look at that boy, you would never have guessed he was your brother. He didn't have that golden tan you'd inherited from your dad (half-Portuguese, you told me, making you a quarter Portuguese and three-quarters 'normal'). Your brother was pale and goofy, and he didn't have that wide rugby-ball grin you had. When your brother smiled, it looked sinister, like he was planning something rotten, which he usually was. His hair was dark, scruffy and distinctly straight while your brown mop glowed golden in the sunlight like a halo. If it hadn't been for your button noses, no one would have guessed you were even related.

When I looked over Jonathan's shoulder I could see the television blazing with grainy images of *Jurassic Park*. There was a sleeping bag spread across the floor with a multipack of crisps and a bottle of supermarket-own cola beside it.

'Where's your mum?' I asked.

The smugness quickly fell from Jonathan's face. I grinned, pleased with my Sherlock-like shrewdness as his face knotted into a scowl.

'She's gone on a holiday and I'm in charge.'

He jutted his chin out, shrugging his shoulders as though this was no big deal.

'I get to be in charge, you see, because—'

'You're older and you're a *boy*.'

He didn't like the way I finished his sentence but I'd heard him say those stupid words so often they sprang from my mouth automatically. For all her wrongdoings I think this was your mother's worst. She repeated these words (*'because you're older and a boy'*) over and over at your brother until he developed a superiority complex – he wasn't just better than us, but better than everyone.

'How long is she on holiday for?' I asked.

'As long as she bleeding well likes,' he said.

'Don't swear.'

'"Bleeding" isn't swearing. It's in the dictionary. Thought you'd know that, seeing as you're *Ravine Ravine Dictionary Queen*.'

He waved his hands in the air as he fairy-danced my name. I stood there, clinging on to the mini dictionary sitting heavy in my robe. After a while, he dropped his hands, releasing a yawn that was so wide I could see the fillings in his back teeth.

'Go away now,' he said and then slammed the door in my face.

I stomped my way back to bed, bubbling with a fury that made me want to shake Amma awake so I could share my outrage.

'Do you know what Jonathan-Weatherboy just *did to me*? Do you know what the *buffoon* just *said to me*?'

31

I climbed back in bed and curled into a foetal position. My fingers were clenched so deep in my pillow I could see the bones of my knuckles pushing up against the skin in little crescent moons. If it hadn't been for his voice, I would have ripped that pillow to smithereens. It was only a mumble at first. I sat up in bed, pressing a glass to the wall and squashing my ear against it.

'You're not crying, are you?' I heard him say.

The tone in his voice was inquisitive rather than mocking. I imagined him standing in your doorway with that scrunched-up expression he had on his face when he thought we were keeping secrets from him.

I didn't hear your reply. I guess it was muffled by the duvet you must have been hiding under.

'But she'll be back soon!' Jonathan cried. 'For shit's sake, Marianne, she said she'd be back soon, didn't she?'

I heard a mumble as you scolded him for his language.

'I suppose you want to come and watch TV now?' he said.

He sounded put-out but the fact he'd invited you, that he'd extended some form of twisted olive branch, was enough to simmer my rage.

Yet something still felt wrong. The crying, the sleeping bag in front of the television and the lack of jabbering through the wall made it hard for me to sleep. I stared up at the cracks along the ceiling and made a pact. With your mother gone, I'd have to step up. Jonathan may have been older and a boy, but he was also an idiot who couldn't be trusted.

Someone needed to protect you, and that person would be me.

Today Amma makes me walk across the landing to the top of the stairs where I stand for five minutes, staring down the steps. She makes me repeat this four times. By the time I'm back in bed, my body is flinching with the repeat feeling of

falling

falling

falling.

In the afternoon she has me sitting at the window, looking out at the estate. This is to remind me that there's a world outside. She comes in every five minutes to ask me what I've seen.

Tower blocks. Clouds. Tower blocks.

Birds. Clouds. Tower blocks.

'No people?' she asks.

'I can't see that far down.'

She helps me stand up, pushes my chair closer to the window then angles my chin down. I push the chair back as soon as she's out of the room.

I'm hoping that with all these new exercises Amma will have forgotten that it's bath day but when she comes in, towel draped over her arm, she has a renewed zeal in her eyes.

'Today we shall get in the bath!' She says this as though it's a brand-new idea and quickly begins levering me out of bed in the same awkward way she does every time. She hauls me onto her small body, her shoulder bone stinging in my armpit as I breathe through the pain.

'Maybe I could walk myself next time,' I say, as she opens the door to the bathroom. 'You know, as an exercise.'

'Good idea,' she says, lowering me down to sit on the wooden toilet seat.

I look at the steam rising from the tub, the bubbles lining the sides. Amma draws baths that are close to boiling.

'In fact, I should probably run the bath next time too,' I suggest.

She smiles down at me as if I've offered to help her with brain surgery.

'Do not worry yourself,' she says, pinching me on my good cheek before leaving.

I stare at the water. There have been times when getting in the bath has caused me so much pain that I've had to bite into a loofah so Amma won't hear me scream, rush up the stairs, quickly assess my curled-up body and immediately call the city council to request the installation of another strange contraption. A seat to swing me in and lower me down like cargo, or a pulley device with a variety of straps and padding that could lift my naked body up and down at the flick of a switch. My mother has a knack for finding the most elaborate and embarrassing equipment. So it's easier to just bite the loofah.

Chronic pain is a bizarre bastard of an illness. There are no symptoms before it strikes, no blood tests to diagnose it, no machine to analyse the level of pain. It is a doctor's nightmare. Repeat visits, negative tests, anger, frustration: and that's just from their side. For some people the pain is localized to the back or the neck, through headaches or stomach cramps, but for me it's in the left side of my hypersensitive body.

It began the night you vanished: 30 December 1999. The night before New Year's Eve. The night my calf was burnt. It was a severe burn, but nothing that wouldn't have healed with time. But the pain signals, designed to tell my brain about the damage and prevent further harm, decided to take a detour. They hitchhiked along the nerve pathways of my entire body then added insult to literal injury by staying switched on long after my recovery.

It's always there, the pain, though its strength varies. Sometimes it's like a dull headache all over. At other times a major limb could be throbbing, deep and monotonous; stinging, like a papercut, like muscles being punctured by needles from the inside out; or, at its worst, it burns. Nothing is as bad as the burning.

Do you remember when we both caught the flu and Amma put us in quarantine in my room? At first we were excited, thinking we were on a never-ending sleepover.

'Let's sing songs and dress up,' you said. 'Let's write stories and figure out how to *fix the world.*'

By the time night came we were both lying immobile in bed, shivering and sweating as our mouths gasped for air. We could barely speak, not even you who spoke so much your mother literally taped your mouth up when she'd had enough.

When the illness was over I remember you telling me, 'It was like dying, Ravine, but *worse.*' I knew what you meant because when you're dying you know it will end. That's how the burning is for me – worse than dying. It's an unbearable heat, relentlessly coursing over my skin, and the fear is that this time it will last for ever.

You'll probably find it difficult, reading about all this pain. Most humans are programmed to empathize, which is why horror movies make them yelp out loud. We feel each other's pain whether we want to or not. Don't worry, there's only one more thing I need to tell you and then all this pain business will be over.

On bath days, when I lower myself into the tub, the pain starts in my hand as I grip the handrail, and then shoots up my arm and to my shoulder. When I step into the water the sole of my foot hits the enamel of the base and makes my whole leg cramp. I drop myself into the liquid quickly, before I keel over, and then curl up into a ball with my arms wrapped around my knees. I try not to look down at my calf. It's not a pretty sight, not even to me, and I should be used to it.

But when I rub soap over my lower leg I can still feel the bumps and knots, the waxy smoothness of each scar along the back. You'd think this would be the most tender part of my body but chronic pain doesn't discriminate.

Or at least it never used to.

This is the thing. Something's changed and it's only today, as I get in the bath, that I realize what it is. This is a big thing so, like a plaster that needs to be ripped off, I'm going to tell you quickly.

I think I'm cured.

Cured, not in the sense of *preparing meat, fish, etc. for preservation by salting or drying*. Nor in the sense of *promoting the hardening of fresh concrete or mortar* but in the standard, everyday use of the word.

> **cured** *v.* to relieve or rid of something detrimental such as an illness or a bad habit i.e. to restore to health.

That's me, Marianne. I've been restored.

The Constellation of Spies

Two days after Jonathan slammed a door in my face, Uncle Walter arrived. We saw him from the fourth floor of Bosworth House, our legs dangling down through the gaps of the railings that stopped us from hurling ourselves to oblivion. Even from up there we could see the enormity of him. As he stepped out of the taxi, we watched it lean to the side then bounce up, released of his bulky weight. His smooth, plastic skin was glazed with sweat, his chin lifted in the air. We thought he was looking straight at us but later we learnt his upturned head was permanent, caused by the unfortunate roll of under-chin fat cushioning his neck. He wiped his brow as he scanned the estate, then waddled to the boot to haul out his luggage. He only had one suitcase, small and boxy in his round, doughy hands.

He didn't have a clue.

At first, not knowing this man was your uncle, we assumed he was a spy. It was an easy assumption to make as he was wearing a shirt and trousers. No one we knew on Westhill ever wore a shirt and trousers, while spies on the television always did.

'Follow me,' you said.

You pulled your legs out of the railings, crouching low as if the sky had dropped. I followed you in this round-backed way – hands fanned out, feet shuffling against the concrete – all the way down to the third floor. Peering through the steel railings to the concrete stairwell below, we heard the slow resonating noise of feet hitting steps.

Ph-lud! Ph-lud! Ph-lud!

This was followed by a pause and laboured panting. When the top of your uncle's head emerged beneath us, thick black hair in a neat businessman's cut, we watched with unblinking eyes as we waited for him to pull out a walkie-talkie or other such spy equipment. He slid his hand into his trouser pocket, our knuckles turning white as we squeezed the bars in front of us, but when he brought his hand out it was only clasping a handkerchief folded neatly in a triangle. He pressed it to his brow, taking in a deep breath.

Everyone knew everyone on Westhill Estate and we weren't the only eyes watching Walter that day. Bradley Patterson and his gang of bicycle goons were standing by the rails at the entrance of Bosworth House, watching your uncle with the scrutiny of a pack of wolves. The gang loved nothing more than standing around propped on their bikes in the most inconvenient of places. Their usual haunt was outside Poseidon's fish and chip shop where they took great joy in leering at girls and terrifying pensioners. Whenever Amma passed by in her brightly coloured sari, Bradley Patterson called out *'but but ding ding'* in what was supposed to be an Indian accent. My mother ignored him. The last thing you ever wanted to do with the bicycle goons was respond. Attention fed them like water feeds a sponge, bloating their egos, making them fat with pride.

It was only when we heard Bradley Patterson's voice singing up at Uncle Walter that we realized the pack had found their latest prey.

'*Who ate all the pies? Who ate all the pies?*'

Being fourteen years old, Bradley's voice was on the verge of breaking. It jittered up the building in half-squeaks and baritones. We saw him nudging his bicycle goons for support. Their chests inflated.

'*You fat bastard! You fat bastard! You ate all the pies!*'

The goons fell into a chorus of mock-manly laughter. We waited for your uncle to pull out a shotgun and pick them all off.

'What the shit are you doing?'

We both banged our heads on the railings in surprise before scurrying to your brother as he stood behind us with his standard frown.

'For cod's sake, Jonathan!' you hissed as we scrambled to our feet. 'Do you want us to get *killed*?'

The laughter from the bicycle goons meant both Jonathan's question and our banging heads had gone undetected. As we stood on the third floor, you explained to your brother that there was a spy downstairs and if we made any more noise he was likely to run up and shoot us all in the head with a pistol. Jonathan shrugged his shoulders as if he didn't give a hoot but kept his lips shut anyway. It was then that we heard the *Ph-lud! Ph-lud!* footsteps coming up the staircase behind us. You grabbed both of us by the arms and dragged us to the entrance of old Mrs Simmons' flat. This was a particularly brave move as Mrs Simmons was a recluse who despised all children. If she caught us playing on the steps outside her flat she'd throw buckets of dishwater, dark and murky, out of her door so that it would swim across the concrete with a menacing speed that made us run away screaming.

Mrs Simmons is long dead now. She was found three weeks after her death when Amma called the council about the rancid stench that greeted her whenever she left the flat. They found her stiff body lying across her living-room floor, covered in bird droppings. From our Bosworth House research, we'd deduced that Mrs Simmons owned two budgies and a parakeet but in truth she'd been housing a whole menagerie. Four budgies, two canaries, a cockatoo; there were even rumours that she was housing a peregrine falcon. When I think of all the faeces she must have cleaned up in her life I'm glad we ran away from that water.

Still, your fear of the spy outweighed any fears of old Mrs Simmons' dirty water. You dragged us to her step, making us squat on the floor with our backs pressed against her door.

'If you don't breathe he won't see you,' you whispered.

Like a fool I didn't question this but held my breath as we waited to have our brains blown out. As I'd given myself the duty of being your protector, I considered whether I could actually, if necessary, leap in front of you as a human shield. When I looked across at Jonathan I could see his eyes swimming wildly behind the lenses of his glasses, as he bit down hard on his bottom lip. I'd been right, he couldn't be trusted. It would all be down to me.

You tightened your grip on my arm as the round figure of your uncle-cum-spy emerged. His forehead was dripping, his shirt circled at the armpits with puddle-sized sweat patches. His face was flushed crab-pink and dappled with white patches that made him look as if he'd caught a rash. He was so distracted by his own physical battle against heat and stairs that he didn't see the blue-faced children crouched down on the other side of the corridor. He paused, preparing himself for the next climb, before glancing over at your door and freezing. He turned to face it with his back towards us, the round mounds of his bottom at our eye level, the flop of his back flesh contained by the thin fabric of his shirt.

He had a lovely body, your Uncle Walter. I remember thinking so at the time. Later, beauty adverts and TV weight-loss programmes would try to convince me otherwise but we found his humongous bulk not only fascinating but spectacular to watch. Even the roll of under-chin fat that caused him so much discomfort was something we marvelled at. So smooth, so glossy; the skin rippling every time he laughed.

Your uncle pulled a piece of paper from his pocket and raised a balled fist as he prepared to strike your door. It was at this point that we lost the battle against holding our breaths to the far worthier competitor of needing air to live. Our collective bodies released a loud splutter that echoed around the corridors and made your uncle spin fast on the spot. He looked down at the three of us on the floor and examined us with a quick scan of his eyes. The sweat was still streaming down his face, his skin was flushed an even deeper red than before, but instead of looking like the fierce monster he should have, his eyes widened with excitement. When he inhaled, his chest expanded like the chests of grizzly bears we'd watched in nature documentaries.

'You're Marianne and John!' he said, as though you were Oscar-winning movie stars. 'Look at you! You're so *big*!'

Upon releasing his booming voice on the landing, the sound of Mrs Simmons filling up a bucket leaked through the door. He looked at us with a stretched grin.

'Is Elaine in?' he asked.

Something is missing. As I lie in the bath I wait for the pain but there is nothing there. No aches or stings, no spasms in my muscles

41

or stabbing in my nerves. For the first time in years my body *relaxes*. It's as though barbed wire had been wrapped taut around each of my muscles and suddenly, it's been snipped free.

I start crying after that, from surprise mainly but also from the feeling of liberation. I wiggle my toes in the water as I continue to sob, stroke the scar across my lower calf and still the pain is gone. I splash so loudly that Amma calls up the stairs to check if I'm drowning.

'I'm fine,' I call back, wiping away the tears.

And I am.

When I get back to my room I begin testing myself. As Amma fries curried fish in the kitchen I lift my arms for ten seconds, then repeat with my knees curled to my chest, then with my legs straightened out. I pinch myself along my body (the shoulder, the elbow, the wrist, the thigh) and feel only momentary pangs of discomfort which vanish as quickly as they come. I swing my body over the side of the bed, jump up, sit down, stand on one foot and nearly topple to the floor. Although my balance is off, my sense of feeling is back to normal.

When I lie back down I try to remember the moment the pain stopped. Was it before my birthday or after I started writing to you? During one of Amma's exercises, or today, at the exact moment I got in the bath? No matter how hard I try I can't grab hold of that moment. It's like finding a lump somewhere it shouldn't be but ignoring it. It begins to itch but you continue thinking it's nothing. This goes on for weeks until eventually you visit the doctor for a minor illness – a sore throat, a cold that won't budge – and find the strange lump you've been pretending doesn't exist has quadrupled in size and now needs a biopsy. It's happened like that for me, except instead of my health getting worse it's got better.

When Amma comes in with her usual tray of flammable foods I get ready to give her the news. I sit up tall, let a smile creep to the corner of my lips, but as she sits down, wobbling her head with her 'I know everything' smile, I stop myself.

'What is it?' I ask instead.

Which is all she needs. Amma leans forward in her seat, holding out a little white card with black type. I take it then turn it over in my hand.

'It is for the general election,' she says. 'You are old enough to vote.'

I look at the card, my name printed in neat letters followed by a row of digits, which apparently is my voter registration number. I feel my smile plunging down into my stomach. It bubbles and hisses into nothing.

'Brilliant,' I say, tossing the card on the bedside table.

Amma sits up tall. 'Don't you see what this means?'

I carry on eating.

'I liked it when you put yogurt in that time,' I say, pointing to the plate.

'I ran out of tomatoes,' she replies. 'But really, darling, don't you see—'

'You should do it again,' I say. 'The yogurt thing, I mean.'

Amma stretches her neck as if doing an impression of a giraffe.

'*Ravine*,' she says. Her eyes are wide now, hands placed neatly on top of each other on her lap.

'OK, what does it mean?' I concede.

She grins, shuffling forward in her seat. 'We have over a month until the general election. We can use that time to get you ready.'

'Ready for what?'

'For getting out of the flat. By the time we are done, you will be able to walk down to the school where the polling station is and make your first vote.'

My eyes twitch as I try to compute what she's saying. I imagine all the paths I'd have to walk, all the eyes watching me, all the memories

43

waiting for me. There's a cramping feeling in my stomach. I place a hand over it as though this will make it stop.

'No,' I say.

Amma frowns. She hasn't heard the panic in my voice so I look down at the curried fish and shrug.

'Maybe I don't want to vote,' I say.

The frown becomes stern. 'People have died for the right to vote, Ravine.'

I shrug again. 'Good for them.'

'*Ravine . . .*'

I keep on shrugging as if I have springs in my shoulders.

'Maybe I don't want to vote. Or leave the flat. Maybe I'm happy as I am and don't want to do all the things you keep making me do!'

I must have shouted the last words because they echo off the walls. We sit in silence, Amma with her arms crossed, chest heaving up and down. I squash rice into fish with my fingers but don't lift it to my lips. My throat is tight. I can't eat.

'It is time to move on, Ravine,' Amma says.

When I look up, her body has softened. She places her hand on my knee.

'You cannot stay like this for ever,' she says.

I lift my tray. 'I'd like to do my exercise now.'

Amma looks at the tray hovering before her. She stands up, takes it and leaves.

There isn't a constellation for pain, but if there were it would sweep over half the sky and be connected by a hundred stars. Next to it would be two stars, brighter but linked by only one line. That would be the Constellation of Truth and Lies. It would seem like nothing in comparison to the Constellation of Pain but it would always be by its side.

After Amma leaves I don't want to look at the black-and-white card sitting on the bedside table. I don't want to think about the secret I'm keeping. So instead I sit on Amma's seat and pretend to do my window exercise.

Children. A police car. Rabid dogs foaming at the mouth and running towards Bosworth House.

After a while I hear a loud beeping noise from outside. Leaning forward in my chair I see a large white van pull up to the entrance of Bosworth House. The Ahmed boys are kicking a ball around. Mrs Ahmed is wearing her usual baggy clothing, her oval face the only flesh on show, but her customary black garb has been replaced with a thin turquoise fabric.

I get up to pull my chair closer to the window. My legs, weak from years of inactivity, wobble from the knees down as I drag the seat. I sit back down, watching as the boys weave between the removal men. When Mrs Ahmed begins shouting and jabbing her hands, they pick up their ball and run down the hill.

'Anything interesting?' I hear Amma call from downstairs.

I lean back in my seat.

'A police car,' I call back. 'And clouds.'

Police cars are as common as clouds round these parts so Amma continues her tasks without further probing. I move closer to the window, watching my breath fog against the glass, feeling nothing but pressure on my elbows as I lean on the sill. Mrs Ahmed stands stiff at the top of the hill. Mr Ahmed walks to her side, gesturing at the boys. What they don't understand, what they perhaps will never understand, is that those boys are happy on this estate and, even though the world might tell them otherwise, they want nothing more than the life they already have.

Seeing them reminds me of us. How we loved this place and

everything it contained. Bosworth House. Bonchurch House. Tewkes-bury House. We both wanted to live in Battenberg House because we thought it was named after the pink-and-yellow cake we loved to eat, with its marzipan icing and square innards. It was only later that I found out our flats were named mostly after Tudor battles.

I feel my muscles sink into the seat as I sit back. I try to absorb the feeling of comfort, to burn it in my memory. If the pain were to come back, I would remember this moment. I hear the beeping of the van as it pulls out. Amma wants me to go back into the world but the truth is I'm not ready. I am a derelict flat. Before I can let anyone in, I need to be repaired.

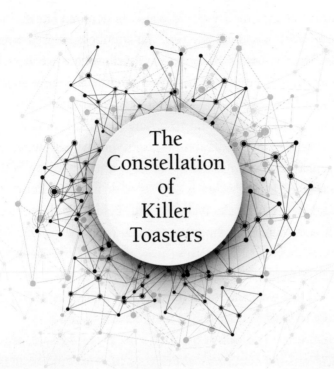

The Constellation of Killer Toasters

Last night I dreamt I was on fire.

I was lying in a bathtub bobbing along the sea. I saw wisps of cloud above me and realized that they weren't clouds at all but plumes of smoke rising from my body. When I looked down my limbs were alight, every inch of me covered with flickering flames. They were red from the core, edged with searing blue lines that curled as the wind fuelled them. Even though I felt the heat of them and the melting of my skin, I did nothing. I didn't scream. I didn't jump in the water. I lay in the bathtub and let myself burn.

I woke up sweating. There was no smoke and the fire was gone.

I lifted a finger, stroking it along the hairs of my left arm. It felt light and as ticklish as silk.

*

It had taken a long time for Uncle Walter to persuade us that he was your uncle. We'd stood outside your flat still convinced he was a spy who was about to turn a pistol on us. It was only when he pulled a photograph from his wallet – him sitting sandwiched between another woman and Mrs Dickerson – that we believed him. Your mother looked young, hair pouffed up in a frenzy, while the other woman was older, with a small quiff and a cigarette hanging from her mouth. Jonathan prodded the image of the other woman.

'Who the hell is she?'

The fold beneath Uncle Walter's chin rippled as he gulped. 'My mum,' he said. 'Your grandmother . . . or at least she was.'

Your jaw dropped as Jonathan frowned. Uncle Walter used his handkerchief to pat his brow.

'She died last week,' he said quietly. 'That's why I came to see you all. I wrote to Elaine about it. She must have told you?'

Jonathan turned to look at us. 'That's not proof,' he said, as though your uncle was not standing right next to us. 'He could be making it all up. He could have forged the photograph.'

You twisted your lips. 'How?'

Jonathan rolled his eyes. 'I don't bloody know, I'm not a . . .'

He looked over at your uncle then back at you, cupping his mouth with his hands as he spelt out the word s-p-y.

'I can prove I'm not lying,' your uncle said, with a loudness that made us all jump. We turned to look at him.

'Elaine's favourite food is spaghetti bolognese. Her favourite colour is peacock blue. Her favourite film is *The Wizard of Oz* . . . though she can never watch the whole thing because it makes her cry.'

'That's true!' I said, pointing at Uncle Walter.

'It is!' you confirmed.

Jonathan remained sceptical as he pulled the front-door key

from his shorts. Yet the proof had been given and he couldn't argue with it.

When your uncle came inside he discovered the full extent of the situation. You gave him a guided tour: Mrs Dickerson's empty room, the makeshift bed Jonathan had made in front of the television and the modest wedge of cash stuck to the fridge with a sticky note reading 'FOR FOOD AND EMERGENCIES ONLY'. Your uncle turned pale and staggered over to the sofa.

'How long did you say Elaine was gone for?' he asked.

Jonathan stepped forward and stuck his chin in the air. 'As long as she bleeding well likes.'

He had his arms crossed over his chest in a tight knot that matched the furrows of his brow. The lenses in his glasses were steamed up with condensation that seemed to come either from the heat of the day or the bubbling of his rage.

'How did she die, anyway?' Jonathan asked. 'You know, that woman in the photo?'

Uncle Walter looked Jonathan straight in the eye.

'Electrocuted,' he said. 'She was trying to fix the toaster with a butter knife and the electric current stopped her heart.'

None of us spoke, startled by your uncle's honesty and the image of a woman poking a butter knife around the element of a toaster.

'That can actually *happen*?' I asked.

Amma warned me of the dangers of everyday household items on a regular basis. The television could blind me if I sat too close to it, the microwave could fry my brain if I didn't follow the instructions, and the toaster couldn't even be switched on without her supervision. If she'd been right about that, what else was she right about?

'They found her in the morning, lying stiff on the floor,' your uncle said.

He made his limbs rigid to demonstrate, arms held straight as poles against the sides of his body.

'Was her hair standing on end?' you asked. 'Like in the cartoons?'

Uncle Walter relaxed and looked up to the ceiling.

'Not standing on end . . . but there was a burnt smell from where it got singed.'

We carried on interrogating him with rapid-fire questions, scared that he would remember at any second that we were children who should be protected from the gruesome realities of life.

In those five minutes, I found out more about your mother than I'd ever known from being her neighbour. Mrs Dickerson had been thrown out of the family home aged seventeen, after a volcanic relationship with her mother led to an almighty fistfight.

'It was like WWF,' your uncle told us, 'but for real.'

Police were called, allegations made and the family was split. Uncle Walter only saw your mum a handful of times afterwards and always without his own mother's knowledge. He would sneak out of the house at night, keeping his head down, trying his best to go undetected.

'I suppose you could say it was like being an s-p-y,' Uncle Walter said, before looking over at Jonathan and giving him an exaggerated wink.

Jonathan's face turned red. He stormed up to his room and slammed the door. Your uncle blinked.

'I only meant it as a joke.'

We both looked at each other.

'Jonathan doesn't like jokes,' I said.

He tapped his temple, logging the fact in the notepad of his mind. Then he clapped his hands together and rose to his feet.

'Who'd like spaghetti carbonara?'

'A spaghetti what?' you said.

I pulled out the mini dictionary from my shoulder bag but the intricacies of Italian cuisine were too obscure for the Oxford University Press back then.

'What is it?' I asked, closing the book.

'It's the best food ever, is what it is,' he said.

Uncle Walter marched into the kitchen, the two of us following behind like baby ducklings.

This is Amma's weekly routine:

Tuesday morning – hop on the bus to the cash-and-carry.
Wednesday – visit the park to feed ducks leftover chapatti.
Thursday – visit the doctor's whether she needs the appointment
   or not.

Amma thinks the body is like a car and needs regular MOTs. I tell her that even a car gets a check-up only once a year, but this means nothing to her. The body is more complex than a car, she tells me, and therefore is more likely to break down.

Do you remember when Amma started wearing trainers? She came to pick us up from school, flashes of white appearing at the bottom of her pleated sari as she walked across the playground. She was wearing a turquoise-and-pink number and it was so hot she wasn't wearing her usual cream cardigan but had left her dimpled arms bare. I tried not to notice how everyone stared. Leicester may have been a multicultural wonderland at the time, but Westhill Estate was slow on the uptake. I was the only Asian person in the school apart from the Singhs, but at least their family had some sense of *subtlety*. They wore western clothes and spoke in accent-free voices. They sprayed their children with deodorant in the morning so they could never be accused of smelling of curry. They dressed them in T-shirts and jeans while I still wore the fashion of seventies Bombay: cutesy puffed dresses and oversized colourful jumpers that buried my small body so deeply I had to roll the sleeves up four times to make them fit. Things are different now; having Yusefs, Priyas and Pytors sitting in the same class is as normal as having cold fish fingers in the dining room. But back in the mid-nineties, to advertise your foreignness on Westhill was as good as putting a 'COME THROW A BRICK AT ME' sign in your window. At times like that, I was grateful to live on the third floor.

When I think of it now I should have seen the trainers as a (literal) step in the right direction. At least they were western. But they only made Amma stick out. When you asked me about them I told you the doctor had prescribed them, claiming they helped people with bad backs. This was true, though I never told you Amma didn't have any back problems. She wore those ridiculous things with air-pockets simply because the doctor had made a fleeting comment about how they helped the alignment of the spine. From then on, flashes of white followed her every step, clashing with her brightly coloured saris. Amma never believed in fashion sense, just common sense, though hers seemed common to no one but herself.

She still wears those white monstrosities. She polishes them with a strange concoction of vinegar and lemon that stinks up the whole flat. I cough and splutter when she starts spraying, until she cries up the steps, 'It is only vinegar, shona. It will not kill you!'

I used to like the fact that, even in these small estate flats, the council built two floors for us to live on. I always thought the stairs made the place feel like a home. They created levels to our lives, gave us depth. But now I've grown I realize how few steps there are and the very small distance they reach. I hear everything that happens, smell every stink. In winter I can feel the draught from the hallway. During the week I hear Amma's telephone conversations in the living room and today, when she comes back from the doctor's, her whispers and mutters as she ushers her companion through the front door.

Amma thinks I don't know about her companion but I smell him every time he walks in. The stale stench of cigarette smoke on his clothes wafts up to me as she rattles with kettles and mugs in the kitchen. I imagine she takes the tea to him in the living room on the same tray she brings me my food on.

As soon as they close the door they begin to speak in a way that hums through my floorboards. He has a low voice that resonates, smooth and deep like the dull drone of a washing machine on a spin cycle. When he speaks, he speaks Bengali. Many of the words I don't realize I know until I hear them; a spark of synapses yanking the memories out. I hear the words '*ji*' meaning '*yes*', '*na*' meaning '*no*', '*shona*' meaning '*lovely*' or '*gold*'.

Amma thinks that her shushing and sneaking is enough to hide her secret from me. But I am the Queen of Secrets and can spot one from a mile away. Besides, Amma's companion doesn't want to be kept secret. After she sneaks him in this morning I hear him coughing theatrically as she guides him to the living room. Knowing they'll have at least two cups of chai before he leaves, I swing my feet out of bed and start testing my body. I pinch myself, stretch my arms out in front of me, clench my fists, march on the spot and roll back on my bed so I can pretend-cycle with my legs. It's the sound of him counting that makes me stop. The way he's doing it, so loud and pronounced, is as though he's playing hide-and-seek. I imagine Amma curled up behind the sofa, the white socks of her feet poking out from behind.

ek
dui
tin
chaar
paach
shoy . . .

As he pummels out the numbers, the memory of Amma counting out sweets for me as a child comes flooding into focus. Her fingers dole jelly beans onto my palm the same way she now doles pills onto my tray. When he stops I feel a peculiar sense of loss.

It's then that I hear a clattering in the room next door. For a moment I think it's the Ahmeds. That they've lost their millions and have been forced to move back. Then I think that it's the boys, running away from their mansion and slipping back in. Before I can decide either way, Amma and her companion start talking again, except this time they're arguing.

I feel their voices reverberate through the walls, Amma *sshh*ing with a gusto that could make the walls cave in. Her companion becomes louder, rattling out strings of words my brain can't compute. The noise grows louder until it culminates in fierce shouts that break from the Bengali.

'But *when*, I ask you? *When?*'

When Amma speaks, it's with shrill, uncharacteristic alarm.

'When she is ready!' she screeches.

A clatter of china is followed by an eerie silence. I get under my covers, bury my head beneath my pillow and try not to scream.

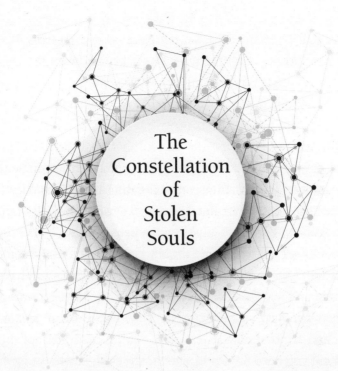

The Constellation of Stolen Souls

If I could give the world one piece of advice from my time in a lifebed it would be this: watch less television.

Amma always believed that, like sugar rots teeth, too much television rots the brain. Before I became ill she'd allow one hour of viewing time per day. She didn't know that when I came to 'play' with you in your flat it was often to watch post-watershed episodes of *Friends* and *South Park*. Everything changed when I came home from the hospital. For the first week, I lay in bed staring up at the cracks in the ceiling, trying not to exist any more. I thought I'd stop being, that the pain would evaporate and you'd come back.

In the second week, Amma decided it was time for me to snap out of it. She bought me toys that would previously have been labelled 'pointless', got me new clothes at full price instead of waiting for the sales and cooked me stacks upon stacks of my favourite (chilli-less) foods. Yet still I remained flat on my back on my mattress. Playing, wearing new clothes or eating would have been admitting that I was real, that everything was real and you were gone.

It was in the third week that Amma hauled the television into my bedroom. As she placed the contraption on my dresser, she began talking through the entire process of setting it up. 'So the lead goes in *here*. And you switch it on *here*. And you tune the channels with *this* button.' She was doing it all wrong and knew full well that the more she prattled on the more irritated I'd get. She then tuned all five of the channels (the only ones we could access in those days before digital) in the wrong order. Then, before she left, my devious, cunning mother switched the TV on, turned up the sound, laid the remote control next to me, and left the screen blazing with the local evening news. She placed her face right over mine, looking down at me with a sweeter-than-sweet smile.

'Tell me if you need anything, shona,' she said, before disappearing downstairs.

I listened to a report about a minor celebrity opening a hospital ward, followed by a story about the county's most intelligent guinea pig. I began banging the buttons of the remote control with the ball of my fist. The voices changed. I rolled my eyes down to the screen to see a re-run of *Sunset Beach*. Amma had banned me from watching this soap, not for any moral reason but because she thought it had a terrible script.

When Amma returned half an hour later I was sitting upright in bed, staring at the scene of a make-up-clad goddess throwing crockery at a muscle-bound fireman. Amma's frown was firm so I made sure to smile widely until she shook her head and left.

Amma had won, but at a cost. In some ways TV brought me back to the real world but in others it drew me further away. I watched pet-rescue programmes when I had no pets, property programmes when I owned no property, endless reams of reality TV shows like no reality I knew. The truth about television is it can teach you everything you could ever want to know but, for the majority of the time, fills your mind with things you don't. The information overload left me exhausted.

So I learnt to limit myself by:

1. Reading library books.
2. Completing crosswords.
3. Listening to Stevie Wonder. ('He is an inspiration,' Amma told me the day she bought the CD. 'Not only was Mr Wonder poor and black when he was growing up, Ravine, he was *blind*. Yet, see how well he's done!' She looked at me as though she expected me to compose a catchy number-one hit on the spot. Instead, I pressed the 'play' button on my remote and let her bounce her foot to the beat. After a few more listens I was hooked.)

The key is to be the controller of the box, not to be controlled by it. It should stimulate the senses, not deaden them. When you live in a lifebed, stimulation is vital. Which is why I watch *The Universe* programmes. They come on every Sunday at eight o'clock, each episode revealing something new about the solar system. The presenter has floppy hair and angular features. He's what your mother would have called 'sex on legs', a phrase we blushed at because 'sex' was about the naughtiest word we knew back then. But this isn't the reason I watch the programmes. While Amma watches with a glint of lust in her eye, which I try to ignore, it's the images that I adore, the concepts and the revelation of how illuminating science can truly be. You always loved the sky at night. You could spend hours staring at it.

'Can we watch some telly now?' I'd say.

You'd look at me dreamy-eyed. 'Sometimes I wish I could be a star.'

I'd cross my arms and huff as you looked back up at the glow.

But now I can see what you saw: not only the stars filling the dark slate above but the history of our universe. You always knew that this life was not all we were. Life was an adventure and, while I was afraid of the monsters that lurked around each corner, you only thought of bigger, greater things. I know you went in search of those things, Marianne, and one day I hope you come back to show me what you found.

Because, meanwhile, all I can think of are the monsters waiting to pounce. You'd laugh if you heard me say that. You'd tell me to stop being so daft. But the world is full of monsters; your brother taught me that.

Jonathan annoyed me in many ways, but one of the things that irked me the most was how he refused to let you abbreviate your names. No Jonny or Marie. No Jon or Annie. No JD or MD and certainly no nicknames. I once called you 'Mop' because of your curly hair. You liked the name but knew it would never pass the high court of Jonathan's judgement so made me vow to never use it in his presence. He was always in our presence. I never used it.

In those days, Jonathan followed us around constantly, pretending that, because he was two years older and a boy, he was duty-bound to protect us. But really he was too strange to have his own friends. He was teased at school because of his out-of-date clothes, his too-big glasses and his obsessive interest in the weather. When we let him tag along on our trips he was both grateful and resentful. Jonathan hated the fact we were all he had, so took every opportunity to undermine and mock us.

He was your brother and I had to pretend to like him because no one else (apart from you) did. But there was something so infuriating about the way he stamped his rules upon you. I wished you'd told him to go away. I wished you'd pretended he didn't exist so that we could have played together without him ruining everything. Jonathan was mean, Marianne. That's the truth of it. Do you remember when he told us about the Soul-drinker? In the woods? The day he put the fear in me?

We loved those woods, although they weren't really big enough to be called woods. They resembled more of a wasteland, patches of unused earth covered in overgrown grass, nettles and a scattering of trees with charcoal trunks. Other than Amma's window boxes, it was the closest to nature we ever got.

We would sneak off there because there were no parks near Bosworth House. A few years ago they knocked down the public toilets regularly used by drug dealers and replaced them with a children's play area. Swings, climbing frames, slides, tunnels; the whole kit and caboodle. You wouldn't believe the changes they've made around here. Youth clubs and drop-in centres, newly planted trees and nature reserves. The youth club is closed most of the time and the trees snapped in two by vandals, but still they're *here*.

I remember that day. We'd been searching for buried treasure by a gathering of rocks and he'd accidentally upturned a stone and unleashed a horde of scurrying insects in all directions. It was the stuff of horror movies – black shiny bodies with wiggling antennae and countless legs scuttling across our path. You and I squealed, hugging each other until our breath ran out. It was a murky day and the shadows looming over us, the dampness in the air, became sources of potential terror.

The incident with the stone reminded Jonathan just how much he loved to scare us. After we'd stopped squealing, he marched us through the woods, searching for a suitable spot, and then pointed at a log for us to sit on. We were both cautious of the huge brown hunk, afraid that it was home to an army of a thousand beasts, but your brother kept on ordering and pointing until eventually we gave in, just to placate him. He liked it when we obeyed him, which wasn't very often, and quickly declared that we would listen to the story he was about to tell us with 100 per cent attention.

'It's a scary one,' he told us, as he paced back and forth. 'So if anyone gets nightmares easily they should cover their ears.'

He eyeballed me and, being the gullible target I was, I sat up straight and knotted my arms.

'It's not about weather, is it?' you asked, shoulders dropping at the prospect of another forecast.

His face began to spasm. 'Let me start and you'll find out.'

Once we were settled Jonathan stepped closer, his eyes wide behind the fishbowl lenses of his glasses. He fanned his hands out as though performing a magic trick and began to speak, slowly and dramatically.

'It's about a man,' he said. 'An invisible man that can only be seen when he decides to show himself.'

'What's his name?' you asked.

'It doesn't matter.'

'Of course it matters. Everyone has a name.'

'Well, this guy doesn't.'

'Why not?'

A furrow developed across your brother's brow. As it wiggled up and down it reminded me of the insects that had escaped from beneath the stone.

'Just listen to the bleeding story, would you?'

We both froze.

'This man,' he said, reverting back to his story-telling voice, 'if he ever shows himself to you, has yellow eyes and black teeth. He lurks in the shadows where you can't see anything and most important of all . . . *he drinks souls*.'

He let the terror of these words sink in.

'Whose souls?' I asked.

He knew the answer to this straight away. *'Little girls'.'*

You frowned.

'Why girls?' you asked.

'Why little ones?' I added.

Jonathan threw his head back. 'For shit's sake! Can I tell this story for more than five seconds without all the bloody *questions*?'

We gasped at the expletives, a reaction that seemed to calm your brother right down. He tried to hide the smirk as he continued.

'As I was saying,' he said. 'This man who drinks souls . . .'

'The Soul-drinker,' you said, clenching your fists against your chin.

I elbowed you in the ribs. You looked at me and clasped your hands over your mouth as we prepared for the onslaught of abuse. But when we looked over at Jonathan his face wasn't devil-red any more.

'The Soul-drinker,' he said, nodding his head. 'Yes, that's his name. He's bad, real bad, and he likes to get little girls best because little girls are stupid, right? Yes, they are, Ravine, it's part of the story . . . Anyway, he needs these souls because without them he *dies*. Like, proper dead. Not like in the films but for real.'

A dark cloud covered us in shadow. You could see the shape of it hovering over the fallen leaves across the ground. It was thick and long, a glimmer of light circling its edges. Beneath my feet I could feel the scurrying of invisible creatures. I pushed my palms into the bark of the log and raised my feet from the floor.

'For example,' he said, 'this girl was going down the stairs one day, like, really high steps on the top floor of our flats. And it was night so it was dark. Along comes the Soul-drinker, without her seeing him because he's all invisible, right? Then, when she doesn't expect it, he *flashes* his yellow eyes in her face. The little girl went tum-bl-ing down the stairs, her bones breaking as she hits each step. *Crack! Crack! Crack!*'

He began performing jerking movements with each part of his body: sticking out an elbow, a shoulder, a hip. The image of him jolting about like this made me queasy. You didn't seem to notice me, sat with my feet raised; you were too busy watching the performance. You swung your legs as Jonathan continued to judder and jolt.

'Why didn't he just push her?' you asked.

Jonathan froze mid-jerk.

'He's not allowed,' he decided. 'He only has a right to your soul if he tricks you . . . It's a rule.'

You nodded, curls bouncing against your shoulders, then held out your hand as if to say 'carry on'.

'And there was this other girl,' Jonathan said, looking me in the eye, 'who was just playing hide-and-seek with her friends but she got lost, because she was stupid, and couldn't find anywhere to hide.'

'Like that time Ravine got lost,' you said.

Jonathan grinned and you grinned back, not realizing the malice lurking behind his glasses.

'*Exactly* like that time,' he said. 'So the Soul-drinker got out this golden trunk. A big one. He told her to hide in it. So this girl got inside because she's so stupid and he locked her in it quick, with a *huge* padlock, and left her there to rot. Fifty years later he came back to claim her soul and when he opened the trunk her skeleton was covered in rats and spiders and all sorts of creepy crawlies.'

You stood up tall, hands balled up on your hips. As you rose I could see bits of bark stuck to the seat of your dress and red indentations across the back of your legs. I wanted to hug your body but was still too afraid to let my feet touch the ground.

'Well I never, Jonathan Dickerson!' you said with sudden force. 'I'm not sitting here a minute longer to listen to your *filth*.'

You stood like that for a few seconds before dropping your arms.

'We'd better go anyway. It's time for lunch.'

You cartwheeled away as Jonathan protested, saying he had plenty more stories about stupid girls who had lost their souls. You just laughed and said he could tell us them tomorrow. I followed behind, examining the nooks and crannies of trees and bushes we passed on the way, waiting to see the flash of yellow eyes. Jonathan caught up with me.

'It *is* only a story, Ravine,' he said.

I shrugged my shoulders and marched on ahead. 'Well, *duh!*'

Neither of you ever knew the power that nonsensical half-story had on me. The thoughts I had, the nightmares. I'd made myself your protector but the Soul-drinker was a far bigger beast than I could manage. What frightened me the most was not being caught by him, or even dying. It was the notion that a man could steal your soul with just one flash of his yellow eyes.

When I got home that day I ran up the stairs to my room and took the mini Oxford dictionary out of the small shoulder bag I carried everywhere. As I flicked through the pages, I tried not to shake as I fumbled my way to *S*. I swiftly ran my finger down the black print, searching for the word that was haunting me.

sought
souk
soul

I kept my finger on the word, not knowing if I should read on.

soul *n.* spiritual or immaterial part of humans; the principle of life, feeling, thought and action.

Life. Feeling. Thought. Action.

I read the words over and over. What else was left if all of that was sucked up by the evil eyes of the Soul-drinker? The answer came to me as my eyes fell down the page.

soulless *adj.* lacking sensitivity or noble qualities; undistinguished, uninteresting.

I don't know what scared me more: the loss of all that made me human or the thought of being uninteresting.

It's easy to forget how many memories you have until you bring one back. But then, like a line of dominoes, the memories are knocked into play, triggering a quick line of collapse. The woods, the story, the hope of reassurance as I searched for meaning in my mini dictionary. As I think back now, the irony is bitter on my tongue. I was so afraid of that word and now it describes me so well.

I am Ravine Roy. I am eighteen years old. I am soulless.

After Amma's companion leaves, I lie in bed making a telescope out of my hands. My two curled palms make a funnel as I peer through the gap. I move my telescope to different angles, catching different images of my room. The edge of the curtains, the beady eye of a bird on the wallpaper, the dark stone midriff of Shiva. I drop my hands and look at the figure's serene expression. Shiva is the god of creation and destruction. In the statue on my dresser he stands frozen in the middle of his cosmic dance, one leg raised high in the air, two of his numerous hands pressed together at the palms. I love that statue, though I won't admit it to Amma. I fake indifference to everything but there are things in the world I want to see, whole libraries of knowledge to learn.

During my GCSEs I actually wanted to know about the nervous system but I found it difficult to study someone else's nerves when there were knives stabbing into my own. Then, on one of the rare occasions I left the flat, I sat in the smelly gym hall for our final exams. I made it through half an hour before dropping my head to rest on the table.

There's little patience for the ill. Students huffed and puffed as I repeatedly collapsed, convinced I was being melodramatic and trying to distract them from their A–C grades. One girl asked what was 'wrong' with me, her expression twisted with such disgust that I was ready for her to spit in my face. I described the whole sorry thing; that I always felt pain, could barely leave my room and that doctors didn't know the cause of, or how to cure, my condition. When I was finished, she looked at me as if I'd told her the world was an egg.

'Bollocks,' she said, pushing a piece of gum into her mouth.

'It's not bollocks,' I said. 'It's a condition.'

She began chewing violently, as though the gum had offended her.

'What's it called, then?'

'Chronic pain.'

She snorted. 'You just made that up.'

'Why would I make it up?'

The school bell rang. She stopped chewing and shrugged her shoulders. 'For attention,' she said, before turning away.

My cheeks burned with the heat of hot coals.

You've got me! I wanted to cry. Bang on the head! I made up an awful, unbelievable illness to get a bit of limelight! I actually *chose* this life! *Chose it!*

But I didn't say anything, just let her saunter off with the idea that people made up crippled lives for themselves. I wonder what she'd think of me now. Probably that she'd been right all along. That I'd made it all up. That I chose this. But I didn't choose to be in pain. And I didn't choose for it to stop either.

'It is time for an assessment,' says Amma, marching into my room.

She's calmed herself down from whatever dispute she's had with her companion, but there's something still ruffled about her. I keep my hand-telescope to my eye.

'I'm swamped at the minute,' I say.

Amma sits down on the chair next to me and brings a piece of paper out from her petticoat waistband.

'You have done your landing walks?' she says.

I drop my hands. 'Yep,' I say.

'You have been looking out the window?'

'Double yep.'

'And you have been practising your crosses?'

I drag a piece of paper from the bedside table and hand it to her. She examines the little rows of crosses I've drawn in preparation for marking my ballot paper.

'These ones look like stars,' Amma says, turning the paper to face me.

At the bottom of the page a series of six pointed stars sit glowing in a line.

'I was being creative,' I say.

Amma shakes her head. 'Voting is not a creative activity, shona,' she says.

As she looks back at her list, I roll my hands into a telescope again, viewing little circles of Amma's flower-print sari.

'I really think we should practise getting dressed soon,' she tells me.

I look at a circle of her lips as they sit wet and expectant. 'I'm not getting dressed,' I say.

Amma pushes my hand-telescope onto my lap. 'You will need to get dressed when you go and vote.'

'Yes,' I say, 'and I only need to do that once.'

I try to lift my telescope up again but Amma keeps it wedged down.

'No, shona,' she says. 'You will need to get dressed when you go to the shops. When you apply for courses. When you go to interviews.'

I can feel my lungs shrivel, my whole body collapse in on itself. The words *shops*, *courses*, *interviews* float about my face like over-inflated balloons ready to pop. I feel an electric bolt of pain in my chest. I try to breathe through it. It stops.

'Right,' I say, as though nothing has happened. 'Maybe tomorrow.'

Amma leans back.

'I know it will be hard, Ravine, but I think if we find you a not so active job—'

'Yes,' I say sharply. 'Tomorrow. Until then, I'll just try going to the toilet, shall I?'

As soon as she's gone I sink deep under my duvet.

We wanted jobs when we grew up. Not to escape Westhill Estate but because our teachers told us that if we worked hard enough, we could achieve anything, and we were stupid enough to believe it. Jonathan was going to be a meteorologist, you were going to be a veterinarian-cum-trapeze artist and I was going to write the new edition of the Oxford dictionary as soon as I figured out how (and if) this could be done. But nowadays you need a qualification to clean another person's bathroom so what hope do I have? There's no point even thinking about it. I look at Shiva. My world is in this bedroom, dancing the dance of destruction with no creation and no way out.

It's then that I hear a clatter through the walls. I look towards the noise but there's only silence. When I look back, Shiva has his brows raised, shoulders pushed into a shrug. I shuffle up in bed so I'm closer to the wall. In total I hear the toilet being flushed four times, the kitchen taps being turned on twice and the vibrating of a mobile phone.

I suppose it's odd that the squatter next door has a mobile phone when I don't. Amma tried to buy me one once but I had no one to call or text so, in the end, she kept it for herself. It wasn't huge and brick-shaped like when we were little but slick and slender with a camera, games and the *internet*. The first time we used the internet at school, teachers were dashing between computers (one between three) as we watched the egg-timer symbol and an inch of colour dropping down the screen to reveal the homepage. It's faster now, and everywhere. Even Amma uses her phone to watch housecleaning tips on YouTube.

I can hear the creaking of springs as the squatter shuffles around on what must be the Ahmeds' old mattress. From the loud, clomping footsteps, I think the squatter is a man and, from the lack of voices, that he's alone. I don't know whether to be intrigued or afraid of this stranger but all the same, I don't tell Amma.

I have a problem with secrets: once I have hold of one I can't let go. It's like our handshake of trust. Whenever we revealed something top-secret, we'd lock that secret away (wiggling fingers, clasping of palms), never allowing one syllable of it to pass our lips again. Since you've gone I've been doing that handshake so often that I'm virtually silent.

The noise of the mobile vibrates again. It's only as it continues to buzz that I realize the squatter hasn't answered it once since he's arrived.

I'm not the only one hiding.

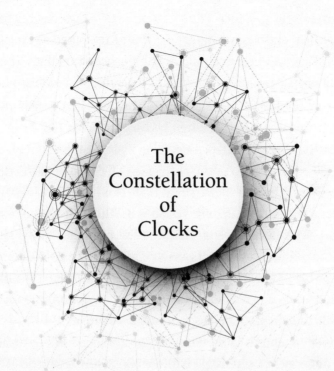

The
Constellation
of
Clocks

For today's exercise I'm made to sit up and down on the bed as Amma times me with a stopwatch. She's drawn up a chart which she's attached to a clipboard, logging my results at one-minute intervals.

I'm surprised at how easy I find the first two rounds. Already I can feel my strength building up, a buzz of adrenalin in my veins. Amma's ridiculous exercises are actually working. But after the fourth round of sitting up and down, I begin to pant and the weakness returns to my legs. I tell her I'm tired.

'Good!' Amma says. 'You must learn to cope with tiredness.'

I sigh. 'What about the pain?' I ask.

Her eyes widen. 'You are in pain?'

I scan my body, feeling an ache in my legs. There's a difference between exercise ache and pain ache, and I of all people know it.

'Yes,' I say anyway.

Amma tucks her pencil under the clip of her clipboard. 'Then we must stop,' she says.

I could tell her I'm not in any pain and therefore this whole business should stop, but I've just won a battle so I don't want to push my luck.

After Amma tucks me back into bed she pulls out the morning letters from the waist of her petticoat. As she rifles through them she tells me she's seen Mr Eccentric at the post office. She doesn't call him that but that's who she means. She then begins reading out a take-away menu for a new Chinese restaurant. This from a woman who refuses to buy takeaway food, claiming she can make any dish more flavoursome than any restaurant could. The same woman who slapped a tray of chips out of my hand when she caught you and me eating them outside Poseidon's fish and chip shop, yanking me home afterwards to demonstrate how 'real food' was made.

As Amma attempts to pronounce the various names of dishes she has no intention of ordering, I think about Mr Eccentric. I try to remember why we gave him that nickname. A hazy memory of Sandy Burke and Mrs Dickerson sitting at your dining table with an equally hazy fog of smoke surrounding their heads comes to mind.

Sandy Burke was a regular at your flat where she liked to a) talk endlessly with your mother, b) drink coffee, and c) eat all the biscuits. Although the two pretended to be best friends there was always an undercurrent of rivalry. Sandy had the loudest mouth in Bosworth House but whenever she was in front of your mother she'd be virtually yelling. Then, whenever Sandy left the flat, Jamaican hair bouncing in a fuzzy globe, your mother would release a torrent of abuse.

'Skinny cow!' she'd cry. 'She's got a mouth the size of the Millennium Dome. God help me if I don't throttle the life out of her. *God help me!*'

On that particular day they were too busy discussing the faults of other Westhill residents to be quibbling over each other's. When they came to Mr Eccentric your mother's top lip curled up, calling him a 'crazy old fart'.

'He's not crazy, Elaine,' Sandy said, as grey clouds circled them. 'He's what you'd call *eccentric*.'

Your mother released a funnel of smoke from glossy lips.

'He's off his bloody rocker is what he is.'

She pummelled the butt of her cigarette into the ashtray as though squashing a cockroach. I remember pulling my mini dictionary out of my bag and skimming the pages until I reached the letter *E*.

eccentric adj. odd, unconventional, irregular

I showed you the explanation and together we decided it was accurate. We kept on calling him Mr Eccentric even after we learnt that his name was Reginald Blake.

'So that is the news for today,' Amma says, getting to her feet.

She stuffs the envelopes and takeaway menu back into the elastic of her petticoat, then points at the tablets on my breakfast tray. I pick them up before she scoops it from my lap. I keep the tablets tucked away in my palm as she glances over at the poll card sitting on the bedside table. When she looks at me again, she squeezes her shoulders tight and lifts her brows before she leaves.

When you're in a lifebed for the majority of your day it's the little things that people look out for. I haven't even voted yet and Amma is as proud as if I've scaled Mount Kilimanjaro solo. I uncurl my hand and look down at the pills.

No pressure, then.

Mr Eccentric lived on the first floor of Tewkesbury House at the bottom of Westhill Estate but, unlike other residents, neglected to put curtains or netting in his windows. Whenever we walked by his flat on the way to the woods we could see him sitting – headmaster fashion – behind a huge oak desk, a mass of clocks mounted on each wall. Round clocks, square clocks, digital and analogue clocks; ones with pendulums, ones without; ones shaped like animals and ones that glowed in the dark. My favourite was the black cat with a dickie bow whose eyes rolled from side to side as its tail swung back and forth. Your favourite was the one shaped like a mushroom with a pensive fairy, chin perched on palm, sitting on top. Jonathan said he had no favourites but rushed home from the woods every Saturday to get a peek at the clock shaped like a raincloud on the back wall. When the hands hit midday, a grinning sun emerged from the side. The way Jonathan beamed at it you'd have thought that sun was smiling at him.

Mr Eccentric was peculiar in every way imaginable. Tall and gangly in body, he had large thick-framed glasses similar to Jonathan's, with wide green eyes behind the lenses. His clothes were caught in a 1970s business-world time warp: pastel suits with flared trousers that were far too tight at the crotch. Whenever we caught him walking up the stairs he would take two steps at a time, with long strides that threatened to rip his trousers in half.

'Twenty-two, twenty-four, twenty-six,' he muttered, joints creaking with each leap.

Most of the time Mr Eccentric kept vigil at his desk, observing the other inhabitants of Westhill through the bare window of his flat, as though they were all murderers. Two years before we were born, his son Bobby Blake had been killed in the hideout he'd built in the woods. It was a decent yet amateur build: breeze-block walls with an open entrance and window, a piece of corrugated iron for a roof. Bobby had even painted the outside camouflage-green and placed a slab at the entrance with 'BOBBY'S HIDEOUT' written across it. Inside, the floor was covered with tarpaulin, some carefully selected logs distributed in a semi-circle to form a seating area, with a metal ashtray the size of my head in the centre (this was later verified when Jonathan made me lie down beside it to compare). Opposite the logs was a wall dotted with postcards from all across the world: tree-covered mountains, towering waterfalls, desert plains with rippling waves of sand. Although the images were faded, the card curling at the edges, they were symbols of Bobby's dreams and soon became ours. We imagined ourselves climbing those mountains, running through those waterfalls, riding camels across the sand as the sun beat down upon our shoulders.

'We were made for adventure,' I said to you once.

'We were made for adventure!' you repeated theatrically, as though this was the slogan of our life.

We tried to stay clear of the hideout, not least because we thought it was haunted by Bobby's ghost. He'd been found there with a knife in his gut, blood pooling across the tarpaulin. Jonathan found it hilarious to routinely collapse on the plastic and begin moaning, zombie-style, while swinging his clawed hands at our legs. We'd scream and tell him if he didn't stop we'd never come back to Bobby's Hideout. But when the clouds darkened and the air became particularly bitter, our promises were blown away in the wind.

For us the hideout was shelter from the rain, but for Mr Eccentric it was Bobby's grave. He visited it regularly, placing flowers upon the doorstep before cutting back the weeds that circled its edges. If he ever caught us huddled inside, he'd shoo us out like unwanted birds in a cornfield, clapping his hands together and demanding we 'get gone!' Bitterness had shrivelled that man into a walking skeleton. Behind his desk he was a chilling figure, but in person he was Death.

Uncle Walter had yet to discover any of this the day he told us we were going to visit Mr Eccentric.

73

'When I was a teenager, Bobby Blake was my best friend,' he told us on the way to Tewkesbury House.

'No way,' you said as we scuttled beside his round belly.

'Yes way,' he replied. 'We built a hideout together and practised survival strategies.'

'No *way*!' you cried.

'Yes way,' he replied.

I elbowed you in the ribs before you revealed our secret and you yelped so loudly I had to elbow you again.

'Survival strategies?' Jonathan said. 'As *if*!'

Uncle Walter spun round, his hand extended in a karate chop that stopped just short of Jonathan's neck. Jonathan froze so still I thought he'd wet his pants. He sulked behind us for the rest of the journey.

As your uncle banged on the peeling paint of Mr Eccentric's front door we all shuffled to the side, hoping that the old man wouldn't slap his hands together with orders to 'get gone!' But when his lanky frame eventually appeared, he only glanced down at us once.

'What do you want?' he asked, fixing his eyes on Uncle Walter's grinning face.

Your uncle seemed confused. 'It's me, Reggie. It's Walter.'

Mr Eccentric shook his head, the wrinkles on his face flapping like the saggy skin on a basset hound.

'I know who you *are*, I'm asking you what you *want*!'

We all looked up at your uncle.

'Well . . .' His eyes tick-tocked from side to side. 'I suppose I came to say hello.'

Mr Eccentric stuck his face out into the hallway, beady eyes skimming back and forth. 'Is *she* with you?'

Uncle Walter forced a grin. His smooth cheeks bulged out like plump cherries.

'Elaine's on holiday.'

'Good riddance,' Mr Eccentric said. 'The woman's a goddamn witch!'

Uncle Walter's smile dropped. He took hold of your hand, then mine. I remember the feel of his squashy palm enveloping my fingers, each digit feeling as though it were sinking into marshmallow.

'Nice to see you, Reggie,' he said before pulling us away.

For a moment Jonathan hovered behind before running up beside us.

'Stay away from Bobby's place!' Mr Eccentric cried as we descended the stairs. 'You don't belong there. *Any of you!*'

The words echoed behind us as we left.

We should have listened, Marianne. We should have done what he said.

I'm testing my body with a series of pinches when Mr Chavda appears in my room. He doesn't seem to notice what I've been doing, striding straight in with his briefcase clutched in hand. Mr Chavda is my tutor, though he hasn't been over to teach me for nearly three weeks. I wasn't exactly heartbroken about this. His lessons are dry, often dragging on far longer than the designated hour. Amma thinks this makes his services even more of a bargain. I think it makes them torture.

Today he stands at the end of my bed, with his briefcase propped on the footboard.

'Good afternoon, Ravine,' he says, as though calling out a school register.

Mr Chavda is a short man with a bald spot surrounded by thin wisps of white hair. When he speaks, his nose turns up to the sky and his eyes droop down at the corners. His face matches the way he speaks. Long, drawn-out words that roll out of his mouth, fringed with a faint groan of disappointment. His main motto in life is that good speech costs nothing. 'A fact,' he likes to add, 'your *neighbours* could certainly benefit from.'

Mr Chavda is not a fan of our *neighbours*. Earlier, as I sat doing my window exercise, I saw him scurrying towards Bosworth House with his head held low, straightening his lapels and patting down his wispy hair as though just walking through the estate would make him scruffy. He picked his way through streams of single parents with pushchairs, men with tattoos, and teenagers walking Staffordshire bull terriers on loose leads, never looking these people in the eye, constantly jumping back in horror as he bumped into them. Each time this happened he quickly hurried on, pulling the cuff of his sleeve over his Rolex. He didn't know the number-one rule of council estates: strutting around like you own the place makes you invisible while shuffling along with wide, frightened eyes makes you instantly suspicious. You could see the visible relief in the sag of his body as he reached the entrance of Bosworth House.

Mr Chavda doesn't visit because of an altruistic need to teach the disaffected inner-city youth. Nor because I've proved to be in any way exceptional as a student (a fact that is evident from my not-so-brilliant GCSE results). Mr Chavda visits our flat for one reason and one reason only.

Love.

Mr Chavda's love story began, like all great love stories, at the cash-and-carry on Melton Road. Amma had been squabbling with a cashier over the dents in a can of chickpeas when Mr Chavda had intervened. As multilingual Hindi speakers the pair began to talk and (after finally replacing the offending can) found themselves sharing horror stories about bad customer-service experiences. Mr Chavda had gone to a restaurant with no napkins; Amma had been refused a refund on a kettle even with a valid receipt. Mr Chavda was given no compensation for a delayed train, while Amma had been left waiting in the doctor's surgery for nearly two hours without an apology.

When they met again the next week, Mr Chavda offered to carry Amma's bags to the bus stop. During their walk he wangled out of her the details of my condition and how, at the time, attending school had become so painful and tiring that I could only manage to go once a week to collect homework. Amma had tried her best to coach me through the basics of the primary curriculum, but when I moved on to secondary education, the sight of quadratic equations made her despair. My grades were flagging and she didn't know what to do. Mr Chavda, seeing his opportunity, swooped in for the kill. He was a retired teacher of mathematics and would give his services for free.

'Teaching is a reward in itself,' he told her.

A statement he's no doubt questioned since.

For as long as he's been 'teaching' me, Mr Chavda has been simultaneously courting the love of my mother. He's always probing for information about her hobbies, her favourite chocolates, whether her plans to never remarry are negotiable. His earnestness is enough to make a girl retch.

'Your mother seems particularly happy this morning,' he says to me today.

This is after approximately five minutes of teaching me the basics of probability.

'She's always happy when she's plotting,' I say.

'*Plotting?*' he asks, as though this is a new word to him.

'She's teaching me how to leave the flat,' I say.

His wispy eyebrows rise high on his forehead. 'You don't know how to do this?'

'Apparently not.'

He begins scribbling in his notebook as though I'm his patient and he's taking medical notes.

'Has she mentioned me at all recently?' he asks.

'She never mentions you,' I say.

His eyes flicker up to mine, then return to his notebook.

I know this is cruel, but the prospect of Mr Chavda as my step-father is enough to make me sabotage any of his efforts. He already nags me about my lack of *Asian-ness*, telling me I should be more reserved, more obedient like the women of my heritage (proving he knows diddly-squat about Amma). He says I'm too bold, that I'm a smart-mouth and have far too much to say about far too little. If he actually came and lived here I'd be turned into a mute.

Through the wall behind me I hear a clanking noise. I try not to flinch as Mr Chavda scrutinizes me. He keeps on looking at me for some time until I begin to wonder if he's figured it out. Maybe my cheeks are more flushed, my body less tense, but somehow he knows I'm better.

'So tell me,' he says, 'have you completed your homework?'

I feel my body sink down into my mattress.

'That depends on your definition of *"completed"*.'

He isn't amused by the comment, and begins to shake his head with the gravity of a priest at a funeral.

'Young girl, we have spoken about this.'

His eyes are wide and unblinking as he sits bolt upright. I cower under the covers, lips screwed up in an expression I hope appears sulky rather than afraid. The subject of my academic abilities is a sore point with Mr Chavda. When he offered his services to Amma he seemed quite happy to 'go back to his roots' by educating me for a short period until my recovery was complete. Unfortunately for us both, this period was not so short. He taught me right up to my GCSEs, predicting that I'd pass at least five. In the end I passed two. He's continued teaching me ever since, not just to be close to Amma, but to rectify this 'clerical error'. Subsequently, Amma has increased her donations from the occasional samosa to full-course meals: dhansaks with rotis, kormas with rice. Mr Chavda seems satisfied with the deal as any time spent with Amma balances out the time he wastes trying to teach me.

'Complete this probability table,' he says suddenly.

He flings a photocopy onto my lap with the headings 'Millipede 1, Millipede 2, Millipede 3' across the top of the paper, with illustrations of the long, winding beasts beneath. My eyes blur, unable to read the words in the question, the legs of the millipedes wiggling alive. I imagine them scuttling clear off the page as if racing to a predestined finish line, then remember, with sudden clarity, the day of our Great Discovery in the woods.

Another clanking noise comes from next door. The squatter either isn't afraid of being caught or is ignorant of the fact I can hear him. Even Mr Chavda glances up briefly before looking back at his wristwatch. Eventually he places it upon his knee, looking me square in the eye.

'How many more legs does Millipede 3 have than Millipede 1?' he asks.

I look back down at the question. The insects have multiplied, filling up the page. I look up.

'Lots?'

Mr Chavda's cheeks expand so wide I think they might pop. He closes his eyes and presses his fingers against his temples.

'Young girl,' he says through tight lips. 'Did you even *read the question?*'

I look at Mr Chavda as my jaw clenches, wondering if he knows about Amma's companion and, if he doesn't, whether I should be the one to tell him.

The Constellation of Slugs

On the morning of our Great Discovery you hit your head on the sideboard and cried out 'God!' when you'd meant to cry out 'Cod!' The rain poured down soon after and you were convinced this was caused by your blasphemy, even though Jonathan told you it was caused by strong winds travelling over the Atlantic.

We sat and watched the rain through your window. It was the thick type that comes down in sheets, hitting the pavements with such violence we felt sorry for the concrete. The sky was a deep violet that reflected off the wet pavement and steel of the handrails. If you hadn't believed you'd angered heaven, we'd have stayed in for the rest of the day and played Uno, but you were adamant we shouldn't suffer for your sin and should go out regardless.

Your brother wasn't hard to convince. He loved all types of weather and always called us sissies when we refused to go out in the rain. Amma dressed me up in four layers of clothing, a navy mackintosh, red plastic sailor's hat with matching wellingtons, and a faded black umbrella that was so big I had to drag it across the floor to carry it. I felt (and looked) ridiculous so you decided to copy my outfit to make me feel better. Your raincoat was buttercup yellow, your wellingtons poppy red and your umbrella, when pushed open, revealed the boggling eyes of a ladybird. You looked amazing, without even meaning to.

Amma gave us strict instructions to go no further than the shops, but the rain was so heavy I was sure we could sneak down to the woods undetected. We crouched behind bollards and litter bins, lacing our way to the woods only to find it was waterlogged when we got there. Huge puddles circled the trunks of trees and if we stopped moving for more than five seconds our wellies sank into the mud. We held the top of them as we pulled our feet free, nearly losing our socks on the way.

Jonathan squelched through the mud regardless, attempting to measure the size of the raindrops he'd caught in his palm with a retractable tape measure from his pocket. He stared up at the sky to check the cloud formations.

'Cumulonimbus,' he said.

He could have been speaking Swahili for all it meant to us.

Already I was starting to see the root of Amma's concerns: even through a mackintosh and four layers the damp was seeping onto my skin. I shuddered, knowing I was further from home than I'd promised. Ready to turn back, I searched for your image through the blanket of rain. When I caught sight of your hunched body it was by a tree stump, the boggling eyes of your ladybird umbrella looking back at me. It was only as I got closer that I heard you yelp.

'Oh my Cod!'

Jonathan and I looked at each other before wading to your side in a manner that would have been highly inadequate in an emergency. I looked over at Jonathan, prepared to push him in the mud so I could be the one to save you from whatever imminent danger was about to swallow you up.

But there was no danger; there were slugs.

I don't think it's an exaggeration to say the slugs were everywhere because they were. Upon the rocks, over leaves, climbing up thick, wide stumps. They were grey and glossy, slithering and squirming in all their translucent glory. Perhaps it was the rain that made them look so magnificent. Or the way they moved; so slow, so considered. Whatever it was, we weren't repulsed or frightened as we had been with the scuttling creatures from Jonathan's rock. We were charmed by this army of fat-bodied beasts and found their every movement fascinating. We picked them up and placed them on our palms, ordering Jonathan not to squish them. We prodded them with our fingers and compared their smells. We attempted to feed them moss and dead leaves, investigating their slime tracks while deciding which ones were adults and which were babies.

'Look at the size of this one,' Jonathan said, pointing to a slug so big that even he seemed reluctant to touch it.

We ran over to him, followed the direction of his finger and examined the monster glued to the base of a stump. It was the size of a chocolate bar and just as brown, with thick, wiggling tentacles and two giant balls for eyes.

The moment I saw it I felt sick. It was different from the other slugs, slimier and peculiar in shape with a humped back that made it seem even bigger than it already was. Because of its size, all its details were magnified. The gloopy gunge, the wiggling veined pattern across its body, the ribbed edge of its foot. It wasn't an endearing creature but you fell in love with it nonetheless, prying it from its chosen home and placing its chubby body on the length of your palm.

'We should call it Walter,' Jonathan said with a smirk. 'Because it's fat.'

You flashed your brother a sharp glare before looking back down at your new companion.

'I'm calling him Stanley,' you said. 'Stanley Slug.'

You stroked the slug as if it were the type of animal that enjoyed being stroked. I felt a pang of jealousy. It was ridiculous, I know. But I was young and egotistical. I thought I'd been replaced.

After a few more seconds of needless stroking you stood tall. 'Slug race at the hideout! Last one there is a giraffe!'

You ran off at such a speed that we barely had time to choose our own slugs. I picked up an orange creature, small and inoffensive, while Jonathan chose four at random. When we arrived inside the hideout you made your brother choose between them. He stuck out his bottom lip.

'Only if I can keep the others as reserves.'

He placed three on a log before naming his chosen slug Storm. I looked at the orange sheen of my minibeast and dubbed it Tangerine.

'That's wrong,' Jonathan told me. 'It hasn't got alliteration like mine and Marianne's.'

I pulled out my mini dictionary, searching for the word *alliteration*.

'*Ravine Ravine Dictionary Queen*,' I heard him mumble under his breath.

I read the definition.

'Sangerine, then,' I said, shoving the book back in my bag.

Your brother slapped his forehead. 'Shit, Ravine, that doesn't even make *sense*.'

You reprimanded Jonathan for his language. He rolled his eyes.

'Get on with it, then,' he said, as though we were keeping him from his business.

We positioned our umbrellas to form a tripod – underneath was the finishing zone – then knelt in front of a log with our slugs held between pinched fingers as we placed them on the tarpaulin. When we counted down 'three, two, one, GO!' the slugs didn't seem to know the race had started. They remained in their positions with only the occasional wiggle. Jonathan tried to flick his slug to victory but even this didn't seem to make much difference. We watched the slugs for a total of five minutes that felt like five hours, until we realized the rain had stopped.

'It's the pressure of an audience,' you said.

'Stage fright,' I agreed.

'Whatever,' Jonathan said. 'Let's go outside and race each other in the mud.'

We conducted a total of eight races, three of which I sat out to adjust my wellies and seven of which you won. On the last race I'm sure you slowed down to let Jonathan win. As he swaggered back to the hideout I restrained the urge to kick him in the shin.

When we walked through the entrance, Storm was where Jonathan had flicked him, looking decidedly shrivelled and motionless. Closer examination confirmed he was dead, a fact that didn't seem to bother your brother half as much as we thought it should. Sangerine was nowhere to be seen but, after a quick search, I followed her tracks to the large metal ashtray where I found her perched on the base. Stanley, on the other hand, was clearly on view. His big fat body was sitting smugly in the finishing zone under the tripod of our umbrellas. He was so smack bang in the centre that Jonathan contested the win. But the evidence was there in the silvery trail leading across the plastic to Stanley's gigantic frame.

'This is a shitty game, anyway,' Jonathan said, kicking one of the logs.

He didn't speak to us all the way home. The rain had begun to spit again and you balanced Stanley on your palm, trying not to let the champion invertebrate slide off. I trailed behind, Sangerine wrapped in four layers of leaves held in the ball of my hands. You told me to hurry up before Mr Eccentric came, but I knew that he never ventured out when it was raining. I was wrong.

A few days later Mr Eccentric came banging at your door. The knocking was so loud that Amma ran to our doorstep convinced that someone had come to harass her. She opened her mouth ready to hurl abuse only to find an empty landing. I stood beneath her arm, the two of us craning our necks round the doorframe to see Mr Eccentric shuffling back and forth outside your door. He was wearing a dusty blue suit with flared trousers, his ash-coloured hair combed over the bald spot on his head. He punched his hands down as he shuffled, muttering to himself in an incomprehensible fury. As soon as Uncle Walter appeared, he stood still.

'They've been at it again!' he yelled. 'Today I found slug trails all over the floor. It's sacrilege, I tell you. *Sacrilege!*'

I pulled out my dictionary as your uncle tried to soothe Mr Eccentric.

'The girls I don't blame so much, but the *boy*. If only he knew, Walter. If only he knew!'

I strained to listen but there were only mumbling noises from your uncle.

'So what if we've already talked about it?' cried Mr Eccentric. '*So what?*'

We heard Uncle Walter trying to quench Mr Eccentric's fire.

'You make deals in this life, Walter, but they get broken just as easy as they get made. Your sister taught me that!'

Mr Eccentric's body flashed past us, a haze of dusty blue.

'The goddamn witch!' he roared before disappearing.

I heard the shuffling of his feet as he hopped down the stairs two at a time.

Of course, on the day of the slug races, I didn't know what the consequences of our actions would be. Would I have avoided Bobby's Hideout if I'd known that Mr Eccentric would come banging at your door? Would I have told you both that we needed to stay home if I'd known what I was going to see that day?

It's easier to think that I'd have been a kinder, wiser person if I had been given all the facts. But really, I don't think I could have changed what happened. You were always going to run after Jonathan that day. I was always going to sulk behind, convinced that my role as best friend had been usurped. I was never going to listen to your cries to hurry up. I was always going to drop further and further behind. And what happened next, it wasn't so much destined as inevitable. The rustling of leaves behind me, my head turning towards the noise. Me catching sight of an image that would fill my nightmares from that day onwards. A dark shadow of a man looking down upon me. Raincoat swirling at the hem as he spun away. The black soles of his shoes as he ran. And his eyes that rooted me to the spot as my wellingtons sank into the mud. Bright. Yellow. Flashing straight into mine.

That was it, Marianne, that was the first time I saw the Soul-drinker.

It's been over a week and still no pain. I want to cartwheel across the rooftop, sing operatically at the top of my voice. Instead I wait for Amma to go out to the cash-and-carry and put on my stereo at full volume. I listen as trumpets blast out Stevie's 'Sir Duke', rocking my hips from side to side, working my arms in a swaying motion as he sings. As the drums speed up, my body erupts into a wild dance, limbs tossing up and down, head twisting in such a violent movement that my hair whips against my cheeks. A thud comes from upstairs. I freeze mid-twist and jump under the covers of my bed. The blood booms loudly through my ears, my cheeks burn. As I realize the thud was a warning from the people above I smooth down my hair and smile.

When Amma comes home she brings Sandy Burke in with her. Apart from Mr Chavda she's the only one who comes to see me now. Even though her voice leaves me with earache, I look forward to her visits. If I was Noah sailing through the floods, she would be the dove, twig in its beak, showing me land was nearby.

When she walks in I can see a small roll of fat protruding over her belt. Sandy used to blame her weight gain on age.

'Age,' she told me, 'is an unforgiving bastard. The older you get the more your body forgets what it's about. Your skin sags. Your sight goes. Your joints conk out like an old car engine. Before you know it your hair's turned white and your fingernails have fallen off.'

Fingernails. If this is ageing then let me stay young for ever.

Sandy opens the window as soon as she comes into my room. She smokes roll-up cigarettes because the factory-made kind always make me cough and leave a strong, chemical smell on the bed linen. When Amma comes in, the butt having already been flicked clear out of the window, she lifts her nose and sniffs for evidence. The last time Amma smelt smoke she pulled Sandy's packet of cigarettes from her pocket and confiscated them in the waistband of her petticoat.

'The girl is ill enough without your second-hand smoke!' she yelled before dragging her out by the arm.

When Sandy returned she was full of remorse, promising that she'd learnt her lesson. She looked so sincere with her deflated afro and her girls by her side that Amma let her in. But Sandy has learnt nothing other than techniques to prevent her being caught. The rollies, the window, the chewing of mints after she's finished. Maybe no one learns their lessons, just ways to skirt around them.

As soon as she's comfortable Sandy begins telling me about her new nineteen-year-old lover who works at Poseidon's fish and chip shop.

'And he's not only handy around the house, he's a wizard in the bedroom,' Sandy says as she dangles her cigarette out of the window. 'Holy mother, sometimes *I* can't even keep up with the lad.'

I try to act indifferent but can feel the burn of embarrassment sting my cheeks. Sandy talks as though I'm as sexually experienced as she is. How she expects me to be anything but virginal after a decade of confinement is beyond me. Does she imagine me sneaking in salesmen when Amma's out feeding ducks? Or canoodling with Mr Chavda during our lessons (the image of this alone could put me off sex for life)? But still, I like the fact she doesn't patronize me. Sometimes, when Sandy Burke comes over, I almost feel like an ordinary person.

'How are the girls?' I ask before she can give me any more details.

'Being little sods as usual,' she says. 'Faith's hair's cut at a wonky angle since she decided to do that *experiment*. And Hope, well she came first in her class for spellings this week.'

She looks at me expectantly as she lets the fact trickle from her lips. I 'ooh' and 'ahh' enough to wangle a smile. I remember the times I used to come first in class for spellings. It was the only thing I was ever good at.

'So Rekha says you're getting out the flat soon,' Sandy says, reaching her hand out of the window to flick her cigarette ash. I watch the embers sail away on the wind.

'Did she now?'

I can't help sounding glum. Sandy raises her eyebrows.

'She seems set on the idea.'

'I'm fine as I am,' I say.

She cocks her head back. 'Stuck in here all day?' she says. 'It must drive you loopy.'

The birds on the wallpaper begin flapping their wings as the My Little Ponies on the curtains laugh. Shiva uses one of his fingers to make a swirling action at his temple.

My body stiffens. Sandy looks away.

'You heard from Walt at all?'

Every time she visits, Sandy asks me the same question. I thought she'd given up the ghost of your uncle years ago but, even with her new wizard of a lover, she can't let him go.

I shrug. 'Not a sausage.'

I look at Sandy as she takes another drag. The tattoo of Death on the side of her neck shrivels as she sucks in. I shuffle upright in bed.

'Have you heard from . . . ?' I struggle to say her name, nodding my head towards Sandy in the hope that she'll finish off the sentence.

'Elaine?' she says. 'Or *Mrs Dickerson*, like you used to call her.'

She smiles as she says this, still hanging her hand out of the window.

'That used to drive her crazy, that did,' she says. 'She wasn't even married! But yes, I still hear from her. She sends me the odd postcard, calls me up once in a while.'

I lean back on my pillow. Even though I've asked the question, a part of me didn't want to know, a part of me didn't want to care.

'She was always so mean to Walt,' Sandy says.

When I look at her she's staring out of the window. She's gazing out across the estate, scratching her nails up and down her tattoo.

'Even when we were little she'd call him horrible names. *Idiot. Fat lump. Lard arse.* He'd just stand and take it, bless his heart. Didn't know any better, did he? Funny, because every time she calls me now she wants to know if I've heard from him. Even after everything that happened.'

She carries on staring out of the window. I watch the fumes spiral out of her mouth, her neck twisting as she turns and leans back against the frame. The way she gazes, eyelashes batting in slow movements, makes her look like a sad Frenchwoman in a black-and-white film. Eventually she turns to look at me.

'You know, you shouldn't blame him for what happened. Walt was an innocent. Really, he was.'

Sandy will talk about the various locations she's had sex with her new toy boy and how Mrs Patterson on the fourth floor is trying to get a breast reduction on the NHS, but never about what happened with Uncle Walter. I try to look quizzical as I shuffle my body up.

'What exactly *did* happen, Sandy?' I ask.

She stands up straight, rabbit eyes scanning the room as though it's filled with spy cameras and hidden microphones. She quickly stubs her cigarette on the wall outside and pulls a packet of mints out of her jacket pocket.

'Best not to go into it,' she says, pushing two squares into her mouth. 'It'll only upset you.'

Sandy is neither the sensitive nor discreet type, so I open my mouth to see if I can push it further. But as she jiggles her foot, shoulders held tight to her ears, my mouth freezes. She's uncomfortable and the only other time I've seen Sandy Burke uncomfortable was Christmas Day 1999, when she came to your flat.

'Well, I'd best be off,' Sandy says, closing the window. 'Can't keep lover boy waiting, can I?'

I shrug my shoulders, bottom lip pouting. She bends forward, prodding my nose with her finger.

'You take care of yourself, missy,' she says with a wink.

Even though the action would be more suitable for a six-year-old, it still makes me smile.

I decide to spend the rest of the day filling out book six of my bumper book of crosswords. I've certain techniques when beginning a new puzzle, searching specifically for clues that have definitions in them. These are just like dictionary definitions but in reverse.

1 across: Too great to assess (12) = INCALCULABLE

15 down: Glove with long loose wrist (8) = GAUNTLET

I scan my brain for every word I've ever looked up. If I get stuck I check in the thesaurus (it's not cheating if you still have to think about it). Clues based on specific knowledge are the hardest.

11 down: Common central spot in fish (8)

31 across: Spotted motorway leading to Yorkshire town (6)

Without becoming a fisherman or travelling to Yorkshire I have no way of figuring them out. Sometimes I just put in any word that fits (still not cheating as I'm only playing with myself).

Later, Amma comes upstairs with my dinner tray and sits down to watch the universe programme with me. As I begin eating dahl and rice I think how nice it was to see Sandy earlier. Her voice wasn't so loud as to give me a headache and when she told me about her twins swapping identities I even found myself laughing. It's surprising that sometimes our friends are just the people who stick around. This is no jibe at you, Marianne, it's just an observation.

As I bring the lentil-and-rice mixture to my mouth the professor informs us that the sun is going to explode. Not any time soon, but explode nonetheless. Just the idea of this would have caused you panic, giving you sleepless nights, started you jabbering away at me through the wall.

'Cod Almight-flea!' you'd scream. 'The sun is going to explode *any second.*'

As the professor explains this revelation I think I hear a rustling from next door. I check to see if Amma has noticed but she is so enraptured by the professor, a supernova could combust in the room and she wouldn't take her eyes from the screen. I press the back of my skull against the partition wall behind me. I think I can feel the slight tremor of movement. I wait for more but my mind must grow bored because I'm soon listening to the professor telling me about the energy of the sun.

He's kneeling down in the middle of a desert, holding a piece of cardboard with a square cut out of the middle. As he tosses back his locks, he angles the cardboard so that a small, illuminated square shines on the sand before him.

'This small square of sunlight I'm measuring has enough power to fuel the whole of the United States for a year . . .'

As the camera pulls back out, I don't look at the professor or the little square of energy on the ground but the sun shining behind him. It's bright and blinding as it hovers in the milky blue sky and I get to thinking about the feel of it. The way it warms your skin. The way it makes you tingle all over as if covered by a woolly blanket.

15 across: The star which the planets orbit (3)

12 down: The giver of life, the source of all warmth, the centre, the middle, the core (3)

As the programme comes to an end, Amma gives me her 'isn't he clever?' expression before she hoists herself out of her seat and leaves. I don't think she notices the sound of the toilet flushing next door.

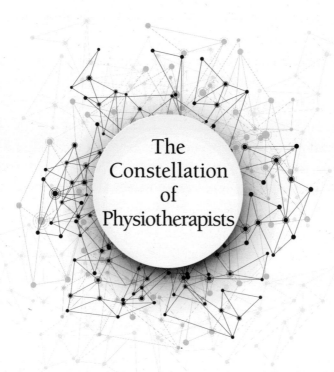

The Constellation of Physiotherapists

Today a physiotherapist comes and tortures me for an hour. He arrives forty-five minutes late and strolls into my room as though I have all the time in the world to wait for him. I do have all the time in the world but still, he doesn't know that.

He asks me the usual questions. If I've been doing my exercises, which I say I have; if I've started any new medication, which I say I haven't; whether the pain has changed or is of the same 'quality'. I tell him it's 'status quo'. He blinks at me for a second, the way people do when I use words they don't expect an eighteen-year-old girl from a council flat to use, before carrying on with his questions. How am I feeling? Am I keeping stimulated? Blah blah blah. If this man knew that he was the only male conversation I have apart from Mr Chavda, then maybe he'd offer something that isn't so bloody dull. Although some people are dull by nature. Interestingly, these people seem the happiest.

He isn't a bad-looking fellow, this physiotherapist. He's tall and broad with mahogany skin so dark and smooth it reminds me of a polished table top. His short afro hair spins in spirals across his scalp and when he gets close enough I can see the same pattern peeking through the V of his unbuttoned polo shirt. They come right up to his collarbone, those little curly hairs, and I stare at them as if hypnotized. When the physiotherapist takes hold of me, pushing my leg back and forth and twisting my ankle in all manner of movements, I can see the muscles of his arm push up against his rich mocha skin, flexing and bulging in a way that makes me blush. When he leans over me to lift my arm, I can smell the woody odour of his deodorant. I feel a tingle all over as though he's sprinkling my skin with the fine spray of his scent. I feel many things when I look at this man; physical urges you'd probably prefer not to know about.

When we were young we wanted to marry pop stars from boy bands but the idea of kissing boys made us retch. Things change as you grow older. Your body wants new things. Boys become more than a mere irritant you'd prefer didn't exist. You have desires. You have needs. You have a physiotherapist you want to grab by the buttocks and pull close to your breasts.

'You seem different this time,' the physiotherapist says, sitting down on Amma's chair. His voice is as rich as his skin, filling every inch of the room.

I frown. 'How?'

He strokes his stubbly cheek with the flat of his hand.

'Almost as though . . . that is to say, you're not *reacting* as much . . . to the pain.'

He must see the irritation flicker across my face because he begins talking rapidly.

95

'Your muscles are less tense, there's more movement in your joints,' he says. 'And you didn't groan as much as you did last time.'

There it is: the future of Ravine stretching out before me. 'You're right!' I'll cry. 'I don't feel any pain!' I'll watch the pride illuminate the physiotherapist's perfectly formed face as he explains the possible reasons for my recovery. Then he'll break the news to Amma in clear medical language she can't interrupt before he asks me on a date in the city centre. He'll coax me out into the Big World Outside, holding me by the hand. I'll fall in love with the physiotherapist, marry the physiotherapist, have babies with the physiotherapist and all will be well with the world because I'll be living a happy normal life like a happy normal person.

But of course this isn't the path I choose.

I lower my chin as he waits for my response.

'So you can feel what I'm feeling?' I say.

The physiotherapist shakes his head. 'Pain is a very personal experience. That's why people who suffer chronically from it find difficulty in—'

'*From that*,' I say, with a severity that's reminiscent of our old head teacher, 'you can suddenly know, through some method of *osmosis*, every sting, throb and *all-consuming agony* I feel each and every minute of my day?'

He drops his head and clasps his hands together. 'There's been studies that have shown . . .'

'Aaaarrrh!' I cry.

He jumps back in his seat. I admit the thrill of seeing this Herculean figure startle at my cry only spurs me on further. I begin to scream, with my head flung back and hands clasped into fists. Scream from the base of my belly to the top of my throat. Scream like a child. I must be beetroot red by the time Amma runs into the room.

'What is it? What's happened?'

I tilt my head forward to see her standing in the doorway with a dripping dishcloth in her hand. I close my mouth and take a deep breath.

'He wanted to hear my pain so I'm letting him hear it,' I say, before flopping my head back down on the pillow.

I've never dated anyone so I'm unaware of the etiquette, but I'm guessing if I'd wanted to impress this physiotherapist the screaming wasn't a brilliant move. In all the great love stories of literature and Bollywood, I can't recall a hero who was seduced by a *tantrum*.

The physiotherapist scuttles over to Amma and speaks to her with flushed cheeks that shine against his dark skin and make him even more desirable. He arranges another appointment which he doesn't even note in his diary and then collects all his equipment in a frantic rush. I try to memorize the feel of his hands on my arm so I have something to reminisce over tonight.

'She has good days and bad,' Amma says to him at the door.

Which is as untrue as a lie can get. I have the same days, over and over again. The same walls, the same bed, the same thoughts carouselling around in my head.

I hear the noise of the birds on the wallpaper squawking, the laughter of the My Little Ponies on the curtains. 'They all disappear,' I mumble as Amma leads my only chance of sexual fulfilment out of the door. 'They all disappear in the end.'

I woke up last night with the sing-song voice of your brother echoing in my skull. It called for me through the hazy blur of a dream filled with mustard eyes and giant slugs.

'*Ravine Ravine, Dictionary Queen.*'

I couldn't shake it off and my mental retort to *Jonathan-Weatherboy* didn't help much. I opened my eyes in a half-sleep and distracted myself with other thoughts: the glow of the streetlamp through the edge of the curtains, the memory of the physiotherapist's hair curling like springs on his chest.

I could still hear the faint repetition of my name. It only went away when I switched my bedside lamp on, hauled myself to a sitting position and began writing to you.

'Ravine.'

You used to whisper my name through the thin partition wall between our rooms, shout it whenever the bell rang for playtime, call it from the top of trees as we played hide-and-seek.

'Raaaviiiiinne!'

It's not a real name. You won't know this because you were used to it, the same way you were used to wearing luminous shorts under your skirts and hearing random weather forecasts from your brother. But you won't find anyone else with this name because Amma chose it at random. In fact, she chose it from a newspaper.

It was on the front page the day I was born.

YOUNG MAN DROWNS IN RAVINE

You'd think the tragic subject matter would have caught Amma's attention rather than that six-letter word hovering at the end of the line, but we all know Amma has her own logic. She'd never heard of this word 'ravine' before and upon sounding it out, took it as her own. It sounded neither Hindu nor English which, considering Amma's history, suited her just fine.

To understand my mother you have to understand her past, a story she has drip-fed me over years, mainly during the worst stages of my illness because this was the only time I wouldn't butt in. Sometimes

I think her life sounds more like scenes from a soap opera than real events, every incident another episode.

Episode One – A Village Scene in Bangladesh

Amma's story began the day her parents sent her to England, aged seventeen, to marry a man she didn't know. Within their small Sylheti community there were growing fears that their once-obedient daughter was Frankensteining into an unstoppable 'individual'. The eldest of six daughters, Amma had become such an unruly character that they were convinced no respectable Bengali man would go within a ten-metre radius of the girl, let alone marry her. She tucked the skirt of her shalwar kameez into her trouser bottoms when racing other children (earning her the nickname Baggy Bum Rekha). She swam in the local river with a plastic bag over her hair. She wanted to attend university and gain a professional qualification. This plan was so outlandish for a daughter of a shopkeeper born into a low and humble caste that her parents began to think her mentally unstable. They were positively dancing when the passport photos they'd sent to relatives in England struck gold. A businessman, fifteen years Amma's senior, was so desperate to marry and create heirs to his empire that he agreed not only to pay for Amma's flight but also to accept no dowry.

Episode Two – Arrival in Strange Lands

My mother lived with her husband (a man she regularly called 'the fool') for a total of seven months. His empire turned out to be a small factory tucked in the backstreets of Leicester, its sole purpose being the production of imitation Rubik's Cubes (aka Roobix Blocks). The puzzle was a hit at the time and his knock-off goods made him enough money to buy a three-bed house in the suburbs. At first Amma had been impressed, not only with the house but also with her new husband, who proved to be polite and courteous and not the great oaf she'd expected. But his best qualities were also his worst. He had lofty ideas and a desperate need to please, a combination that proved an expensive mix. He'd routinely buy Amma red tulips, unaware that such gestures were wasted on a woman who hated things that had no practical use. Then, when she called him a fool for repeating the act, his eyes welled up.

'He always had this face,' Amma told me, 'as though he would cry at any second. No wonder no English woman would marry him! But it was a deceiving face, Ravine, to make me think him innocent when really he was nothing but a toerag runaway.'

Episode Three – The Strange Disappearance of Roobix Man

My father vanished ghost-fashion three days before Amma discovered me in her womb. It was the scenario every wife fears: my father left the house in the morning to get some milk and never returned. Despite being ruffled by his vanishing, she was free! A woman in her own right in the land of the religiously liberal and morally ambiguous! And with a three-bed semi to boot!

However, my father had left for a reason.

The popularity of Roobix Blocks had dwindled dramatically and, in his panic, he'd gambled away all of his assets. My father was so deeply embroiled in the gambling world that he was being hunted down by a gang of muscle-bound loan sharks. Within a matter of weeks my mother was abandoned, pregnant, homeless and penniless in a country that was not her own.

Episode Four – The Aftermath

Amma was never one for convention but being a Bengali single mother in pre-millennium Britain wasn't easy. She had no money to buy herself a ticket home and my grandparents conveniently didn't answer any of her calls. With no other choice Amma took action. She secured herself a series of small cleaning jobs, taught herself English through scattered overheard conversations, while at the same time handling the day-to-day racism and sexism that was (she tells me) commonplace at the time. With the help of a translator to fill in the forms, she got herself a council flat along with a little extra money from the government to subsidize her pitiful wage. The money was there to help her until she qualified for a better job and I was old enough to snap up a swanky graduate position.

Amma tells me that the world is exploding with opportunities. She says that it's never been so good for Asian women: educated at the top universities, taking senior positions in business and politics. She never had those opportunities and I can't enjoy any of them. Or won't enjoy any of them. Because of this, I am Amma's biggest disappointment.

Episode Five – . . . ?

The truth is I am Episode Five. I am the new storyline in Amma's saga and with my addition the whole production has come to a halt. She wants to direct the rest of the story. She's been setting the scene for the denouement (cut to folded piece of paper pushed into ballot box) but it doesn't matter how many plans she makes, how many new exercises she gives me because I am the lead and I am refusing to turn up to set.

Amma gave me the name Ravine to break from her past. She wanted me to be something different, something *new*. But it plagues me, this name, because I can never live up to it. Everything is the same for me now. Besides, I don't want to be different. I don't want to be the Ravine girl stuck in her flat with chronic pain syndrome. I don't want to be the Ravine Ravine Dictionary Queen your brother sang about. I don't want to hear that same song whirling around in my dreams and then hear that name being called through the partition wall of my room when I wake up.

'*Ravine?*'

I can hear it so clearly. Then again.

'*Ravine?*'

It's like a ghost calling for me from the afterlife. But once I've blinked myself awake, my eyes adjusting to the blankness, the voice has gone. I begin to feel that it's happened, I've become (as you used to say) 'doolally'. When I look over at Shiva, he looks at me with sorrowful eyes that seem to agree.

When I wake up, Amma's face is hovering over mine.

'And how are you today, shona?' she asks.

Without even letting me answer, she begins to feel my forehead with the back of her hand.

'You look pale,' she says.

I'm about to tell her that I haven't slept. That I've been hearing voices calling my name. That guilt is obviously eating me up and it's time to tell her the truth. But she carries on before I can speak.

'I suppose screaming at the physiotherapist has tired you out.'

She pulls out the junk mail from her petticoat.

'I didn't scream,' I say.

She sits down on her chair. 'Yes. You did.'

'It was part of the therapy. You know, "primal scream" and all that.'

She looks at me from the top of her eyes with an 'oh please' expression.

'It's a real thing,' I say.

Amma carries on looking at me, ripping an envelope open as she holds my gaze. 'He was shaking when he left,' she says.

When she tells me this I feel the same hurt that I used to feel when you took Jonathan's side all the times I was clearly in the right. I was embarrassed and ashamed, but most of all, I was irritated.

I dig a finger in my chest. 'I was shaking too,' I say.

This seems to pique Amma's interest. She places the mail on her lap. 'And why was that?'

I drop my hand as I try to stop my chin from trembling. The irritation is being overridden by the embarrassment and shame.

'Can we not talk about this?' I say.

She pauses, nodding slowly. 'Then what would you like to talk about, shona?' she says.

I think about this for a second. It's hard keeping all the emotions in. I've built a dam up around me but clearly the walls are starting to crack. I look into Amma's eyes, deciding if I should do it. If I should tell her the truth.

'Nothing,' I say.

When she leaves the room Amma's shoulders are stooped. I feel hollow, like she has scooped out a part of me and taken it with her. When I hear her rustling around in the kitchen I creep out of bed and kneel slowly before the statue of Shiva. There must be an answer to all this, a solution to make everyone happy that doesn't involve me leaving the flat and facing the Big World Outside. A solution that doesn't leave Amma disappointed.

I press my palms together and close my eyes.

'Dear Shiva,' I say, and then realize I'm not writing a letter. 'O great and mighty one,' I say, which feels forced and stupid. 'God . . . ?'

I drop my hands and open my eyes to see Shiva giggling into one of his many hands. I roll my eyes, wondering why Amma didn't teach me some pujas when I was younger.

I used to think that all immigrants were as lax with religion as Amma, but the Ahmed children went to the madrasa every day after school. Some nights we could hear their father doing his namaz through the walls and one time, Amma saw the family go crazy when a dog began sniffing at their shoes when they passed it on the stairs. Mr Chavda is a strict Hindu and attends the city temple daily, while the Singhs, who went to our school and wore more Western clothes than you could fit into a shopping centre, carry out fasts during the holy days, eating only nuts and fruit, drinking only water and milk. Once, when you were ill and not at school, the young boy Singh brought in a huge drum he'd used at the Vaisakhi parade to show off in assembly. He banged it so loudly that everyone was sure he'd be told off and applauded when he wasn't.

Since her childhood in Bangladesh, Amma has refused to take part in any rituals. Yes, she keeps pictures of the gods around the flat as tokens of nostalgia and yes, she gets binoculars out at Diwali, searching for the Melton Road fireworks from the fourth-floor balcony.

'But I will never,' she tells me, 'become a slave to the dogmas of religion and tradition!'

She said I could choose what I wanted to believe for myself. I wish she'd decided for me. How am I to know if going to church on Sundays, fasting during Ramadan, lighting divas for Diwali pleases God or *enrages Him*?

Or Her.

Or It.

Sometimes all you want is just one answer.

I look at the statue of Shiva again and my stomach begins to cramp. He's looking smugly at me now, as though godliness is oh so easy, oh so effortless. Then I hear footsteps coming up the stairs.

'Do you want a chai, shona?' Amma calls.

I turn Shiva to face the wall then leap back into bed.

'I'm fine,' I say in a loud I'M-BUSY voice.

I pull the sheets up to my chin as her steps retreat, imagining what she would have thought if she'd caught me knelt in front of Shiva. Or, even worse, if she'd caught me jumping back in bed; no shaking, no wincing, no pain.

The Buddhists believe that life is suffering. I read this in a library book once. I thought that with its calm and meditative approach to life Buddhism might be the religion for me, but after reading that statement found myself slamming the book shut and throwing it on the floor. I didn't want life to be suffering. I was suffering enough already and the idea of it never ending was enough to make me scream. But maybe the Buddhists are right.

Life is suffering.

Life is a struggle.

Life is crisis after crisis thrown straight at your unenlightened head.

The Constellation of Rabbit Heads

Uncle Walter was a successful man, though we weren't to know this until the unlikely detective duo of Amma and Sandy Burke decided to investigate. Sandy came banging on our door one morning with her twin girls buckled into their car seat carriers. She balanced them one on each arm like a set of scales, asking Amma outright if she knew what was 'going off' in the flat next door now that Elaine had gone. To her own annoyance, Amma found she knew nothing. She called me to the door and tried to wheedle information out of me by pinching my cheeks and making me stare into her eyes. After intense interrogation she found I knew as much as her.

Sandy jiggled the carriers on her arms as the girls began to whine. The balls of her eyes protruded from her shrunken face as she shook her head and clicked her tongue. This was in Sandy's beanpole days when she was made more out of bone than of flesh.

'Can we *trust* him? That's all I want to know,' she said. 'You know, what with his problems?'

Amma's eyes widened. 'Problems?'

Sandy let the question hang in the air then stuck her chin out. 'Not my place to say,' she said.

Amma looked down at me with narrowed eyes, placing her hand on my scalp as though checking – through some subtle vibration – for the truth.

'Ravine, can this Walter fellow be trusted?' she asked.

I shrugged my shoulders.

'Suppose,' I said.

Amma dropped her hand instantly and rushed to the kitchen. When she came back she had a tub of leftover lentils in her hand.

'This will not do,' she muttered to herself as she stepped outside and rapped her knuckles against your front door.

Even though I usually let myself into your flat, Amma wouldn't let me go in until Uncle Walter opened up the door. When he did, Amma shoved her offering into his chest, which Uncle Walter accepted with so much enthusiasm you'd think he'd been starving for the last week. We remained fixed on the spot until he finally began to nod.

'Come in, come in!' he said. 'I was just about to put the kettle on.'

Sandy Burke pushed past the two of us and made her way to the same dining table she used to sit at with your mother. She placed the girls by her feet and began rocking their carriers with the toes of her trainers, leaning back in the chair as though it, and the whole flat, belonged to her.

You were sitting at the table yourself with a chessboard in front of you while your brother read a meteorology book on the sofa. You seemed unfazed by the sudden appearance of Sandy and it wasn't until I came and sat next to you that you snapped out of your gaze.

'I think I've nearly cracked it, Ravine,' you said, then lowered your head as you pressed a finger on each temple, staring down at the pieces.

You'd won the chessboard in the school raffle that summer. All prizes had been donated by parents and checked by teachers (bottles of vodka and old pin-up calendars withdrawn), which had left a dubious yield. Out of a bounty of one-eyed dolls and broken toy cars, the chessboard had been one of the superior items and, even though the box was battered, two pawns and the instructions were missing, you still treasured the game as if it were brand new. But without instructions we were lost. We didn't know where the pieces went, how many moves you were allowed or even what the different pieces did. Uncle Walter knew the names of the pieces but nothing else, while Jonathan claimed to know the rules but refused to teach us them because 'any fool could figure it out'. We'd been trying to do exactly that for the last month.

As you tried to communicate with the knight via some form of telepathy, Amma began her investigation. She sat up straight, bangles clanking against the table top as she folded her arms. Her questions were swift and direct. Where had Uncle Walter been living previously? Where did he work? How long was he planning to stay? I watched this back-and-forth for some time, perplexed by the things adults wanted to know about each other. The only question we'd asked Uncle Walter was how many stars he thought were in the galaxy and even then he wasn't able to give us a solid figure.

At last you connected with the chess piece. You sat up straight, picked up the queen and balanced her on top of the knight as though recreating the act of horse riding.

'No, no,' you mumbled as the queen fell off. 'That can't be it.'

I pushed the pawns around the board in a fashion I thought fitting, hoping Jonathan wouldn't get up from the sofa to look at how we were screwing up this foolproof game. He remained indifferent, his book fixed in front of his face, two swirling images of clouds peering out from the cover like a pair of spinning eyes.

We kept our heads low as Amma continued her Q&A, managing to maintain the appearance of not listening. This is an art mastered by the young, achieved solely by the adult habit of forgetting you exist. My mother hurled an arsenal of questions at your uncle while he responded without aggression or force but with a steady smile and the pure charm and grace of a diplomat. He had no reason to be polite to this nosey neighbour and for this I'm grateful to him. If my mother is anything she's fair; when your uncle treated her with respect she saw no reason but to treat him the same.

Sandy Burke was a harder nut to crack. She leant back in her seat, looking at Uncle Walter through the slit of her eyes as though he were a suspect in a murder investigation. As she rocked her twins with her toes, Tony Blair's eyes flashed up on the back of the carriers. The more she rocked, the more the bumper stickers were revealed. *New Labour. New Britain.* I pictured people in orange overalls labouring away at British coastlines.

'So, Westhill is good enough for you now?' Sandy asked.

There was spite in her tone as she sat, arms folded in a python grip around her chest. Your uncle, on the other hand, grinned so heartily that his round double chin shone like glazed doughnuts.

'It's like coming home,' he said.

'It *is* your home!' Sandy snapped. 'Or at least it would have been if it hadn't been for your stupid cow of a mother, God rest her soul.'

Her chin wrinkled even with the 'God rest'. She leant in close to Uncle Walter.

'I know where you've been all this time, Walt. Elaine told me everything.'

Uncle Walter's face began to flush. 'Everything?' he said.

Sandy shrugged. 'Sure,' she said, in an offhand way that seemed to relieve him.

I looked over at you as you continued to stare at your chess pieces. I checked your face to see if you were absorbing all this vital information. But your attention was fixed on the wooden objects, your eyes not shifting one millimetre.

I looked back and watched Sandy Burke shove an escaped dummy into the mouth of one of her twins.

'What have you been up to, anyway?' she asked. 'How come you never came back?'

Uncle Walter looked up at the ceiling. 'Well,' he said, 'I guess it all began at army camp.'

Sandy stopped rocking the carriers. 'Army?' she said, cocking her neck back. '*You?*'

Uncle Walter smiled. He had, so he told the panel, been working in the army for the past six years, based in a camp in Italy. This was where he'd perfected his survival strategies and had picked up the nuances of the Italian language. Since leaving he had written a book on the knowledge he'd obtained and was currently negotiating deals with both British and Italian publishers. He was hoping the book would be released in early March 2000. We were all dumbstruck.

We'd heard Uncle Walter speaking in quick-tongued dialogue on the telephone, gesticulating with his hands up in the air as he spoke in a language we thought was made up. We only found out it was Italian when you asked him outright. After that you attempted to copy his gestures whenever he spoke it, repeating the words in a fumbled, bumpy manner. The only foreign phrases you'd known before then were '*jaldi*', which my mother used when hurrying us up, as well as '*c'est la vie*', which you said when the mood suited you, even though you weren't 100 per cent sure of its meaning. At the time we hadn't thought much of the fact your uncle had this bilingual talent – we never realized it was an *asset*. My mother knew Bengali and Hindi, and that had never seemed to help her. But your uncle's bilingualism combined with his expertise in survival strategies had brought him success. By the end of the conversation, Amma was looking down at her bowl of leftover lentils with sudden remorse.

'I have made a mistake,' she said, pulling the Tupperware to her chest. 'I have brought you the wrong tub.'

She looked over at me with large eyes made all the wider by the black kohl liner she used to circle the edge of her lids.

'Ravine, shona, go fetch me the lamb biryani from the pot in the kitchen.'

She moved her head forward in goat-butting movements as though this would hurry me on. I put my pawns down, knowing full well that the biryani she'd made that morning had been intended for lunch and dinner that day. If she gave our food away now maybe we'd have something *without* chillies in it later.

'It's just like when we were younger,' said Sandy, arms loosening. 'You and Bobby always messing around building trenches. Trying to camouflage that shed of yours.'

'Hideout,' you corrected.

Uncle Walter looked down at you before you quickly began moving chess pieces around the board.

'You remember that?' he asked.

'Of course!' Sandy said. 'The two of you were glued at the hip. He was always so mardy, though, that Bobby. Took everything so *serious*. Him and all his plans.'

When I looked at Uncle Walter his chin had dimpled, eyes glazed with a sudden wetness. Sandy shook her head.

'Who would have thought it would actually *lead to something*, though?'

Your uncle released a small laugh as he rubbed his eyes, at which point Sandy, remembering her cynicism, wound her arms back into a vice grip.

'*Ravine*,' Amma hissed as she poked me in the side.

As I slid off my chair, you slid off your own and followed me. Jonathan temporarily emerged from behind his book. He snorted loudly at our inability to do the smallest task without each other.

'You coming, Jonathan?' you asked.

'I'd rather eat my own snot.'

I glanced over at Amma, who had never been shy in reprimanding your brother, even in front of Mrs Dickerson, but she was too busy grinning manically at your uncle to notice the comment. As we left the flat I found myself smiling too. I'm sorry to break it to you, but Amma wasn't the biggest fan of your mother. Yes, she acted civilly to her in passing but within the privacy of our living room her true feelings came out. Mrs Dickerson was an 'irresponsible fool'. Mrs Dickerson was an 'egomaniac'. Mrs Dickerson was an '*alcoholic*'. I looked up all these words in my mini dictionary and found none of them were complimentary.

But things were different with your uncle. That day in the kitchen, my mother's neck was straight, every betel nut-stained tooth on display, as she sat in the glow of your uncle's success. She was not being civil when she smiled at Uncle Walter, she was being adoring. And that was a miracle in itself.

The bunny-killing spree began in the summer of 2007 in the hutches and back gardens of Ruhr Valley, Germany. Rabbit bodies were found stretched out on lawns, drained of blood and beheaded. At first the murders were put down to a rogue fox or large dog. But after the numbers of deaths increased, it was clear that the killings were caused by human hands. Satanists, experts speculated, using Google Earth images to identify their targets.

The murders caused a panic throughout the city, rabbit owners withdrawing pets from outside and heightening security measures. Many other Germans were alarmed by the massacre, fearing where the killer might move next. As for me, I remained indifferent until the day Amma decided to update me about the matter over a curried-lentil breakfast.

'Fussel was just three years old when he met his horrifying fate,' she read from the newspaper spread over her lap. 'The pet rabbit was snatched from his cage in the western German Ruhr Valley along with his sister Marianne. Both were decapitated and bled dry. Their lifeless bodies were left behind for their distraught owners to discover the next morning.'

If I'd been using a fork, I would have dropped it. Instead, blobs of yellow dripped from my hand and splashed back into the dish as Amma, oblivious to my shock, continued to scan the newspaper for more horrifying news.

The rabbit had been called Marianne, a ridiculous but true fact that had disturbed me to the point of making me tremble. It had been years since I'd heard the sound of your name, never in connection with such barbaric acts. My mind began reconnecting history like pieces of a broken jigsaw, cramming them together whether the picture matched or not. The day you disappeared in December 1999 you'd fled the country, gone into hiding in the form of a German rabbit, found sanctuary with a kind-hearted buck named Fussel who agreed to be your replacement brother, living a happy, carroty life together. Then, one night you'd been pulled from your refuge and

113

slaughtered by a satanist. Fussel had sunk his bunny teeth into the ankle of the perpetrator but he too had his head chopped clear off his body.

I blame repeated viewings of *Watership Down* for my imaginative reworking. Although technically a children's cartoon about bunnies it was the most brutal and realistic film we'd ever been exposed to. As I imagined heads being ripped from fluffy bodies, I comforted myself with the image of your black, rabbit-shaped soul bouncing over the hills as Art Garfunkel sang 'Bright Eyes'.

But even Garfunkel couldn't stop the nightmares that night. Bunny heads lying across my bedroom carpet and rolling around the sheets. Blood from their severed necks seeping into the white of the bed linen as their large, black eyes stared out at the wall.

Stop! you yell. *Enough with the decapitation and blood!*

I mention this all for a reason.

This morning I had the same dream about decapitated rabbits' heads, except this time there were also cats. Not decapitated but full-bodied ones lying on their sides with knives stabbed into their guts. Around them the birds in the wallpaper were squawking and flapping their wings. Their flapping was so vigorous they looked ready to attack the corpses, every beat of their wings promising the possibility of escape from their paper prisons. It was only when I woke up, the noise of them still ringing in my ears, that I knew to dismiss it as a nightmare. But then a memory of Sandy Burke made me realize that the dead cats were not completely plucked from the ether.

Memories pretend to leave you but they're always there. Always ready to catch you off guard, to remind you that life is never as simple as what you happen to be dealing with at the time.

There is always the past, waiting to pounce.

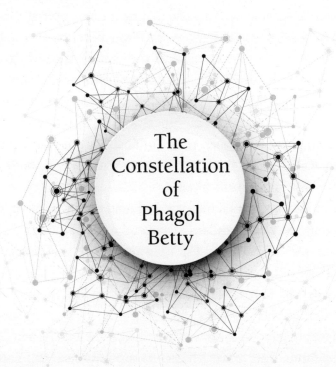

The Constellation of Phagol Betty

It took us a while to realize Sandy Burke was smitten with your uncle. She had a strange method of courtship that involved being snide and distant whenever Uncle Walter was in her presence. It was only on the day of the stabbing that we realized the truth.

To teach us survival strategies, Uncle Walter had been pretending to be a bear in your living room. Since we'd discovered he was a survival expert he'd taught us the basics of how to escape killer bees and what to do when lost in the desert.

For our lesson about bears we'd moved all the furniture to make him a den and put on our hunting gear, which consisted of fishing hats and green poster-paint smeared over our cheeks as camouflage (Amma had screamed when she saw me later, mistaking me for a goblin). We'd crouched behind the coffee table as your uncle pretended to be asleep, scratching his belly and itching his nose with the back of his hand as he held a jar of honey in his arms. Whenever we crept up to his cave, he began to toss and turn with a loud grumble, making us jump back and return to the safety of the coffee table. Then, when we got close enough to reach out for the honey, your uncle would wake up and roar with such viciousness that we instantly fled, holding on to our hats as we squealed like animals caught in a snare.

'No, no, *nooo!*' he said in alarm. 'You don't run away from the bear unless you want it to run after you.'

'But it's so *hard* not to run away,' you said from behind the coffee table.

'It's *instinct*,' I added.

Your uncle shook his head. 'Do you want me to chase after you?'

We both agreed that we didn't.

'Then you need to lie down and be still. Remember, *lie down and be still*.'

When we attempted the reconstruction again, I was the first one to scream and run. Your uncle chased us around the living room in large, plodding steps. He scooped us up by the waist, dangling us upside down as he roared, 'LIE DOWN AND BE STILL!' We could feel the rumble of his chest as he bellowed, quickly repeating the words 'LIE DOWN AND BE STILL!' until eventually he released our chuckling bodies and returned to his makeshift cave to begin the whole process again.

It was during this bear-hunting activity that Sandy Burke came knocking at the door. Jonathan, who had confined himself to his room because of 'all the stupid racket', emerged with a smug grin.

'Oi, *bear*, are you going to answer that door or what?'

Uncle Walter uncurled himself from his sleeping position.

'All right, Mr Grumpy Pants,' he said, before hauling himself to his feet and making his way through the living room.

It always took a long time for Uncle Walter to walk anywhere, not just because of his weight but because of the unfortunate angle of his head, which meant he could see very little in front of him. When he walked it was belly first, legs, then head. It was as though each body part was testing a different layer of the room, checking for any items he might trip, bump or knock into. By the time he made it to the door Sandy Burke was banging it like a drum, but Uncle Walter still looked through the spy hole. He'd been tricked by Bradley Patterson and his bicycle goons one time too often, opening the door to have them hurl abuse at him before running off in hysterics.

'Fat bastard!' they'd cry. 'Marshmallow Man! *Flabber jabber*!'

When Uncle Walter eventually inched the door open, Sandy was quick to push her way through, balancing the twins in her arms as they lay in their carriers.

'Did you hear?' she cried, voice gasping. 'Did you hear about the stabbing?'

Each strand of her afro bounced up like exclamation marks on her head. Mascara had stained her sunken cheeks with grey trickle marks and her skeletal body was shivering so forcibly we could hear the chattering of her teeth. She looked at the chaos of our living room and temporarily broke out of her panic.

'What the hell are you doing?' she said, as Uncle Walter walked past her and pulled the overturned sofa back into place.

Sandy shoved one carrier into your arms and the other into mine, and didn't wait for an answer as she sat on the sofa and blubbed. We placed the babies on the floor and rocked them back and forth as we crouched down in front of them. They were round and plump as tomatoes, dressed in a ridiculous pale pink, floral headbands placed over their wispy hair. But even the cherubic faces of the twins could not distract us from Sandy's disturbing news. It had been she who

117

had found the body stretched out behind the rubbish bins, a kitchen knife punched into the belly.

'I was just walking to the shops when I saw it,' she said, wiping her nose on her sleeve. 'Just to get some milk, that's all I wanted. I wasn't expecting it. I know it's rough round here but no one expects to see *that*. Right there in front of me, a furry black tail sticking out from the bins.'

It took us a moment to compute.

'An animal?' Jonathan said. 'Is that all?'

Sandy Burke's shrivelled neck whipped to the side as she eyeballed Jonathan.

'Animals are people too,' she said with a mild hiss. 'I thought your mother would have taught you that.'

Jonathan opened his mouth to object but Sandy produced a look so vicious that he snapped it closed again. Sandy Burke was the only person who could shut your brother up. I never knew if it was because of your mother's friendship with her or because of the tattoo of Death on the side of her neck.

'It gives him the willies,' you told me once, sticking your palm out for the handshake of secrecy. I would have given anything to have rubbed the fact in his face but when I shook your hand the secret was locked away.

As Uncle Walter brought over a box of tissues and patted Sandy Burke on her bony shoulder we listened intently, waiting for the gruesome details.

'It was a cat. A black and white tabby. Poor little sod. I can't stop thinking about it, Walt. What if they go after my cats next? What if they don't stop there? You know this is how serial killers start, with small animals? It could be the twins next. Lord knows, it could be any of us.'

Despite Jonathan's blasé attitude, you and I were petrified by this news. We'd never known anyone to be murdered before, and the fact

118

that a cat was the victim made little difference. As Sandy sobbed into your uncle's chest, you looked over at me with genuine worry.

'What if they go after Stanley?'

I rolled my eyes. I wasn't worried about that disgusting fat slug but the yellow eyes of the Soul-drinker. I didn't tell you at the time but I was convinced he was the culprit. He had begun his spree of soul-catching and I was the only one who knew.

We waited for Sandy to give us more information but as she clung on to your uncle her thoughts seemed to wander.

'I don't know if I can take it, Walt,' she said, squeezing her arms around the mounds of flesh that made his belly. 'This is just like what happened to Bobby.'

She began rubbing her hands all over your uncle's torso. His back stiffened, his face flushing raspberry red as he glanced over at us.

'We shouldn't talk about that,' he said. 'It'll only get you upset.'

She looked up at him with blinking eyes.

'But I can't help it, Walt. It was done in the exact same way, wasn't it? Knife to the gut.'

To demonstrate, Sandy clenched her fist and punched it into her lower abdomen. I watched as her hand bounced back up, imaginary blood spurting across the room.

Uncle Walter began to squirm, the folds of his body jiggling up and down.

'We shouldn't be saying this in front of the kids,' he said, nodding towards us.

Considering the fact your uncle had told us about the electrocution of his own mother, we were surprised by this statement and opened our mouths to protest.

'You're right,' Sandy said. 'Why don't you kiddies go to Jonathan's room and play with the girls, eh?'

Jonathan scowled. 'Why my room?' he asked.

Sandy raised her chin, the hooded image stretching tall along her neck. When we got into Jonathan's room he flopped on his bed and crossed his arms.

'Stupid cow,' he murmured. 'Who does she think she is?'

At first we heard very little from the living room and were quite happy to play with the twins. Even Jonathan got involved as we swapped their headbands and asked him to guess who was who. Eventually we swapped so many accessories that nobody could identify them. We began calling out their names, as if they were puppies, seeing if they would respond.

'Hooope . . . Faaaith.'

They were as confused as we were and it was only when we heard the yelling that we tore our attention away from their lopsided bows.

'Typical! Bloody *typical*!' Sandy cried.

We heard her flat feet marching across the living-room floor. There was a mumble from Uncle Walter followed by a grunting noise from Sandy.

'When *are* you going to be ready? I'm a woman, Walt. I have needs . . . And to think I've been trying to defend you!'

We crept back downstairs, placed the twins in the hallway and got down on our knees. Crawling to the living-room door we prised it open and arranged our heads along the gap. As we peeked through, we saw Uncle Walter sitting on the sofa with the top few buttons of his shirt undone, his hair ruffled into a bird's nest. Sandy was leant over him, the zip of her hoodie pulled down to reveal a fuchsia push-up bra beneath. She dropped her voice and began pointing at him.

'There's been rumours, Walt. You'd be stupid to think there wouldn't be. Louisa Cartwright came up to me the other day and told me she had full intention of calling the social services about Elaine running off like that. She said you shouldn't be allowed to look after the kids, what with your problems.'

Uncle Walter began shaking his head. Sandy pressed her finger in her chest.

'You know what I did, Walt? I *lied*. I said she hadn't run off, was just on holiday while you took care of the kids. I said she'd told the council all about it, that it was all legit, and the stories she'd heard about you weren't true anyway.'

Uncle Walter was now muttering under his breath, eyes blinking like a flickering computer screen on overload. Sandy gripped her hipbones.

'And why did I lie, Walt? For myself? For that two-faced cow of a sister of yours? *No bloody way!* It was for your sake. For *you*. Lord knows, I wish I hadn't bothered now!'

Sandy tossed her head back before getting to her feet and charging towards the totem pole of our eyes.

'Sorry, kiddies,' she said as she pushed the door open, toppling our bodies to the floor. 'Apparently I'm not welcome here.'

She began muttering to herself as she grabbed hold of the two carriers. As she stood tall I could see that the New Labour bumper stickers once plastered across the back of the carriers had been ripped off, leaving a trail of teeth-shaped paper remains glued to the blue plastic.

'Not *ready*?' she cried back at the living room. 'You've never been bloody ready for anything *in your life*, Walter Dickerson!'

She slammed the door behind her, making the banister in the hallway shake. We looked at each other then ran into the living room.

'What the flip happened?' you said, then froze at the sight of your uncle sitting on the sofa with his head in his hands.

He was rocking back and forth, wet patches circling his shirt.

When we got closer we could see beads of sweat all over his clammy skin and hear rapid muttering.

'*But I didn't mean to . . . You can't do that . . . You can't!*'

'Uncle Walter?' you said.

He carried on rocking.

'*Don't say that. No, please, no!*'

'Uncle Walter?' you said again, voice getting high.

He only seemed to become more panicked, his skin freckling with white spots. Suddenly his hands were punching at his gut the same way Sandy had punched at hers.

'*Bobby, no! Bobby——*'

'HEY, WALT!'

Jonathan's voice roared so loudly it made us all jump, including Uncle Walter. His head snapped up, his whole body sitting upright as though jabbed in the back. His eyes searched wildly around the room, swimming round his sockets like fish pulled out of the water.

'Uncle Walter?' you said for a third time, but he didn't seem to hear. He wasn't mumbling any more but his eyes were still searching.

You turned to look at me. Your tanned forehead crinkled with worry.

'What's wrong with him?' you asked.

I looked over at Jonathan, eyes wide behind his glasses. I hoped he might know what to do, but he only looked back at me with a shrug. I stepped forward, knelt down on the floor and grabbed your uncle's hands.

'Remember your survival strategies,' I said, squeezing deep into his palms.

Uncle Walter's eyes focused. I could see ripples of brown weaving through the emerald of his irises as his pupils locked on to mine. He squeezed my hands back, then sucked in a deep breath.

'Survival,' he said, inhaling deeply. 'Survival.'

'Yes, yes,' you said, kneeling down beside me. 'Remember your survival strategies!'

Uncle Walter carried on sucking as though he'd come up for air from a deep-sea dive. Beside me I felt Jonathan crouching down on the floor with us. He didn't say anything but the blood drained out of his fingers as he gripped on to his knees.

Uncle Walter let go of my hands and flopped back on the sofa. He sat there panting for a while but when he looked up, his eyes were no longer searching. He pulled out a handkerchief from his pocket and began patting his wet skin.

'It's OK,' he said. 'Everything's OK now.'

We carried on looking at him sceptically. He cracked a small smile.

'Thanks, kids,' he said. 'I don't know what I'd do without you.'

Amma comes into my room with her 'I know everything' smile. She seems different somehow and it isn't until she pats the bun at the nape of her neck that I realize the white streaks that normally flow in waves down her scalp have been replaced with the matt darkness of burnt wood. It isn't flattering, this dyed hair; in fact, it emphasizes Amma's wrinkles. Suddenly her skin is saggy, her eyes less vibrant against this mock-colour that is so fake it makes her look as if she's wearing a wig.

'Why have you gone and done that?' I ask.

Amma's smugness is replaced with a stern surprise that makes her chin stretch low, cheeks hollowing in.

'I never taught you to be *rude*, Ravine,' she says with a coolness that instantly shushes me.

Amma rarely gets cross with me and as soon as I see her expression I know I've overstepped the line. I sit quietly as she reads me the junk mail and say nothing about the black stains on the tips of her ears.

123

The only other time I've seen Amma look that severe was when I decided I didn't want to be your friend any more. You won't know about this because Amma got to me before I said anything, but if I'm unearthing our past I'll have to tell you everything.

Slugs and all.

Ever since your victory at Bobby's Hideout you'd kept Stanley Slug in a large jam jar lined with leaves and twigs. He sat proudly in the corner of your bedroom while I had to keep Sangerine III in an old biscuit tin, holes punched in the top, beneath my bed. I was afraid that Amma might find her and, thinking her a pest, squash my breed slug underneath the sole of her white trainer. I'd already lost two slugs and couldn't face losing a third.

The first Sangerine went missing in action after one of our slug races was interrupted by Jonathan falling backwards off a log and hitting his head. He sobbed all the way back to Bosworth House as though his brain was spilling out. When Amma told him he had a graze that required no stitches, he demanded that his head be wrapped in layer upon layer of bandages. By the time we returned to the hideout, Stanley was once again sitting proudly in the finishing zone of our umbrella tripod. Sangerine, on the other hand, was nowhere to be seen.

Sangerine II had a less mysterious departure. We'd decided to have a picnic in the woods and, while you were sensible and kept Stanley tucked away under the safety of a jam-jar lid, I'd opened my biscuit tin with the idea of giving Sangerine II some fresh air. As we were halfway through eating marmalade sandwiches and salt-'n'-vinegar crisps, a crow – so large it was big enough to eat *me* – flew down by the biscuit tin and gobbled Sangerine in one. The swiftness of its landing, the quick peck and tilting back of its feathered neck before it flitted off into the trees, was enough evidence for me that the crow had circled our innocent picnic and planned its attack beforehand. You can't trust anyone, not even the birds.

Sangerine III was found beneath the soggy bottom of a drinks carton and was so small and grey you could have mistaken her for a wood-louse. I had an affinity with small things but on reflection it would have been wiser to pick a gigantic creature somewhere close to Stanley's size so that it would at least have had a *chance* of winning. As it was, your slug had a four-centimetre head start before we'd even said 'GO!'

It was that winter, upon noticing Stanley was distinctly slimmer than usual, that you became convinced he'd caught a cold. You wrapped an old scarf around his jar and dropped cough sweets inside until you realized he was beginning to turn the same plum purple as the loz-enges. You had to use tweezers to pull them out of the jar, trying your best not to stab the fat creature in its bulbous sides. You loved that slug like it was a baby; it was ridiculous. And, with the feelings of a first child, I resented the attention you gave it because it meant there was less attention for me.

When your birthday came I decided I'd punish you for your lack of attention by giving you none in return. I sat on the sofa in my pyja-mas and, when Amma told me it was time to get dressed in my whipped-cream party dress, I refused to budge.

'I'm not Marianne's friend any more,' I said.

Amma's cheek twitched. If she'd been a different type of parent she would have picked me up and thwacked me across the backside. She let the brutality of her glare smack me instead.

'Give me one good reason why this is the case,' she said.

I crossed my arms. 'You wouldn't understand.'

'One good reason!'

It's a credit to you that Amma didn't, for one second, consider you the cause of our break-up. Girls of our age were constantly falling out but you were made of sturdier stuff and my mother knew it. As she looked down at me I frantically began to consider my reasons. Amma knew nothing about our races in the woods but even if she had, I could never admit that I was jealous of a slug. So instead I sighed dramatically.

'It's *confidential*,' I said.

Amma placed her hands on her hips, the folds of her sari billowing in and out. Behind her the birds on the wallpaper were frozen in mid-flap as they sat between repeat-print thistles. When she eventually spoke, Amma's voice was low and growling.

'You only have one life, Ravine,' she told me. 'And you don't know how long people will stay in it. They can disappear. Poof! Out of the air!' She spread her fingers out to demonstrate the 'poof'.

It took years for me to realize how right she was. I thought you'd stick around for ever. I thought our friendship was guaranteed. Then, one day you were gone. Poof! Out of the air.

Amma bent over me with piercing eyes.

'If you do things, you do them with good reason. Give me your reason to be a bad friend to Marianne or go put on that dress and eat birthday cake!'

Suffice to say, I went and put the dress on.

Later, when we were playing Twister in your living room, Jonathan sitting with bandages still wrapped around his 'injury', I forgot about my reasons for not wanting to be your friend. We laughed and drank cherry pop as we watched *Pokémon: The First Movie*. Not once did you mention Stanley.

After this morning's hair-dyeing debacle I don't hear very much from Amma. A faint rustling of material filters through the hallway along with the smell of vinegar and lemon as she buffs her trainers. When she comes back an hour later she's dressed in a new sari covered in elaborate paisley swirls. Amma hasn't bought a new sari for ten years and I have to admit, the yellows and purples look dazzling against the sparkling white of her trainers and her newly dyed hair. She has kohl pencilled around her eyelids, a purse clasped in her hand and her mackintosh draped over her arm. Even though it isn't a cash-and-carry day or feed the ducks day or doctor day, I don't ask her where she's going or tell her how good she looks.

'I don't feel well,' I say instead.

Her face twitches with alarm, wrinkles rippling, eyes blinking. I regret the words instantly, though not enough to take them back.

'Is it the pain?' she asks.

I tense my body, grimacing the way I used to on the worst days. I nod.

'Out of ten?'

I keep my body tight.

'Eight and a half.'

She instantly drops her bag and throws her mackintosh on the chair.

'Don't worry, my dear shona,' she tells me, feeling my forehead with the back of her hand. 'I shall get a cold flannel.'

As my muscles relax, I feel a weight in my stomach as though it's filling with rocks. Downstairs I hear Amma muttering to herself. She paces up and down the hallway before picking up the phone.

'No, no,' I hear her say. 'I shall take care of her. We can meet another time.'

The wallpaper birds look at me with beady eyes. They know all my secrets, see all my lies. They laugh at me, scorn me, judge and hate me.

I lie flat on the bed and close my eyes. Do I feel guilty? Yes. Am I expecting the pain to come back twice as hard for the lie I've just told? Yes. But more than that I feel relieved. You only have one life, Marianne, and you don't know how long people will stay in it. I plan to cling on to my mother for as long as my strength will let me.

She's the only person I've got left.

Before the illness, Amma and I had a ritual. On Fridays, after a busy day of cleaning other people's toilets, she would sit on the sofa with feet outstretched and I would treat her like she was the great Maharani of Westhill. I would bring her fruits and biscuits, putting them on flowery plates before spreading them out on our coffee table. The table, bought in a clearance sale, was far too fancy for us: thick legs with curved feet, elaborate carvings in the drawers and edging. It looked ridiculous in our small, mediocre living room. But on the nights when I set out her mini banquet, Amma would look at that table like it was a piece of art.

'This is most splendid,' she'd say in her most regal maharani voice.

After spoiling her for approximately half an hour, she'd let me come and sit on her lap so we could watch game shows together. It's only now when I look back on it that I realize how, on those nights, Amma only ever ate the fruits on the table, leaving all the biscuits for me.

'Ravine.'

The voice comes hissing through the wall. At first I pretend it's the kettle boiling, or the pipes rattling, but then it comes again.

'Raviiine.'

My body stiffens. It's the same voice that woke me from my sleep, the same sing-song tune that made me think I was going crazy.

'Here it is,' says Amma as she strolls into the room. She places the cold flannel straight on my forehead and squeezes her body tight beside me. With the feel of her warm cushion of a body squashing into mine I relax but still the voice bounces around my head.

I inhale the scent of Amma's perfume. The whiff of rose and incense is so strong my vision blurs and for a moment I feel the sting of fresh tears in my eyes.

'Have I told you about the time that I ran barefoot over a snake?' she says as she strokes the back of my head.

I blink the tears from my eyes and, even though she's told me this tale so often I could recite it, I shake my head.

'It was back in Sylhet in the dried-up reservoir by the village shops,' she says. 'It was so dry that just walking on it covered your clothes in red dust, but we raced all the same. I was a good racer, a lot better than those loudmouth neighbours of mine, and a lot of the other children were jealous. Jealousy is an evil thing, Ravine; make sure it never takes hold of you.'

I think of Stanley, your scarf wrapped around his jam-jar home.

'They would tease me, the other children,' Amma says, 'because I tucked my shalwar kameez into the waist of my trouser bottoms.'

'Baggy Bum Rekha,' I mutter.

My mother clicks her tongue at the memory. She adjusts the pillows around her, sinking in their fatness as she tells me how the children jeered at her right through the first two races. Still she went on, qualifying for the next race and then the next, until it came to the end of the day and there was only her and two other boys left. They combed their greased hair and congratulated themselves on their excellent running abilities as Amma carried out her stretches. Workmen arriving home were circling the edge of the reservoir. They sat down with legs crossed and lungis tucked behind their ankles, drinking chai as though watching a cricket match. When Amma looked up to see her father watching from the crowd, she began to feel the pressure. His grim face had an expression that said: *how will my wayward daughter disgrace me this time?*

129

The two other finalists continued to mock Amma as they stood at the starting line. They pulled at the long plait dangling from the back of her head, laughed loudly in her ear as they ran around her, swapping sides and stepping on her toes. But my mother was steadfast in her focus. She looked straight ahead to the end of the reservoir, ignoring the smell of mangoes and bhelpuri as street vendors saw their chance to feed the ever-developing crowd. She held her racing pose even as the girls giggled, telling each other how foolish she looked. But when the starting cry beckoned, Amma was ready, pounding her feet into the red dust.

Even with her speedy start, the boys were quick to catch up. No matter how fast she pummelled her feet she couldn't regain her lead, and as they neared the end of the reservoir and the crowd cheered louder and louder she thought she was done for.

That was when she saw the snake.

'No grass snake, I tell you,' Amma says. 'It was a *naja kaouthia*. Pale and poisonous with a long body, lying across the dust in front of us.'

One of the boys screamed when he saw it, stopping dead in his tracks before running in the opposite direction. The other boy looked back at him in confusion, continuing to run until he too saw the long body lying across his path. Amma could feel the boy looking over at her in panic but she wasn't stopping for any creature, man or beast. As her last opponent fled back in defeat, my mother's foot trod on the body of the serpent. It jumped and contorted, but her ankles were too quick for its venomous fangs as she continued her run to victory.

'What did it feel like?' I ask as Amma sits erect on the bed, the pride rippling across her face even after all these decades.

She contemplates this for a moment. 'Squishy,' she says.

'And your father?'

She exhales loudly. 'He thought I had spooked the boys with some kind of voodoo,' she says. 'Even when the others told him about the snake, he said I was phagol for running over it.'

'Phagol,' I repeat, a smile creeping to my lips.

'Crazy,' my mother says.

'I know,' I say, nudging her in the hip. 'You used to call me that all the time.'

My mother smiles as she pats me on the cheek.

Some of the villagers thought that she was crazy too; others that she was blessed. To step on a snake and not be bitten was truly the act of a god or at least (for the Muslim contingent) the hallowed-by-God. She was treated with both reverence and fear from that day forth and became famous throughout all the neighbouring villages.

'Your father had even heard the story,' Amma tells me. 'When I told him about it he said they had nicknamed me at his school as *the crazy Bengali girl who ran over a snake.*'

Again she grins, the title hanging round her neck like a medal.

I repeat the words my mother used to chastise me with. 'Phagol betty,' I say.

Loosely translated as *'crazy woman'*.

Amma looks down at me with raised eyebrows. After I developed a distinct disinterest in my mother tongue, Amma too found she used the language less and less. At first, when her companion came to visit, she spoke very little Bengali but as time has passed she's eased back into it. There's a fluidity in her voice that she's unable to conjure in English; a speed far more suited to her character. When I hear her speak Bengali it's akin to watching someone swim in water after trying to trudge through mud for thirty miles. A part of me is happy to see the sudden freedom of her tongue, while another part of me is afraid that it will swim off, along with her body, all the way back to the land of her birth.

I can see Amma is encouraged by my simple use of 'phagol betty'. Her eyes twinkle in the light of the bedroom lamp and soon she's singing the Bengali national anthem.

She told me the translation once.

My golden Bengal, I like you lots and lots . . .

I listen to the softness of her singing and, remembering the squatter next door can hear us as clearly as I could hear him hissing my name, I begin to join in. As my eyes blink slowly to sleep, I wonder if he's covering his head with a pillow.

Your brother was never a fan of my singing.

The Constellation of Sandwiches

After Uncle Walter arrived at Bosworth House the two of you became much cleaner. Not that you'd been filthy before, but things had changed from when Mrs Dickerson was in charge. On days when Amma combed my hair into elaborate plaits that weaved over and behind my head, yours remained so wild and unkempt that spiders could have lived in there. Jonathan often came to school in the same clothes he'd worn all week, large splash stains multiplying with each day. On PE days you both had to pull stinking items out of the spare-kit box – mismatching plimsolls, shirts so big they covered your knees – because Mrs Dickerson never washed your own. When Uncle Walter came, your clothes began to match, your faces were scrubbed clean, you handed homework in on time and had your reading records signed every day. On parents' evening Mrs Jenkins leant in to talk to Uncle Walter with such enthusiasm it looked like she might grab him round the neck and kiss him.

Yet this wasn't enough for Jonathan. At the time I thought he was being a brat, but on reflection I suppose it was his mother's absence that made him such a miserable sod. He never smiled at Uncle Walter, never laughed at his jokes. When your uncle made up elaborate names for meals – Penguin Stew, Butterfly Salad, Unicorn Stroganoff – Jonathan would shove them away, saying no name was going to stop them looking weird or smelling funny. Sometimes he was out-and-out spiteful, 'accidentally' drenching your uncle's favourite recipe book with sticky cola, pulling a chair away as he was about to sit down. But I'd also seen his fingers clinging to his knees the day Uncle Walter had an attack, and once caught him peering over the top of his weather book as your uncle taught us how to survive killer bees. His hatred of Uncle Walter was as put on as his insistence on blood and guts in our emergency-room games. Or at least I thought so until the incident with the sandwich.

Jonathan came over to my flat that morning particularly disgruntled. Uncle Walter was teaching you Italian and Jonathan had found the drone of foreign words unbearable. When Amma opened the door, he wore his sulking expression with his bottom lip sticking out, arms knotted at the very top of his chest.

'*Raviiine!*' Amma cried at a volume that was completely unnecessary as I was standing right behind her.

She'd grown edgy during that time due to a string of heavy-breathing nuisance phone calls. We suspected Bradley Patterson, but without evidence Amma was growing fraught. She'd gone so far as to place a foghorn next to the phone.

'I don't want Ravine,' your brother was quick to interject.

I felt a small stabbing pain as he said that, but I didn't let it show. Jonathan lifted his chin as he looked at Amma.

'I want chilli powder.'

Amma put her hands on top of each other neatly, placing them on her midriff with a look you never want to be given by my mother. Jonathan gulped, the muscles bobbing up and down his throat.

'I mean, can I have some chilli powder, please, Mrs Roy?'

Amma lifted her chin but only a fraction. 'What for, young man?'

'I'm doing an experiment and I need hot chilli powder,' he told her. 'The *really* hot stuff. You know, the one that makes us all choke like we're about to die.'

I could tell Amma was reluctant because she didn't move from her position for a good few seconds. But after nights of disturbed sleep from nuisance calls, she soon caved in and walked into the kitchen. She measured out a teaspoon of chilli powder (far more than anybody could need) then delivered it to Jonathan in a sandwich bag. The vibrant orange of the powder shone through the plastic. He stood, holding it to the light as though examining a precious jewel.

'Can I watch your experiment?' I asked, following Jonathan back to your flat.

'No.'

'Why?'

'Because you'll ruin it.'

His response shouldn't have fazed me – it would have been stranger if he'd said I *could* watch – yet his words still stung. While Jonathan slunk off to the kitchen, I followed the noise of indecipherable chatter and sat down heavily beside you and your uncle in the living room.

'*Bagno*,' you were saying over and over again. '*Bagno, bagno, bagno.*'

You were using what you thought was an Italian accent but was actually more akin to Welsh; mouth moving in an elastic fashion, eyes so wide they looked ready to pop.

'What does "*bagno*" mean?' I asked.

'Bathroom,' you said, before widening your eyes again. '*Bagno, bagno.*'

Jonathan began rattling things in the kitchen but we were more interested in the way Uncle Walter was showing us how to position the tip of our tongues on the roof of our mouths. All three of us sat there with fleshy veins of tongue-undersides on display as Jonathan strolled up to the sofa with a saucer in his hands.

'I made you a sandwich,' he said, looking at Uncle Walter.

There was a trio of clicks as our tongues flopped back into place. Uncle Walter pressed a finger into his own chest.

'*Me?*'

Jonathan nodded so firmly that his glasses nearly dropped off his face. As he stepped forward, a smell saturated the air. It was strong and so spicy it made our eyes water. Soon you started to choke, placing a cushion over your face to stifle the fumes. I don't know if Jonathan had used all the chilli powder but the orange smudges pressed into the surface of the white bread indicated he hadn't been sparing. There wasn't even a piece of lettuce to prove this was a genuine food offering. Jonathan was serving a chilli sandwich and he wanted your uncle to know it.

And of course your uncle knew it. Anyone with a sense of smell would have known it. Yet he said nothing. He took the plate, picking up the orange spotted slices between his fingers and turning them back and forth in his hand.

'Smells good,' he said, nodding as though this was actually true.

'I made it myself,' Jonathan said. 'It'd be rude not to eat it.'

'Jonathan Dickerson,' your muffled voice came from behind the pillow.

You let your eyes hover over the edge but they immediately welled up with the chilli fumes and you had to pull them back down again.

Jonathan scowled. 'Mind your own beeswax, Marianne.'

I opened my mouth.

'That includes you, *Dictionary Queen*.'

He yanked an imaginary zip across his lips with the same swiftness as someone drawing an imaginary knife across their neck. I closed my mouth.

'Don't get cross, Jonathan,' your uncle said. 'It really looks great. Thanks a lot.'

I covered my mouth, not because of the chilli smell (which I was used to) but because I knew what Uncle Walter was about to do. Your brother looked confused because he also knew what your uncle was about to do and it hadn't been what he'd expected. Your eyes were buried in the cushion, but just as he brought the sandwich to his lips, Uncle Walter looked over at your no-good brother, tilted his head and gave him a wink.

The bite was big. Uncle Walter's thick square teeth sank into the bread and tore away at it in a way that caused panic even in Jonathan's eyes. When he began to chew I squeezed my hands even tighter over my mouth, anticipating the heat of the burning inferno in his mouth.

'Ummmm,' he said, jaw working up and down. 'Not bad.' He swallowed his mouthful and stuck the remainder of the sandwich out to your brother. 'Want a bite?'

Your brother looked down at that sandwich with clenched fists. Red blemishes bloomed across his neck like deadly flowers. There was more heat in his anger than any amount of chilli powder could serve.

'You're a bloody fat shit and I hate you!' he cried before storming up to his bedroom.

You lifted your head immediately from behind the cushion.

'Jonathan Dickerson!'

You ran after him, pausing at the bottom of the steps to look at us. 'He didn't mean it,' you said.

'YES I DID!' Jonathan screamed.

As you ran upstairs, Uncle Walter sighed, placing the remainder of the chilli sandwich on the table. I watched him pull a handkerchief from his breast pocket and decided that years of survival training had obviously served him well. They must have deadened his taste buds the day he signed up to the army or built up his resistance to spice by feeding him whole chillies. As I opened my mouth to ask him if there were any other foods he was resistant to, Uncle Walter dabbed his forehead and looked me in the eye.

'You couldn't get me a glass of milk, Ravine?' he said, eyes bloodshot. 'I'm not feeling so good.'

He's come back. The voice I thought was in my dreams, the chants of 'Ravine Ravine Dictionary Queen'. It was all your brother.

Jonathan-Weatherboy has come back to torment me.

I've resurrected his ghost. For years I tried to forget you and now that I'm remembering, your idiot brother has turned up. I've summoned the characters of our childhood just by writing to you. Yet still, I keep going. Maybe the more I write the more chance there is of you reappearing in my life.

I heard a rustling noise this morning and just the knowledge that this rustling was coming from Jonathan set my head in a spin. What was he rustling? Why was he rustling it so loudly? Was it for my benefit? To finally drive me crazy?

When Amma comes up with my curried breakfast, I can barely look her in the eye.

'How are you feeling out of ten?' she asks.

I try to calculate a number that's both believable and non-alarming.

'Six,' I say.

Her eyes widen a fraction.

'Five and a half?' I say.

Her lids relax.

Lies follow lies. And the worst of it is you can almost convince yourself that you're doing the right thing, protecting your nearest and dearest from everything they can't handle. But all the while there's a twisting of your inner organs, the feeling of bile rising up to your tongue.

Amma cups my face gently. 'You are such a brave girl,' she says.

I feel my cheeks grow hot. Next door, I imagine your brother keeling over with laughter.

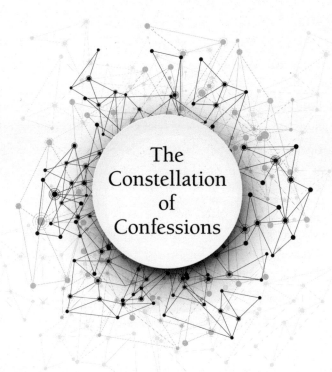

The Constellation of Confessions

It's time I confessed.

There are lots of things in my life that I probably shouldn't have done, one of which is writing our life down for you. It's made me remember everything with an intense vividness that's left my eyes sore, my head aching. And now Jonathan's next door and all I can think of are the things I've done wrong. The things that make me ashamed.

Confession number one: I was once so cross with your brother I gave him a sweet that I'd found on the landing. It had pieces of fluff, grime and remnants of Mrs Simmons' dirty bird water on it but I just wiped off the disgusting parts and handed it straight to him. He was ill for two days afterwards.

Confession number two: I'm a murderer.

Don't disagree, you don't know the whole story yet.

I had motive. I had intent. All I didn't have was the guts to tell you at the time. Which is why I need to tell you now.

It happened the day Stanley recovered from his cold. He was ready to race again and you were excited, swinging your legs as you sat on my bed, heels banging against the sides. Stanley was in his jam jar, which sat on your lap as you watched him slither and gunk all over the leaves inside. The light shone through his fat brown body, making him glow like a fresh dog turd. As I set up a game of chess on the carpet you gave him a pep talk.

'You can do it, Stanley,' you muttered. 'I believe in you.'

When I'd placed the pieces in the random order of my liking, you made me promise we'd go for a race after one game.

'Because he's mentally prepared now,' you said, 'and if we leave it too long he might forget everything and I'll have to say it all over again, and if I say it all over again that will mean waiting even longer, and if we wait any longer . . .'

I rolled my eyes. 'OK, OK!' I said. 'But we have to finish *one whole game.*'

Unfortunately for me we grew bored after two minutes.

'Come on, then!' you said, grabbing Stanley's jar and racing to the door.

'Wait!'

You froze, legs spread apart, one hand clasped on the door handle as the other hugged Stanley's jar. I didn't know what I was going to say, though I knew I'd had enough of this slug-racing business. Losing each race, losing a handful of marbles every time you won, but, most of all, losing your undivided attention. You had read that a slug could live up to fifteen years in captivity. *Fifteen years.* I couldn't wait that long. It was simple. I wanted you back and I wanted Stanley gone, and (like Amma and the snake) I was so focused on the goal I didn't stop to think about the consequences.

As you hovered at the door, I asked you, in what I believed was a sceptical doctor-like manner, if you knew for sure that Stanley was better. You looked down at your jar and nodded.

'A hundred per cent better,' you said.

I frowned, rubbing my chin with the tips of my fingers.

'But is he *a hundred and ten per cent* better?'

You looked at me confused because, even though you weren't the best at maths, you knew this wasn't a regular percentage. I began packing up the chess pieces with a casual air.

'I just happen to know something that can make him *a hundred and ten per cent* better, is all.'

You gasped. '*A hundred and ten per cent?*'

I looked up from my chess pieces. 'For definite.'

Your hand slowly relaxed its grip from the door. You looked down at Stanley and considered the worth of 100 per cent compared to 110 per cent before craning your head towards me.

'What is it?'

I continued to look you in the eyes. 'Salt,' I said.

It was an evil thing to do, I knew it even then. But there was a thrill running through my veins fuelled by nothing more than my own selfishness and a part of me that wanted to test you.

You believed my salt lie with enthusiasm. You asked me where we had some and I strolled out of my room, down the staircase and straight to the spice rack by the kitchen sink. The salt was kept in a cellophane bag tied in a knot at the top and was the same salt I'd seen Amma using on the slugs that invaded her window boxes. I watched her, Marianne. I witnessed the whole procedure. I knew full well what would happen to Stanley that day.

You brought the beast into the kitchen and placed his jar on the table. You were wearing a summer dress with daisies on it, and when you sat down the skirt pushed right up to your waist revealing the bright green of your shorts. I stood by the sink with the bag of salt in my hand and watched as you swung your feet back and forth beneath the table. You looked over at me and smiled.

'Maybe he'll be even *quicker*,' you said. 'Then we could enter him into the Slug Racing Championships.'

I nodded my head, not questioning if there was such a thing, and watched as you unscrewed the lid of the jam jar and scooped Stanley's fat body out with both hands. He seemed bigger than ever, his thick jelly body sliding from your wrist to the top of your peach palm. I didn't want to see his wiggling tentacles, that huge hunched back of his, so I angled my face away.

'Come on, Ravine,' you said with a backwards nod of your head. 'Strike when the ironing board's hot!'

Your whole face grinned. I didn't even try to correct you.

It was at this point that I had a realization. With your hazel eyes shining at me, I saw my scheme for what it was. I realized what was about to happen and, more than that, I knew it to be wicked. Amma had been right all along: you didn't need priests and temples to teach you morals, you needed a conscience.

'Marianne . . . ?' I began as I stepped forward.

'Quick,' you said. 'Before he slides off.'

You were rolling your hands in front of each other to catch Stanley as he glided forward. You had such urgency in your voice that I felt driven to make a decision. The problem came when I looked down at him. He was so repulsive; I couldn't understand why you loved him so much. His thick slimy body, those patterned indents covering his strange skin, his large foot covering your palms in filth. I looked down at Stanley, curled my top lip and opened the bag.

Admittedly, pouring out the whole contents of the bag was not such a good idea. I was imitating Amma, tipping white piles over each culprit in her box, swift and merciless, without thought or feeling.

For a moment there appeared to be more salt than slug and you looked up at me with your wide grin, eyes squishing into thin slits as your cheeks took over your face.

Then he began squirming.

My skin became so hot that I thought I'd caught a fever. My knees shook as my entire body prepared to collapse with the evil I'd just committed. When Stanley squirmed, it was in jerky violent movements that made the smile drop from your face and your eyes widen so I could see the whites around your irises.

'What's wrong?' you asked.

I didn't answer. I was too consumed by the sight of Stanley's trunk beginning to shrivel, as though the very life of him was being sucked out. For a second I thought I could hear him screaming, tiny slug lungs releasing a small weak cry. You stood up, chair dropping behind you, as you raised his body to your ear.

'We have to give him CPR,' you said.

I looked at you with a blankness you couldn't compute.

'Don't you want to know what CPR is, Ravine?'

I didn't reply and it was then I think you knew. I stood rigid as Stanley's body slipped from your hands and onto the floor. Our heads dropped as he dropped, looking down to watch him die on the kitchen linoleum.

I don't know what I'd expected but it wasn't this. As his body ceased to move, his giant mass collapsed in on itself and dried into a brown blob. I looked up, searching for any glimmer of a reaction from your face. Your head remained down. All I could see were curls of your hair and slumped daisies on your dress.

'I think I'll go to your room now,' you said.

So now you know. I killed Stanley. I murdered your slug.

Later that day, I stood outside my room, convinced that I'd lost you. I pressed my ear to the wood of my door, waiting for you to smash chess pieces against the walls. I didn't hear you crying but, when you came out, the rims of your eyes were raw and your tanned cheeks as shiny as a plastic doll's. You sniffed and wiped your nose on the back of your hand, gulping tiny shots of air that made your shoulders jump. I could already feel my chin trembling, eyes blinking quickly to stop the wetness spilling over. I balled my fists inside my oversized jumper and prepared to stick my head under the collar as if I were a tortoise.

You stood in the doorway staring at me. Your expression was empty, as though asleep, and when you blinked the movement was so mindless it was hard to tell if you could see me at all. Eventually you shrugged.

'*C'est la vie*,' you said.

At first I thought I'd heard wrong, that I was only hearing what I wanted to hear. But as I looked at you I saw there was no anger or bitterness in your teary eyes, but a simple acceptance. I'll never forget the feeling when you forgave me. It felt like falling off a cliff. I could feel myself dropping, hurtling to the ground, the wind rushing past my body, the panic seizing me by the throat. But then, as I prepared myself for the pain, I was scooped up to safety by the wings of a dove.

You were the dove, Marianne. You saved me.

You never told anyone about what I did to Stanley. When people asked, you said he'd suffered a tragic case of slug influenza.

'I had to stay by his jam jar all night, patting his brow and feeding him fresh leaves. Like Florence Nightingale with the soldiers in that war. At the end, when he started turning blue, he looked up at me and smiled. It was like he was saying, *"Thanks, Marianne, you've been a really awesome nurse, but now it's time for me to go."'*

Uncle Walter let you wear black for the rest of the week. Even Jonathan was sympathetic. He'd always thought Stanley was 'just a dumb slug' but after his death never said this to your face. When we had the slug burial in the woods with the shoe box, spinach leaves and speeches, he only rolled his eyes once.

Yet somehow Jonathan knew the truth. When you told people your slug influenza story he looked at me sideways through his glasses, studying my expression so carefully that I had to look at the floor. When you were particularly down and I wrapped my arm around your shoulder or gave you all my black Jelly Babies because they were your favourite, he'd stare at me with a look that said, 'Stop making a fool of yourself. You wanted him gone.'

But I didn't care by then. After that day in the kitchen, all I cared about was protecting you. I had seen evil now, felt it in my blood, and would never let it near you again. I tried to be a comfort to you even when it made Jonathan suspicious, even when it made me a hypocrite and a fool. And you let me comfort you, which is more than I ever deserved.

When I look out of the window this morning, the buds on the tree-top outside, once fat and round, have uncurled into emerald leaves. They're dotted along the branches like handprints across a mural, light flashing in sparks along the edges. When Amma comes up with her tray of curried potatoes I eat the whole lot without complaint and even make some noises of interest when she reads a menu for a new Indian restaurant.

Her eyes narrow.

'Never as good as home-made, of course,' she says, before moving on to the bills.

In the past, the attacks of severe pain have not only lasted days but have taken me days to recover from. So Amma looks at me sceptically when I tell her I'm feeling better.

'Four out of ten for pain,' I say. 'Maybe less.'

After much fussing, administering pain relief and testing my temperature, she decides to venture out to the cash-and-carry. I wave her goodbye, pulling out my crossword book to begin a new page.

It isn't that I think I'm forgiven; what I did to Stanley was unacceptable. But having written it down, having confessed to what actually happened, I can't help but feel the lightness on my neck as the albatross is lifted (*The Rime of the Ancient Mariner* was my GCSE text, a poem Mr Chavda stated was 'beyond my comprehension'. Ha!).

But enough of that. I have to tell you about Jonathan.

After Amma leaves for the cash-and-carry I begin to get into a flow with my bumper book of crosswords. Sometimes when this happens I can complete a whole puzzle in less than ten minutes. The letters criss-cross in front of my eyes and for a second I reach my own personal moment of Zen and all is one. I'm in one of these moments, scrawling the letters down wildly on the page, when I hear Jonathan's voice through the wall.

'Ravine,' it says. 'Can you (*mumble*) me?'

I sit with my pen poised over the squares. He speaks louder the next time.

'I know you can hear me, Ravine!' he says.

I can hear the exasperation in his voice. The same 'for goodness' sake' tone he used when we were children. But your brother's no longer a child; he's a twenty-year-old man. When I remember him back then I see a messy-haired, pale-faced brat with glasses three times too big for his face. When I think of him now I see the same brat, but taller. It's irrational, I know, but in the same way that you'll never age in my mind, neither will he.

I can hear a few more mumbles but his voice is low. I reach for the empty glass beside my bed and place it against the wall with my ear on the base. I catch the odd word (give, never, now) until suddenly his voice is loud again, as though he's right up against the wall.

'All I want to do is talk to you!' he says.

I don't reply, putting the glass down and trying my best to read the next clue on the list. He begins tapping the wall.

'Ravine!' he shouts. 'I'm not kidding about!'

I roll my eyes. As if he, the great grouch of Westhill, was ever known for *kidding about*.

The tapping gets louder, faster in pace. The thudding in my chest joins in with the beat. I grow irritated. He's ruining my good day. Already I've lost the flow with my crosswords and I'm beginning to get a headache. He was always a ruiner, your brother. Always finding ways of spoiling, wrecking, destroying. He thinks he can still do this. He thinks he can push me around like I'm still a little girl.

I look over at Shiva, dancing his cosmic dance of creation and destruction. I think how fitting it would be for me to pick him up by the waist and hurl him through the wall so that he'd smash through the partition and crush Jonathan's skull.

The noise stops.

'*RAVINE!*' Jonathan shouts. '*RAVINE!*'

I drop my pen as he screams my name. It's so loud that I duck down and bury my head beneath the covers, hoping if I stay under – plugging my ears with my fingers – I will never hear that voice again.

'Go away,' I mumble into the mattress. 'Go away, go away, *go away*!'

He stops screaming. I bite my lip, hoping he hasn't heard.

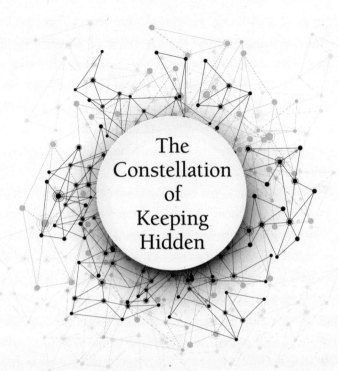

The Constellation of Keeping Hidden

Amma has her companion over again today. It's been so long since his last visit that at first I think the gasman has come to check the meter. Soon the familiar rumble of his voice rises to my room.

'*Bala asini?*' he says, standing in the hallway.

'Fine, fine,' Amma replies, ushering him quickly into the living room.

Last night, when Amma came home from feeding ducks I heard her speaking on the telephone. As she was speaking Bengali I assumed she was talking to her companion, but as the conversation continued I realized her tone was too formal, the repeating of phrases almost official. I listened in and tried to pick out the odd few words of English.

'*Airport,*' I heard her say. '*Bangladesh . . . Tickets.*'

So there it is: Amma is going to leave me.

After the mollycoddling of my 'lapse', the story of her stepping on a snake and the singing of the Bengali national anthem, I'd hoped that we'd grown closer, but she's pulling away from me faster than ever. No wonder she's been so keen to get me out of the flat, no wonder she's been pushing and pushing for me to move on with my life. She wants to leave the flat herself, to get on with her own life. I know I deserve this. I know I should let her be happy. But seriously, what am I going to do without Amma?

I listen to her companion's voice as it vibrates through the floorboards. At one point I even hear them laughing. It stings me, that laughter, like the sting of being chosen last in PE.

After he leaves, Amma comes up to my room. She sits in her chair with a colander balanced on her knees and begins shelling peas with a look of pure innocence on her face.

Bangladesh. It never occurred to me that Amma would really go back. There was talk when I was younger of her taking me there to 'discover my roots', but when I got ill all hopes for that were dropped. But things are changing. She speaks so loudly to her companion now, it's almost as if she *wants* me to hear.

Maybe I should tell her the truth. Drop it on her the way the truth of those tickets was dropped on me.

I'm not ill at all!

I sulk for a while as she shells peas, the flesh of each pod snapping as she ploughs her way through the heap. The bursting flesh fills the room with a fine sweet fragrance I can't appreciate. I try to remember the news update she gave me a few days ago about the volcano in Iceland. It had caused mayhem for European air travel due to the enormous ash cloud that was spouting from its mouth. Was it still spouting? Would all her crazy travel plans be thwarted? Suddenly I wished I'd listened more when she gave me updates, instead of deciding the information was useless to a body unlikely to travel further than this room, let alone out of the country. I look over at Amma as green pearls pop from her fingers.

'What do you *want from me*?' I roll my head back and stretch my arms across the bed. I hold my palms up to the ceiling as though lying on a crucifix.

I can see her look up from her peas out of the corner of my eyes but the shock I thought would be stamped across her face isn't there. She shakes her head.

'It is not *me* who wants anything from you.'

She continues shaking as I remain in my crucifix position. Eventually I roll my head forward. 'Well, what does *he* want then?'

Again, no shock.

'To see you.'

'What *for*?'

Amma's eyebrows spring up as though I've asked her the million-dollar question. I drop my head back.

'Never mind,' I say. 'I don't want to know.'

When I shift my gaze towards her she doesn't look angry but tired, as though the very act of speaking to me is draining.

'You cannot hide from the world for ever, Ravine,' she says as she stands up with her half-shelled peas.

From the periphery of my vision, I watch her leave. Amma is giving up on me. I can see it in her drooped eyelids, in the way she barely argues with me any more. She has her companion who she dyes her hair and buys new saris for. She's in courtship; a concept that makes me nauseous. Soon she'll tire of me completely and begin her own life.

And she should. I am useless. I am ungrateful. But worst of all I am a liar. As soon as she finds this out, what reason will she have to stay?

I cannot hide for ever. That's what Amma tells me. Yet I lie here wishing I could.

The second time I saw the Soul-drinker was in the cash-and-carry. Amma had taken me there on an 'educational trip' one Saturday morning. This was like the times she took me to the park, the market, the Gas Museum or the library. On Amma's educational trip list, places with free admission ranked at the top.

'If you can't learn from life, then what can you learn from?' she said, shovelling scoops of red lentils into a transparent bag.

I didn't mind going to the cash-and-carry. It was a colourful place full of exotic items you'd never see in the corner shops of Westhill. This was the place where the Asian community congregated and held their meetings. It was a gurdwara, a temple, a mosque and church all in one, with the added bonus of selling cheap imported goods. When I entered the store I'd gaze at the brown faces wandering down the aisles as though I was an alien who'd just found its home planet. I never resented being the only Asian girl on the estate. Apart from the occasional 'but but ding ding' from Bradley Patterson, I was left alone and only noticed the odd confused stare at Amma and her sari-and-trainers combo. Even at school the other children seemed oblivious to my skin colour. The only exception was Luke Judd who once called me a 'Paki' during playtime. I looked at him and rolled my eyes.

'I'm not from *Pakistan*, I'm from *Bangladesh*.'

This statement truly baffled him and it was only later when Mrs Jenkins made him deliver a sour-faced apology that I realized he had been trying to be insulting.

But in the cash-and-carry there were too many people for Bradley Patterson and Luke Judd to offend. There were hordes of other Ammas wearing brightly coloured saris and trench coats, their hair tied neatly into buns. There were men too, hair jet-black against their dark skins, round pot bellies underneath short-sleeved shirts tucked neatly into trouser waists. One of these men could be my father, I thought. All I'd have to do was find a man with a bunch of red tulips and a face that looked like it was about to cry.

Another reason I liked the cash-and-carry was the fact that Amma didn't mind if I wandered off by myself. On the estate I always had to hold on to her hand which, at the age of eight, was becoming embarrassing. In the cash-and-carry she became so absorbed with canned chickpea offers and examining mangoes that she didn't notice when I wandered off to look at chilli crisps.

I think you would have loved the cash-and-carry. I wish I could have taken you. It was different from the neat Western supermarkets with their aisles perfectly stacked and straight. The cash-and-carry often had boxes of stock lying in the middle of aisles, flickering lights above the checkout and huge towers of goods piled precariously by the door. Spices sat in barrels with huge scoops, spiky vegetables lay in boxes by chest freezers full of pre-made samosas and frozen okra. The Asian population liked their products in large quantities and I'd often find myself measuring my small body against the sacks of rice, drums of sunflower oil and string bags filled with onions that rose as high as my shoulders.

The day I saw the Soul-drinker I'd been reading the label on a sack of gram flour, trying to find (with little success) the word '*besan*' in my mini dictionary. When I glanced sideways I saw him hovering in the chutney aisle. He was wearing the same short-sleeved shirt-and-trouser combo as the other men and would have gone undetected if it hadn't been for the strange way his shoulders were hunched over as he huddled behind the shelves. He was pretending to read a jar of mango and lemon pickle but all the while his eyes were peering over at Amma rifling her way through a box of green chillies. His yellow glare was fixed on her and right then and there I knew that the Soul-drinker was not only after my soul but the soul of my mother.

I stared at the Soul-drinker with my mini dictionary held tightly in my hand. I held my breath as though your phrase 'If you don't breathe he won't see you' was actually true. His skin was as dark as coffee beans, tiny dents that looked like craters all across his cheek. He was chewing his bottom lip with vigour, the even little squares of his teeth stained red with what was either the remnants of paan juice or blood. Standing by the gram flour, I assumed it was the latter.

I don't know how I got his attention – whether I screamed, dropped my dictionary or if he sensed my eyes staring at him with his super-natural powers – but in the next moment the Soul-drinker was looking at me. Under the shop lights his yellow eyes were as bright as traffic lights, widening with surprise. He glanced over at Amma and crouched down behind the aisle.

The cowering body confused me for a second before I realized what had happened. I'd caught the Soul-drinker off guard and, in doing so, had drained him of all his power. I released my breath, nearly tripping over a broken coconut and price sticker gun, as I ran squealing to Amma's side. She barely flinched as I pulled at the fabric of her sari.

'We have to go, we have to go!' I cried.

I glanced at the chutney aisle, seeing the head of the Soul-drinker bobbing up to look at us. I looked away so his eyes wouldn't drain me of my soul, while continuing to tug at Amma's sari. She whipped the fabric from my hands, carrying on searching through a pile of shelled peanuts.

'We still have ten minutes until the bus comes,' she told me. 'Go get yourself a lollipop.'

When I looked back at the chutney aisle the Soul-drinker had gone. I could see his shirt billowing out behind him as he ran through the sliding doors of the exit. He disappeared within seconds, Amma none the wiser, and even through my relief I was irritated that I'd been the only one to see him.

'But he was just there,' I said, pointing to where his bobbing eyes had been watching us.

Amma looked down at me and shoved a fifty-pence coin in my hand.

'Go wait at the till,' she said.

As I sucked on a cinnamon-flavoured lollipop on the bus ride home I couldn't help but stare out of the window in case I caught sight of the yellow eyes following us. Amma chattered on about the rising price of kidney beans as I deliberated our close call. We'd been lucky this time but I couldn't be sure if we'd be so lucky again. It was then, as we drew nearer to Westhill Estate, that I decided I would do what Uncle Walter would do. I would devise a survival strategy to protect us from the Soul-drinker.

Last night I dreamt I was at sea. When I looked over the boat's edge I saw ripples in the water as clear as diamonds, a thousand tropical fish swimming near the surface. When I sat up, I saw the coastline drifting away behind me, a cut rope trailing in the water like a drenched tail. I was free. At last I was free.

But then I woke up and realized that I wasn't.

Secrets are carnivorous. The longer I stay floating on that sea, the sooner those fish will come jumping on board to eat me. Not that there'd be much left to eat. I've been shrivelled down to a Stanley-sized blob. Karma, my mother would say, even though she doesn't believe in such things. But if the Hindus are right, I'm destined to be reincarnated into a wet, slimy slug lifetime after lifetime.

'*Ravine, I know you can hear me,*' your brother said through the wall this morning. '*Please talk to me.*'

I turned my face, trying to hide my tears from the wall.

Please, he said to me, and it made me cry. I've never heard Jonathan say that word to me before.

The Constellation of Getting Dressed

I haven't been able to write to you because I'm waiting for a new notebook. You should see Amma's face when I ask her for it. The bindi rises so high on her forehead it almost disappears into her hairline.

'You've finished the one from your birthday?' she says. 'Already?'

'I like to doodle in it. It helps me solve crosswords.'

Another lie tumbling like rocks off a cliff. Amma sits back in her chair and sighs.

'I have paper you can *doodle on*. Newspaper and old envelopes.'

'That won't be enough.'

Amma looks puzzled, as though I've delivered her a genuine conundrum. She holds a finger in the air.

'I have that toilet paper that is too hard to use. I bought it cheap at the cash-and-carry and they won't take it back.'

I hear your brother sniggering through the wall.

'No, Amma,' I say loudly. 'I want writing paper. Something that *won't fall apart.* I'll even pay for it myself.'

She looks at me with wide eyes as I wave to the dresser drawer. She pulls out the piggy bank I made when I was six, ears chipped, snout more like a trunk with an uneven red glaze that makes it look sun-burnt. I've put all the money I've ever been given for birthdays in that bank, as well as the pound a week Amma gives me as 'pocket money'. (It isn't real pocket money because it never goes into my pocket. As soon as she places the coin on my palm Amma watches me put it straight into the piggy bank.)

I reach my hand out for Amma to pass me the pot but she holds it tightly between her fingers.

'I thought you were saving.'

The more I stretch out, the tighter she holds on. Eventually I drop my arm.

'Saving for what? Besides, a bit of paper isn't going bankrupt me.'

Amma continues to look down at the pot. I know I have at least £480 inside so can't understand her hesitation. She gently pats the head of the pig before placing it back in the drawer.

'No, shona. You will need that money. I'll pay for the paper myself.'

She's gone before I can object, marching straight down the stairs and spraying her trainers with vinegar and lemon before leaving for the shops.

If the same thing had happened a week ago I wouldn't have thought twice. Amma is the type of person who'd save for a rainy day if she lived in the middle of the Sahara Desert. But I know about her plans now and suddenly her words are more sinister.

You will need that money.

When Amma comes back I hear her shuffling about downstairs before coming up with a new notebook in her hand. Before I can thank her she pulls out a bunch of rolled-up election flyers that have been sprouting like carnations from her petticoat and begins to grin at me. As pills rattle against the plastic tray, Amma delivers me election promises. Labour will halve the budget deficit by 2014, the Conservatives will give the unemployed a 'hand up, not a hand out' by reducing welfare dependency and the Lib Dems will scrap university tuition fees. According to the flyers each party is the best choice and all opposing parties are intent on steering the country to rack and ruin. Gordon Brown is miserable and hot-headed, David Cameron too posh to sympathize with us plebs and nobody even knows who Nick Clegg is.

I'd been hoping to get some sympathy from Sandy about Amma's forced-voting scheme. She'd come to visit, cigarette hanging out of the window, when I began my defence. But as soon as I mentioned the word 'voting' she lit up like a lamp, telling me she was the only one of her friends on Westhill who ever voted.

'People say there's no one worth voting for,' she said. 'I ask them if they're *abstaining*. They look at me like I've gone loopy but I watch the politics on Sundays, see. You've got to know the system, Ravine. Got to know what they're doing at the top. I've learnt my lesson from those God-awful Blair years.'

It popped all the air out of my balloon to have her supporting the voting plan.

'I'm voting Cameron, for sure,' she continued. 'He's a posh boy but he can't do worse than this government. My benefits will be safe under his watch, mark my words.'

Sandy is highly protective of her benefits. She's convinced that Cameron won't cut hers because of her legitimate clinical depression, unlike Mrs Patterson who says she has a bad back but still goes to Zumba every Wednesday. Sandy's been living on benefits since she was sixteen. It's the only way she knows how to function. It's the same as me and this room. You might be stuck in a pit but when you've never seen the light of day, it's more comfortable to stay in the dark.

As Amma reads through the flyers I look at her casual expression and wonder when she's planning on telling me about her return to Bangladesh.

'Do you want anything from Laser's car boot?' she asks, tucking the flyers away.

My shoulders drop. 'I wish you wouldn't call him that.'

'But it is his name.'

'His name's Ian. And it's not a car boot, it's a knock-off goods stall.'

Behind Amma I can see the leaves of the tree fan around her head in a green halo of innocence. She shakes her head, smiling at me as though I've made a simple mistake.

'Laser assures me all his products are above board and of the highest quality.'

'*Laser's* also been in prison for fraud so I wouldn't trust everything he says.'

Amma blows her cheeks out as though I'm being deliberately contrary. She told me the same thing herself about Laser when I was younger, and only changed her mind when he gave her a discount on a set of stainless steel saucepans.

'I've always had a soft spot for exotic ladies,' he said through a gap-toothed grin.

While any other woman would have found this repellent, my mother began giggling manically. She was always a sucker for a compliment and a discount, and the double whammy left her senseless. Now she won't hear a word against the person she once referred to as '*the lying cheat man*'.

After my mention of Laser's prison sentence Amma becomes stiff.

'Do you want something from him or do you not?' she says.

'I do not.'

'Very good.'

She places her reading glasses on the tip of her nose and begins opening her bills. I carry on ripping chapatti between my fingers, wondering if I can somehow sneak down to Laser's stall without Amma noticing. Maybe if I go out by myself now, going out to vote with Amma later won't be so bad. Besides, I could do with some new crossword books and could maybe rifle through his collection of second-hand CDs from the discount box he always keeps on the floor.

Knowing Amma, she'll go down to Laser's straight after breakfast to get first dibs on his 'high quality' goods and from there to the park to feed ducks. I'll have a good one-and-a-half-hour window to scuttle downstairs, have a quick look at what's on offer and make my way back to my room. I try to visualize the plan, rushing down the pissy concrete steps and out into the light of Westhill. I imagine looking down at the pavement, the shield of my hair concealing my identity. I'll scan the crowd, locating the faded jeans and Tommy Hilfiger jumper that is Laser's uniform (on closer inspection the words spell Tommy Hill*finger*). I try to visualize walking up to his gap-toothed grin and opening my mouth in greeting but when I get to that part of the scene I feel a twisting pain in my chest that snaps me out of my thoughts. The pain is sharp, as though a tiny hand is wrestling with my oesophagus. I think it's the chilli in Amma's chickpea curry but even when I gulp down the mango juice the pain grips tight, the light of the room becoming dazzlingly bright, making me dizzy.

'I have some news,' Amma says abruptly.

When I look at her she has her chin buried deep in her chest, eyes fixed to the envelope in her hand. Just seeing her there, ponies dancing across the curtains behind her, makes the pain soften. The world of the estate is a far-off place again, stuck behind the walls of our flat.

'News?' I say, trying to keep my voice indifferent.

'About Mr Chavda,' she says.

She keeps her eyes fixed on the envelope, leaving me to assume the worst. I stuff chapatti in my mouth and think of all the times I haven't listened to Mr Chavda and rolled my eyes at him. Of all people, he's the type to die and come back as a ghost just to spite me. Sailing around my room at night, wailing times tables at me.

'What's wrong with him?' I say.

Amma begins to rip open the envelope and, in her fury, tears the corner of the letter inside.

'Nothing,' she says, shaking her head and pulling out the mutilated bill. 'He's just being a big baby.'

'What do you mean?' I ask.

Amma purses her lips. 'Never you mind.'

I drop my shoulders. 'Then why tell me?'

She glances up at me for a second then looks back down at her bill. 'Because he won't be teaching you for a while. He's too busy sulking.'

I don't press any further as Amma is clearly in no mood for explanations. Besides, I've already guessed the reason for Mr Chavda's sulk: she's told him the news of her return to Bangladesh and he's reacted with a temper tantrum. Amma (who never responds to such tactics) will have refused to talk to him until he apologizes and Mr Chavda (who I imagine hasn't apologized to anyone in his life) will be waiting for the same.

'What exercise shall we do today?' Amma asks, still ripping her way through the junk mail.

'How about staying in bed?' I suggest.

She drops her chin. 'You do enough of that already . . . I know! We shall time you sitting up and down again. We will see if you can beat your record.'

I groan, letting my body deflate with the noise.

'Can't I do the window exercise?' I say. 'I'm getting really good at that one.'

She doesn't seem to hear me, distracted by the electricity bill.

'The price of fuel is very high now,' she mumbles.

I bet it's cheaper in Bangladesh, I think, stuffing chapatti in my mouth before the words come out.

I must have fallen asleep because, later that day, my eyes spring open at the sound of Amma's voice.

'You cannot hide for ever, Ravine. You cannot hide.'

She's whispering in my ear, repeating the words at juggernaut speed until I fling my head back, ready to tell her to give it a rest. But she isn't there. As I look around I hear the front door click shut and realize she's gone out on her errands.

I sit up, my head feeling like a broken-up jigsaw. It tries to piece itself together as I rub my eyes, shoulders aching from all the tossing and turning. Amma has left a lunch tray on the bedside table but when I look at the lamb pieces buried in grains of yellow rice my stomach remains indifferent. I glance at the crossword books on the table, the zig-zag stack of library books on the floor, the upturned television remote at the bottom of the bed. Nothing tempts me. Eventually I come to a conclusion. I'm going to do something different today. Something I haven't done for a long time. I'm going to get dressed.

The last time I got dressed was four months ago when I had a hospital appointment. Of course I've had clothes on since, but only in the form of pyjamas or old shalwar kameezes covered in gaudy paisley patterns. They are comfortable at night but not exactly suited for estate wear.

I swing my feet out of the bed and plant them on the carpet, carrying out little pinches on my arms, then clenching and releasing different parts of my body. I go to the wardrobe in the corner of the room and open the doors. Before me is a collection of office wear, party gowns and nothing in between. Suits, waistcoats, shirts and skirts. Prom-style dresses, glittering saris I have no idea how to put on, slinky satin evening wear and ruffled items that easily rival the whipped-cream dresses we wore aged seven. Amma has been renewing my wardrobe each and every year and, judging by the contents, expects me to be attending job interviews and award ceremonies. It hasn't occurred to her I'd need everyday items – T-shirts, day dresses, *jeans*.

In the end I decide to put on one of the less flamboyant dresses: a short-sleeved crimson smock reaching down to my ankles and tucked in just beneath my bosom.

I go to the bathroom to brush my hair and wash my face. As I stand at the sink I see Amma's kohl eyeliner and attempt to press the waxy tip on my own lids. I'm left rubbing the black marks off, the smudges giving me panda eyes and leaving the edges so red raw it looks as if I've been crying for the past hour. I think maybe I can correct this with some talcum powder but decide against it. I don't plan to be out for long.

I begin my descent down the stairs. It's the first time for years that I've made it down unaided and I have to lean my hand on the wooden rail, trying not to go *Crack! Crack! Crack!* down the steps like the girl in Jonathan's Soul-drinker story. My legs are not as unsteady as I thought they'd be, Amma's exercises having built up some strength in my thighs and calves. When I get to the bottom of the stairs I'm only a little out of breath, pausing for a moment before I slip into a pair of Amma's plastic sandals. When I turn my head I see the full-length hall mirror. I used to press my face against the glass, blowing hard so I could form condensation marks around the shape of my lips. I barely came halfway up the mirror back then and now I'm at full adult (or at least Bengali) height. It scares me to see myself so tall and dressed up. I look like some other person. A grown-up person with long flowing black hair and a surprisingly large bosom. I place my hand on the knob of the Yale lock and, leaving the door ajar, step outside the flat.

A chill breeze hits me square in the face. I crane my neck out to scan the landing. When I see it's empty I creep out from the front door, keeping my head ducked down. I step sideways to what used to be your door and look down at the mat the Ahmeds had left behind. It's a straw mat, the word WELCOME printed against the background of a Union Jack. It was a declaration of the family's dedication to its new country and a polite request to please not egg their door.

A few days back, your brother spoke to me through the wall. I couldn't understand him at first. I thought he was saying, 'Give me the hat, Ravine, the hat.' Then, when I put a glass against the wall, I realized he was saying, '*The key's beneath the mat, Ravine, the mat.*' He wants me to come and visit him.

It's clear that, for whatever Jonathan-shaped reason, your brother is in hiding and has decided to reveal himself to me and me only. I suppose this is flattering in a way but I'm still unsure. I haven't seen your brother in over ten years and our last meeting wasn't a particularly happy one.

He'd come to visit me in the hospital with a lady from the social services. His pale face sat on top of a rigid body and if it hadn't been for the lady's subdued voice, the room would have been filled with nothing but the beep of hospital equipment. Jonathan was going into foster care, she said, until what was best for him could be decided. He didn't look at me as she explained this, not once, but kept his eyes glued to the end of my bed as though my hospital chart was the most fascinating image he'd ever seen. When he left, I made sure to call out, 'What's the weather, Jonathan-Weatherboy?' even though the pain was shooting up my jaw with each word. I said it without malice, hoping to elicit a reaction from him, for him to chant '*Ravine Ravine Dictionary Queen*' and perform his fairy dance. For a moment he stood there, shoulders hunched over, but then he kept walking.

I bend down to the Union Jack and pull the key out from beneath. I wonder what Jonathan will make of me in my Little Red Riding Smock. Then I begin to wonder what he looks like now, no longer a little boy in too-big glasses but a fully grown man. Is he handsome and broad or as weedy as ever? Does he still wear those thick-framed glasses or a slim pair that give him the air of a university professor?

I turn the key. The lock clunks open. I push the door forward. There's the shuffling of feet. His feet. Your brother's feet.

I don't know why that sound makes me panic but it does. I yank the door shut, shove the key under the mat and dash back into my flat, up the stairs and into bed. I lie under the sheets with sandals still on my feet, the red smock twisted around my legs. And it's then, as I lie still, that the pain strikes. When I look over at Shiva, his chin is pressed down, face full of disapproval.

5 across: Faint-hearted. Yellow-bellied. Chicken (6)

I watch the walls closing in, a little white crossword box drawing up against my body. There are no clues linked to me, just a sea of black around each edge. As the darkness narrows in I try breathing deeply, waiting for Jonathan's voice to come through the walls.

I can hear him moving, but he doesn't say a word. Then, a noise comes shrill and brutal. Crockery smashing into the brick on the other side of the wall, a sound so sharp it makes my body jolt and my ears ring. I hold on to my knees, waiting for the walls to come tumbling down. But there's no more crashing, no more noise. Nothing but the silence, surrounded by the dark.

The Constellation of Disappearing Suns

When I watch the universe programme with Amma, the professor is viewing a solar eclipse in Varanasi. He stands on the banks of the Ganges as throngs of spectators wade in the river up to their waists, with a multitude of saris and bare chests. I sit transfixed at this image of India. The lush greenery, the colourful garments, the hot glowing sun, and I realize that these must be the things Amma misses most about Bangladesh. I wonder what our lives would have been like if she'd never been shipped out of the country and flogged to the first man with a decent offer. If she'd stayed she might have defied all convention and become a lawyer or an academic. She might not even have had me.

I watch in silence as the disc of the moon travels over the orange globe of the sun, listening carefully as the professor tells me about the amazing coincidence that allows a solar eclipse to occur.

The moon is approximately four hundred times smaller in diameter than the sun, and the sun lies approximately four hundred times as far from Earth as the moon. This twist of fate means that when the three bodies align during an eclipse the distance between them creates the perfect effect of the moon covering the entire mass of the sun. The professor takes a green coconut and a lime from a cart and lines the objects up to the camera lens until the coconut is obscured by the roundness of the green sphere.

'This proves,' he says, 'to be one of the most remarkable coincidences in all of nature, and a truly breathtaking vision for any spectator to behold.'

Varanasi becomes covered in darkness. The crowd cheers.

I hear the creaking of bedsprings next door. I glance over at Amma. Her hands, which have been kneading chapatti dough in a metal bowl, are now frozen as she watches the professor. It isn't until the end credits roll that she becomes reanimated, jumping to her feet with floury hands and a shaking head.

'That professor is a very clever man.'

I smirk, knowing full well she doesn't watch for his cleverness, then let her kiss me on the cheek before switching the screen off. When she leaves the room, I hear a tapping on the wall. I glance towards the door as Amma's feet plod down the steps. I've been worried your brother would stop speaking to me after yesterday. That he'd be in one of his almighty sulks. I told myself I didn't care – I'd survived all these years without Jonathan Dickerson, I could manage a few more – but still I quickly spin my body to a half-kneeling position and use my glass to listen through the wall. Eventually I hear his deep voice vibrating through the plaster.

'Ravine?'

I gulp down the saliva in my throat and close my eyes.

'Yes?'

Even with this one syllable I can hear my voice shaking. I press hard onto the wall to steady myself. There's a pause.

'What did it look like?' he asks.

I glance at the TV and frown.

'Better than that other one,' I tell him. I remember the day he missed out on a (partial) solar eclipse. We'd all gathered on the top floor of Bosworth House. I imagine his frustration at sitting so close to another eclipse, even if it's only a televised one. To hear the applauding and cheering of a thousand Indians and see nothing himself.

I hear the patter of two palms being pressed against the wall. I almost pull away at the thought of him so close.

'Better?' he says.

I lean my ear into the glass and try to think of the most appropriate synonym.

'*Phenomenal.*'

A pause. 'Can you describe it?'

I think about this for a second.

'Well . . .' I say. 'When the moon was completely covering the sun, there was still this glow around it. Fuzzy and white.'

'The sun's corona,' your brother says.

I roll my eyes. He always was a know-it-all.

'Whatever,' I say. 'And the sky was totally black. The moon was totally black. Everything black except for this fuzzy white disc in the sky. It was so . . . *clear.* Back when we were kids you could only see clouds.'

There's another pause. I let my hands slide off the wall as I sit back down on my heels.

'You could probably find it on YouTube,' I say.

It takes a moment for him to reply. When he does, it sounds like 'Thanks.'

I look at the wall. 'You're welcome.'

Which must be the most civil we've ever been to each other.

The day of the 1999 solar eclipse was the day of Jonathan's transformation.

For the majority of the country the eclipse was a pretty understated affair, as the narrow track of total coverage was limited to the lower stretches of Cornwall. Even then, it was only a partial eclipse, but this didn't stop the BBC streaming the message 'WARNING: STARING AT THE SUN CAN DAMAGE YOUR EYES'. In response, Amma searched through her drawer of cereal-packet gifts and fished out two pairs of 3D glasses, claiming that by putting the two shades together, green plastic against red, red against green, my young eyes would be protected.

Much like the assembly of the Dome in London, the solar eclipse was a signpost on the road to the Millennium. The Y2K bug had made us all edgy (we expected planes to fall from the sky on the first stroke of midnight). We were entering a new era and anything seemed possible, a fact reinforced by the disappearance of the sun.

Jonathan didn't even try to hide his excitement. As the overseer of weather, the sun was the closest thing he had to a friend. He even used all his pocket money to buy three pairs of solar shades from Laser's car boot for you, him and Uncle Walter. I, on the other hand, was left stuck with Amma's cereal-packet invention.

On the day of the eclipse everyone gathered along the balcony of the top floor of Bosworth House. When you have little to no money, the best things in life are indeed free, and nothing proved this more than the mounting excitement brewing that day on the fourth floor. People brought folding chairs with them, cartons of juice and sandwiches in tubs. They left the doors of their flats open so they could be regularly updated with live news coverage from Cornwall, giving us the countdown to the great event. The whole occasion would go down in Westhill history as the unifying moment that demonstrated the power of small inner-city communities. Or at least it would have, if it hadn't been for Bradley Patterson.

He was standing with his goons against the doors behind us. Minus their bikes they were so small and insignificant that we barely noticed them. It was only when they began chanting that we turned to see their scowling faces.

'Who ate all the pies? Who ate all the pies?'

They sang this low and quietly to begin with, repeating the same lines over and over, even though they knew that Bradley's mother was sitting on a deckchair two feet away. Not that this made any difference. Mrs Patterson had become desensitized to the callous nature of her son and, though vocal on larger issues such as theft and arson, allowed smaller offences to pass unnoticed. When Bradley pushed his way to the front of the balcony to mock Uncle Walter at close range, she barely raised an eyebrow.

'What's that stink?' Bradley bellowed. 'Can you smell that fucking *stink*, lads?'

'Chicken and mushroom?' one duck-faced boy suggested.

'Liver and onions?' another threw in.

They all began to chortle as they doled out pie filling after pie filling. We, unsure of how to react, looked up at Uncle Walter's sweating body as each insult was flung. His face sat propped on the fat beneath his chin. We could see him wince with each butt in his belly from the straggly-haired boy's elbow.

After a while, Bradley seemed to get bored of his pie joke. He glanced up at your uncle as he stuffed a ribbon of chewing gum into his mouth.

'Oi, *Walt*,' he said, jaw grinding. 'Mum tells me you're a nutter. Is that true?'

Uncle Walter's eyes dropped down for a second. It was a tiny movement, barely noticeable. Bradley grinned as his gang began to chuckle.

'She says you went mental after your friend got shanked,' he said. 'Got locked away cos you had a *breakdown*. Did they feed you too much? Is that why you're so *fat*?'

Bradley's laugh was so loud that no one could even pretend not to hear him any more. The crowd didn't join in, but then they didn't stop him either. This was the power Bradley held over the estate. Just looking at him made you yellow.

I looked up at your uncle as I waited for him to use a survival strategy: squealing loudly to make Bradley's ears bleed, pulling out a stun gun to jab him in the ribs. Instead he stood rock-still as Bradley began pushing into his round belly, harder and harder. Eventually he pushed him so hard that Uncle Walter stumbled, holding on to the railings to steady his footing. He kept facing forward as he clung on.

'That's enough now,' he said.

Bradley scowled. 'What you gonna do? *Eat me?*'

As the goons released a peal of laughter, Mrs Patterson looked over from her chair and smirked. It's true. I saw the little dimples in her cheek. Next to Mrs Patterson, Sandy Burke sat with her lips sucked in tight. Ever since she had failed to seduce your uncle, she'd refused to speak to him. As she sat by Mrs Patterson, Sandy smirked too but it was half-hearted and twitchy. She kept her gaze averted, unable to look any of us in the eye.

As the boys continued laughing, Uncle Walter whispered discreetly into Amma's ear. She nodded, touching him gently on the arm before he shuffled away to the staircase. His eyes were glossy and round, like those of a child watching a horror movie.

Bradley Patterson strode back to his wall as though he'd just defeated Goliath. He clasped hands with the other boys in a manner I assume he thought was impressive, then leant back on the wall with the stance of a gangster.

Jonathan was furious. He hissed and muttered, his face turning devil red. Having bought the solar shades from his own pocket money, he was clearly sore at the prospect of a pair going unused.

'I don't see why Uncle Walter had to go,' he mumbled as he looked back at the wall. 'He wasn't even doing anything.'

It was the first time Jonathan had referred to Uncle Walter as 'uncle'. If it hadn't been for his furrowed eyebrows and snarling mouth it would have been sweet. He carried on glaring at the boys before crossing his arms.

'They're not even watching.'

You tried to reason with your brother. Uncle Walter *wanted* to go back to the flat. He was creating some form of snare to catch Bradley Patterson so he could torture him and find out his secrets (we never shook off the notion that he was a spy). Yet the more you spoke the more your brother's eyes narrowed in that way they did when he was planning something rotten.

The sun was almost hidden behind the thick grey cloud above us. We donned our glasses and looked at the small white globe through our lenses, standing on tiptoes and squinting as we edged closer to the brink of the balcony. Even Sandy Burke and Mrs Patterson rose from their chairs as the black rim of the moon began to skim the sun's edge.

Just as we thought we could see the dark circle biting into the cake of the sun, we heard the scream. We turned around, each one of us whipping off our frames, to see Jonathan huddled on the floor with his own solar shades smashed beside him. Blood covered his small squat nose as he lay at Bradley Patterson's feet.

Mrs Patterson threw her cigarette to the ground.

'What have you done, you little shit?'

Bradley put his hands in the air. 'I didn't touch him.'

Jonathan wailed, large tears rolling down his cheeks as he clutched his dented nose. Mrs Patterson ran over to his heaped body.

'It's all right, lad,' she said, helping him up as he sobbed. She looked back at Bradley. 'For God's sake, boy! He's half your size!'

'He did it to himself,' Bradley said.

'They could press charges, you idiot! You're already in enough trouble with the filth.'

Bradley Patterson drew a deep breath. He looked back at his goons, now mute, then back at his mother's bloated face. When he spoke it was with the slow consideration of a person giving evidence on trial.

'He came up to me out of nowhere. I didn't say a word to him, he just came. Then he threw his glasses on the floor, smashed them with his shoe and began beating the shit out of himself. It's the God's-honest truth, Mum.'

He held his palms up to the sky to show his hands were clean of the crime. Mrs Patterson laughed.

'Pull the other one,' she said, dragging him by the collar back into her flat.

The rest of the goons stood agog as their leader was manhandled by a five-foot-two woman with large breasts.

Half an hour later, Mrs Patterson hauled her son down to your flat and made him apologize to Uncle Walter for the crime he insisted he hadn't committed. His body was hunched over, his eyes red raw as he sniffled his way through an apology. Your uncle listened calmly as Mrs Patterson pleaded a bargain. She swore to personally make sure Bradley stayed away from the whole family if he promised not to press charges.

'He hasn't got many chances left, Walt,' she said. 'If you can't do it for his sake, do it for mine. There's only so much grief a woman can take.'

Amma was still giving first aid to Jonathan's bloody nose as Uncle Walter negotiated with the Pattersons. We both watched in fascination as the crimson liquid continued to flow down your brother's face. As he winced with each prod and poke, I wondered if it was really possible that he'd done what Bradley Patterson had accused him of. The same Jonathan who cried like a baby when he got his school jabs. The same Jonathan who had his head bandaged with metres of dressing after a minor fall. Could this same Jonathan have caused the damage to his face with his *own fist*? It seemed impossible.

It was only when Uncle Walter came into the dining room that I knew for sure. He looked exhausted, as though he'd scaled the steps of Bosworth House a hundred times over. He poured himself a glass of apple juice and sat down at the table to recover. As Amma continued to mop up blood, Jonathan looked over at the bundle of red cotton wool beside him. He caught your uncle's eye and nodded in the manner of a mafia don.

'Don't worry, Uncle Walter,' he said. 'Those boys aren't ever going to bother you again.'

I spoke to your brother again last night. The smell of Amma's cooking had leaked through the kitchen window to his flat and he was curious to find out what I was eating.

'Vegetable dhansak,' I told him.

He asked what vegetables were in my dhansak. I looked down at the mixture on my plate. Colourful cubes poked out from the sauce as I jabbed at the meal with my fingers.

'Potatoes, carrots, peas, sweetcorn. Chillies, if you count that as vegetable . . .'

'Fruit,' he said. 'Because of the seeds.'

I rolled my eyes.

'What does it taste like?' he asked.

I frowned before scooping the mixture into my mouth. 'Hot.'

I carried on eating as he fell into silence, realizing with each mouthful that there was more to this meal than mere heat. I moved the pieces around my mouth, detecting a delicate blend of spices: cumin, turmeric, cardamom and chilli. My tongue felt the softness of each vegetable chunk as it collapsed against the roof of my mouth, blending into the richness of the coriander-laced sauce.

'Your mother (*mumble mumble*) good (*mumble*),' he said.

'Good what?' I said loudly.

'Hook,' he said.

'Hook?'

'COOK.'

I frowned, remembering how Jonathan screwed up his face whenever Amma put a plate of curry in front of him. He'd ask for a pint of water and gulp it down with each mouthful, beads of sweat dotting the lines of his crinkled forehead. I stared down at the food before me, steam rising like smoke from a chimney pot. I can't imagine the Ahmeds left much food in the flat and I haven't heard Jonathan leave for provisions since he arrived.

I washed my hand in the bowl of water Amma had left and wiped it on the tea towel beside it. When I heard Jonathan mumbling again I drained my glass and held it up against the wall.

'Does it hurt very much?' he asked.

I didn't know how he knew about my condition. Amma hasn't heard from him in years and Sandy has never mentioned him.

'Yes, it hurts a lot,' I said.

Another lie. Another wrench to the gut. But I couldn't blurt out my secret to him. If I owe anyone the truth it's the woman who's nursed me for the past ten years, not your prodigal brother who should be pleased I'm even talking to him.

'It sounded bad when the doctor came round.'

I tried to think of what doctor, then realized he meant the physiotherapist.

'You shouldn't listen in to other people's conversations,' I said.

'It's hard not to when someone's screaming their head off.'

I huffed through my nose; an action I realized was lost on him as soon as I performed it.

'Hey, Ravine,' he said, slower now, tentative. 'I keep meaning to ask you something . . .'

I waited, breath held tight.

'Can you play something else on your CD player? You know, other than Stevie Wonder? It was all right at first but now it's driving me mental.'

If he'd been in front of me, I would have punched him in the face.

'How long are you staying?' I asked.

I'd meant to stun him and, as desired, he remained quiet for a few seconds. When he did respond, Jonathan's voice was so faint I had to ask him to repeat himself.

'*Not sure!*' he yelled.

I rolled my eyes. 'Typical.'

I could have asked why he'd come back, what he was after or who he was hiding from, but I didn't ask because I didn't want to know. I'm not ready to be involved in Jonathan's life again. Not yet.

I knew that Amma would come to fetch my tray any minute. I leant my body over the bed and from the darkness below I pulled out a biscuit tin, the same that had housed Sangerine I, II and III. I've washed it out since, in case you were wondering, and have been using it to store the throngs of vitamin supplements, painkillers and other medication Amma gives me each day. I want to know if I actually need them any more. It's been three weeks now, the tin's half full, and even though there have been moments of pain, it's nothing like what I used to feel.

'Ravine . . . ?' your brother said through the wall.

I sat up. 'Want to know what I'm having for pudding now?' I said.

I heard him snort. Then Amma's feet came shuffling to the bottom of the stairs.

'Are you saying something to me?' she called up.

'No,' I called back.

I cupped my mouth as I leant into the wall. 'I think she's coming up.'

I put my ear back on the glass.

'OK,' he said. 'But Ravine . . .'

He paused. I leant into the wall, one ear cocked in the air waiting for the sound of Amma's feet on the stairs.

'*Yes?*' I said as the silence continued.

He remained quiet and for a moment I thought he was trying to provoke me like he did when we were children. Prodding me, teasing me. I heard the thump of feet on the staircase.

'I'm sorry I never came to visit,' he said just as Amma reached the top.

I put the glass on the table and shuffled down under the sheets.

'I swear those steps get higher each year!' she cried, holding on to her back as she waddled into the room.

I glanced back at the wall.

'They must be growing,' I said as she collected my tray. 'Either that, or you're shrinking.'

Amma made a *tsk* noise. I watched the folds of her sari swish from side to side as she left the room, hoping she hadn't seen the smile plastered across my face.

Later that night, when Amma is tucked up in bed, I creep down the stairs and into the kitchen. When I open the fridge I see the stacks of Tupperware she keeps in case of a crisis. Judging by the quantity, Amma clearly imagines biryanis and fish curry will be enough to guarantee our survival in the apocalypse. I pull out the top tub and shut the fridge door carefully so it only makes a squeak. With the tub and a fork in hand, I creep to the front door, creaking it open before placing the food on the WEL of the WELCOME mat outside your flat. I rap my knuckles hard against the panels of the door and slip back into my flat with the speed of a ninja. When I sneak back up the stairs, each step slow and steady, I try my best not to breathe as I enter my room. As soon as I'm under the sheets, the springs of the mattress creaking as I slide in, I hear a voice through the wall.

'Cheers, Ravine,' it says.

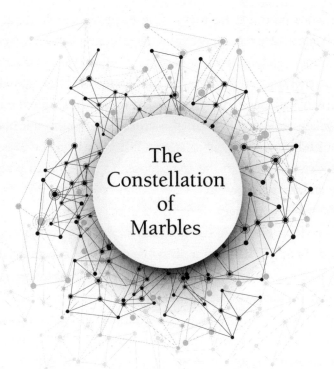

The Constellation of Marbles

Seeing the Soul-drinker twice had made me vigilant. His yellow eyes and dark face haunted my daydreams and nightmares. To protect not just you but Amma too, I squeezed a whistle into my shoulder bag and wore a bracelet made of jagged beads upon my wrist. On shopping trips to the cash-and-carry I would stand on guard beside Amma's hip, ready to blow the whistle if I spotted any sign of him. If he grabbed hold of me I planned to use the jagged bracelet to gouge out the yellow of his eyes and drain him of all his power. These were my survival strategies and I was certain they'd keep me safe.

When we went to the woods I made sure we were never left alone and that we stopped playing hide-and-seek. Jonathan grumbled about it at first but eventually shrugged his shoulders. He was tamer during that time. Since the incident with Bradley Patterson and the solar shades he didn't have anything to prove. He no longer spoilt Uncle Walter's recipe books or fed him chilli sandwiches. He no longer fussed about the food in front of him but instead assisted your uncle in the kitchen: peeling onions, cooking pasta, washing up dishes, all acts which had been considered 'not for real men' in the days of Mrs Dickerson. He ate his meals without complaint and joined in with our Italian lessons, albeit from a distance.

On a few occasions he went so far as to play football with Uncle Walter on the patch of grass at the bottom of the flats. He was nifty with the ball, always ready for a tackle, while your uncle was surprisingly speedy, considering his size and the fact he could barely move his head. Bradley Patterson and his goons stood by, pretending not to watch, but whenever Jonathan gave them one of his googly-eyed stares they would quickly saunter off, muttering 'nutter' as they left.

I liked this new version of your brother. He was less grumpy towards me and even lent me his book about weather so I could read all the words in the glossary. On days that we went to the woods he no longer pulled rank, letting us play our 'sissy games' while he went in search of woodland creatures. He wanted to catch a boar, though he wasn't sure what one looked like, and tried to devise a multitude of traps out of twigs and netting. We helped him occasionally, and when he gave us instructions it wasn't with rolled eyes and loud exhalations but with calm, considered advice. Your brother had realized your mother was never coming back and relinquished the idea of being in charge, handing the reins to your uncle. It seemed to relieve him, this passing of responsibility, and with this relief your brother became a bearable person.

Until the incident with the marbles.

We'd been using marbles as prizes for the slug races in Bobby's Hideout (which you always won) but ever since the slug homicide that was Stanley's death, we'd begun to use them in a more traditional manner. We rolled them along drainpipes, bashed them hard into one another, swapped them and won them and then sold them back to the highest bidder. I owned the largest collection of marbles, mainly because they were on a two-for-one offer in the pound shop and Amma had bought me six bags 'just in case'. I shared out the bags equally between the three of us and heard Jonathan whisper, 'Cheers, Ravine' when he thought you weren't listening.

Because we couldn't play on the uneven muddy floor of the woods we decided to have our battles on the smooth tarpaulin of the hideout. We managed to get away with this for some time until one morning we heard a shrill voice shouting at us.

'*Sacrilege!* Have you no respect for the *dead*?'

We'd been crouched down on our knees and, after one glance at each other, began collecting the scattered marbles in panic. We filled our pockets but found the slippery balls tumbled straight out. You lifted your skirt and gestured for us to fill it up with marbles.

'Shit, shit, shit!' Jonathan said.

'Cod, Cod, Cod,' you said.

'Sacrilege, sacrilege, sacrilege,' I said, trying to remember the word so that I could look it up in my mini dictionary.

We'd gathered half the collection when Mr Eccentric's crow-like head appeared through the open window.

'Out!' he shouted at us. 'Get *out!*'

You hugged the hem of your skirt to your chest and hobbled out of the door with the swollen belly of our goods. The marbles fell from your skirt almost instantly.

'Marbles!' I cried, dropping down to the floor.

Everything blurred. All I could see was coloured glass rolling through my fingers. I felt a hand on my shoulder. For a moment I thought it was Mr Eccentric but when I looked up, Jonathan's square glasses were pointing down at me.

'I've got it covered,' he said. '*Go*.'

I scrambled to my feet and out of the door while Jonathan snatched the marbles. Mr Eccentric's ridiculous scarecrow frame stretched tall as he grabbed hold of the window ledge.

'Listen, boy, this is no place for games!' he said.

Jonathan paused to look up at him. 'Listen, *fella*, I'm only going to be a minute. Keep your bloody hair on.'

We stood outside and watched as Mr Eccentric stood puffing up his chest before striding inside Bobby's Hideout and hauling Jonathan out by the ear. You stood with a belly of marbles and your luminous shorts on display. I brought out my whistle and began to blow. The whistle (bought from Laser's car boot) released a pathetic trill so you decided to help out by screaming.

'Let him go, let him go, let him go!' you yelled until your cheeks were crimson.

Mr Eccentric stood at the entrance of the hideout with his chin raised in the air and his fingers still clamped on Jonathan's ear. If he hadn't had an armful of marbles I'm sure your brother would have thwacked Mr Eccentric hard in the stomach, running off before the old man had a chance to realize what had happened. As they stood next to each other, with too-big glasses and the same twitching scowls, they looked like younger and older versions of each other.

'Now, all of you listen to me,' Mr Eccentric said over the din of my whistle blowing and your screaming. 'We're going to make a deal . . .'

'Run, for shit's sake!' Jonathan cried out. 'Get Uncle Walter!'

For the first time in our lives we listened to your brother's order. We ran out from the trees, dropping marbles across the muddy floor as the voice of Mr Eccentric faded behind us.

'Get back here at *once*!' he cried as we checked the road three times and then ran across.

We found Uncle Walter in the living room, eating a tub of ice-cream. He had his arm wrapped around the carton and a dessert spoon stuck in his mouth. We rarely ever caught your uncle eating like this and it was only as we saw his startled expression that we realized it was a secret. When we told him what had happened, his alarm quickly vanished and his hands balled into fists. He stood on his feet and marched out of the flat with us hopping down the stairs after him. We'd never seen your uncle angry before.

'*Non preoccuparti, sii felice!*' you cried.

'*Non prick-co-part-seee . . .*' I tried to repeat.

It was only when we got to the bottom that I asked you what it meant.

'Don't worry, be happy,' you said before running off.

When we arrived at Bobby's Hideout there was no sight of Mr Eccentric or Jonathan. We tried to pick up all the marbles from the floor as Uncle Walter scanned the breeze-block walls. He seemed distracted, examining the postcards of worldwide destinations before staring down at the huge ashtray in the middle of the room. I saw his skin fade to grey and worried that he was going to have an attack like the day Sandy tried to seduce him. Instead, he peered at us over his belly, placing his hands on our shoulders. He was Gulliver looking down on the town of Lilliput and we were his Lilliputians.

'You shouldn't come here, girls,' he said. 'It's not right.'

When we marched back to the estate, Uncle Walter didn't look back at the hideout but kept his eyes on Tewkesbury House. As we approached the building, you held on to my arm.

'Maybe he's turned him into a clock,' you said.

The idea made me grin. Images of your brother as a pocket-watch dropped in my bag soon filled my head. I imagined his scowling mouth shouting at me as I brought him out from the depths, slamming the watch door over his fuming face.

'What's the weather, Jonathan-Weatherboy?' I'd whisper through the hinges, knowing full well that he couldn't reply.

Then I remembered how he'd just saved us from Mr Eccentric and my grin fell from my face.

But when we arrived at Mr Eccentric's flat we could see that Jonathan was still very much a boy. Through the front window we saw him sitting on one side of Mr Eccentric's huge oak desk with the man himself seated opposite. A plate of sandwiches lay between them as pendulums swung back and forth on the wall behind.

'It isn't right,' your uncle muttered as his breath became louder. 'It isn't right.'

'*Non preoccuparti, sii felice!*' you said, even though you seemed unsure of the sentiment yourself.

When we entered the flat, Mr Eccentric lifted his chin and acted as though the abduction of a child was an everyday occurrence. He escorted us into his living room of clocks and brought seats out for us with a courtesy we'd only ever observed in costume dramas.

'Why thank you, kind sir,' you said, pulling out the sides of your skirt before planting your derriere on the chair.

When he spoke, Mr Eccentric's voice was calm like trickling water and not the shrill, harsh screech we were used to hearing. He asked us if we wanted any drinks and to help ourselves to the sandwiches on the table. You picked one up eagerly but Jonathan looked over at you, shaking his head with such mournful weight that you placed the triangle straight back on the plate.

'Can we speak outside, Reginald?' Uncle Walter said, as tears of sweat rolled down his face.

'Certainly,' Mr Eccentric replied, before following him out of the door.

If we'd been smarter we'd have listened to their conversation through the flimsy walls of the flat. But instead we asked Jonathan what was in the sandwiches.

'Sardines,' he said, before clutching his stomach as though he was about to throw up.

'I've never had sardines,' I said.

Jonathan rolled his head towards me. His skin was ashen, his body slouched in a manner that made him look seasick. 'You're not missing out.'

He didn't speak much after that but we were happy enough to gabble to each other about the room of clocks. Every wall was covered from top to bottom with the ticking machines. Round clocks, square clocks, standing clocks and mounted ones. Even the strips of wall by the window were lined with them, positioned with precise care above one another until they reached the cornices. That room was not just a room but a gallery of items through the ages from traditional round clocks with Roman numerals to modern irregular pieces shaped like bottles, dragons, flowers and hearts. One clock was shaped like a pizza with pepperoni slices for the numbers; another like a triangular pool rack with different-coloured balls. We stared at these clocks and gave them marks out of ten.

'Eleven out of ten,' you said, pointing to a clock in the shape of a cow.

'You can't do eleven out of ten,' I said, before looking over at your brother. 'She can't do eleven out of ten, can she?'

Unimpressed by the Museum of Time, Jonathan didn't look up. He kept his eyes on the sardine sandwiches in front of him, seasick in his chair. I put it down to the ticks and tocks working against each other in the room. Even you were swinging from side to side as though the rhythm had taken over your body.

'Do you think Mr Eccentric is actually a clock?' I asked.

You thought about this for a second as you bobbed this way and that.

'Most *certainly*,' you said, still in Period Drama Mode.

'*Indeed*,' I replied.

You held a finger in the air. '*Quite!*'

I searched my mind for a suitable synonym, holding my finger in the air and giving it a shake.

'*Undeniably!*'

Jonathan sighed loudly.

'For shit's sake,' he mumbled. 'Give it a rest.'

When we looked over at him his face was twisted in its old bitter expression. He looked sad and cross at the same time. You leant in close to my side, keeping your voice a whisper.

'*Unquestionably*,' you said, before giggling into your hand.

'Mr Eccentric's my grandfather,' Jonathan said.

We both looked at him. He was paler than ever and when he looked over at you his eyes were wide behind his glasses.

'Don't worry, he's not yours,' he said. 'Your dad's the one in prison. Mine is the one that's dead.'

'*Dead?*' I said.

'Dead,' he said, pretending to stab himself in the gut.

Your face was crinkled with confusion but for me the truth became clear.

Mr Eccentric's son was Bobby Blake. Dead Bobby Blake. Bobby Blake + Mrs Dickerson = Jonathan Dickerson with Mr Eccentric's looks.

'I see,' I said, nodding at Jonathan.

'Exactly,' he said, nodding back.

Your face was still confused as Uncle Walter opened the door and told us it was time to leave. We all slid off our seats, Jonathan lagging behind with a bowed head. We kept looking at each other, trying to process what we'd been told. You opened your mouth but nothing came out. I opened my mouth but nothing came out. When we got to the doorstep Jonathan glanced up at Mr Eccentric then at Uncle Walter. He put out his pale-pink palm and shook Mr Eccentric's hand. It was a short, firm shake, as though finalizing a deal. We both looked at each other as though we'd just seen a pig fly over Westhill Estate.

Jonathan said nothing as we left Tewkesbury House and kept his head low as we made our way back. When Uncle Walter placed his arm over Jonathan's shoulder Jonathan slid straight out from under it and began marching ahead. You tried to catch up with him.

'How do you know Mr Eccentric's your grandfather?' you asked.

He shoved his hands in his pockets. 'He's not Mr Eccentric, he's Reginald Blake.'

Your brows knotted together. I caught up with you.

'How do you know *Reginald Blake*'s your grandfather, then?' I said.

Your brother looked over at me with a scowl. 'None of your beeswax,' he said. 'Now bugger off.'

The reign of peace in Jonathan's kingdom was shattered.

I have a surprise visit from Mr Chavda today.

'I take my commitments very seriously, Mrs Roy,' I hear him thunder from the bottom of the stairs. 'I do not allow personal matters to interfere with my professional work.'

Amma speaks quietly. I sit up in bed, inching close to the foot of the mattress in the hope of hearing her muffled words. One time, Amma stood in the hallway listening to the heavy breathing of a nuisance caller for a solid eighteen minutes. She remained standing, smoothing down the folds of her sari, as the minutes ticked by. When eventually I asked her what was going on she simply raised her hand and continued to listen. The caller buckled first and after Amma had made sure the line was dead, she placed the receiver down and strolled into the kitchen, destalking okra with a thin knife as though nothing had happened.

It will be the same with Mr Chavda. No matter how much he ruffles his feathers, Amma will not give in. He comes marching into my room, releasing short shots of air from his mouth.

'*Phfft! Phfft! Phfft!*'

He carries on making the noise as he straightens his tie, then places his briefcase on the end of my bed and clicks it open.

'Let's begin,' he says. 'I have selected some multiple-choice tests for you to carry out. They are to decipher what level of understanding you have reached so we can decide the next steps in your education.'

He pulls out a wad of booklets and begins rifling through them. Throughout this whole exchange he hasn't looked at me once, so I take the opportunity to flatten my bed hair with the palms of my hands, pinching my cheeks to fake the appearance of alertness. When he passes me the first test he still refuses to look me in the eye, sitting down in Amma's chair and pulling out his silver Rolex to time me. There's no use forcing tears in an attempt to wiggle my way out of this one.

'Two minutes gone!' he barks as he taps the glass face of his watch.

I try my best with the test, but it's early in the morning and the first question is about quadratic equations. I work my way through but after ten minutes find my eyes wandering across the room and back to Mr Chavda. He sits lax in Amma's chair, the Rolex held loose in one hand as he rubs his chin absentmindedly with the other. He's straightened his tie so much that it sits halfway up his neck and when

189

I look at the buttons on his shirt I see that they're fastened out of order. I follow the track of his eyes out of the bedroom door. Maybe he's expecting Amma to come drifting in, white flag in hand. The large lids of his eyes are drooping and for a moment I think I see a tear sparkle in the corner of one eye.

I look down at the test paper and flick back to the cover sheet. The examination length is one and a half hours. I know Mr Chavda is all too willing to wait the maximum time permitted. I place my pen neatly across the sheet.

'I think this test is too hard for me, Mr Chavda.'

The sound of my voice snaps him out of his gaze. He looks down at his Rolex and pushes himself into an upright position.

'Young girl, I don't believe they're designed to be *easy*.'

Although the tone is sharp, the sadness in his bleary eyes stops me from getting irritated. All these years and I've never considered that Mr Chavda has *feelings*. Of course he's been cross with me, indignant on occasion, but these shows of teacher-type behaviour have always felt staged. Similarly, his courtship of Amma has always had a touch of the hammed-up about it. He seems to do things because he thinks them right, not because of any burning desire from within. It's only as I look at his watery eyes that I realize perhaps his love for my mother has not been entirely mechanical. That there is genuine affection.

Mr Chavda, sensing I'm ogling this private side of him, readjusts his expression into a severe scowl.

'It seems the problem is you find *all* tests too hard.'

Again, I feel no pang at his jibe.

'Then I guess that says something about me,' I say.

Mr Chavda lifts his chin. 'And what would that be exactly?'

I shrug. 'That I'm not academic.'

He's startled by the response and a silence ensues as he tries to think of a suitable retort. Eventually, he makes a spluttering noise with his mouth.

'But your English language skills are impeccable.'

In all his years of teaching, Mr Chavda has never given me one compliment and the fact he just has makes his cheeks blush.

'You write very good sentences,' he mumbles, 'even if the technical knowledge within them proves questionable.'

I watch his hands shaking as he fiddles with the strap of his watch and secures it around his wrist. I look at the circle of white hair around the circumference of his head and see that it's been brushed in a hurry, the strands criss-crossing each other.

'Are you all right, Mr Chavda?' I ask.

He snaps his neck straight, looking at me as though I've asked him if he's an imbecile. He narrows his eyes.

'I suppose you know all about this Rikesh fellow?'

I frown. 'Rikesh?'

As soon as I say it, I realize who he means. Amma has never told me the name of her companion and I'm startled to hear it on my own lips. All the same, Mr Chavda is enthused.

'So it's not just me she keeps in the dark!'

He glances momentarily at the door then leans his body towards me.

'I caught them in the park,' he says in a low hush. 'They were feeding ducks together and . . . *holding hands*.'

The surreptitious whisper of Mr Chavda's voice, the way he leans in with manic eyes, makes my stomach heave. He throws his hands in the air with sudden exasperation.

'The man wasn't even wearing a tie!' he says. 'When I confronted her about it, she told me I was overreacting, that she could do as she pleased. What about the smiles she's given me? The food? She's been treating me like a fool and all for a man who doesn't even polish his shoes!'

He flings his hands in the air again before falling back in his seat. He looks at me from the corners of his eyes.

'They have plans for you too, you know?' he says. 'She told me so. *"We are grateful for your services, Mr Chavda, but we have other plans for Ravine now."* The nerve of it!'

'Plans?' I say. 'What kind of plans?'

'In the park so everyone could see. I never thought your mother would be so *brazen*.'

Swans have been known to break people's arms when protecting their nest. In the same fashion, I find my humility vanishing, my spine uncurling as I prepare to flap.

'Well, I suppose that's her business, isn't it?'

Mr Chavda's eyes widen, wiry hairs poking out from the centre of his brows. It isn't what I've said that's shocked him but the way I've said it. Firm, self-assured. For ten years the man has treated me like a child but now he's looking at an adult.

'Of course,' he says, resuming his upright position. 'Now back to your test.'

He taps the booklet on my knees as if to reinstate his authority. I look down at the questions and tick-boxes before pushing the paper away.

'No more tests, Mr Chavda.'

Again his eyes widen and again he is defeated. A look of hurt ripples across his face. He quickly stands to his feet and collects his papers, telling me he's too busy for this foolishness and has other things to do anyway. I envision his journey back to his car, his feet scuttling along the pavement as he keeps his head down, his body crashing into single mothers and pushchairs. Loneliness can make a person build defences. I know this better than most people.

'Come round for tea sometime,' I say before he leaves. 'You know, for a chat or something.'

He looks over at me as he straightens his tie, eyes blinking as he computes my words. He seems to be considering whether he should be insulted by this offer. His chest grows round as he draws in a deep breath.

'Perhaps,' he says, before storming out.

I don't hear him say goodbye to Amma. Instead he shuts the front door in a way that is loud enough to be noticed.

'Idiot,' Jonathan says through the wall.

I stare at the 2010 calendar still attached to the back of my bedroom door. It's slipped to a crooked position.

'Stop eavesdropping,' I tell him. 'And don't call him an idiot. You don't even know the man.'

The reprimand silences your brother for approximately four seconds. When he speaks again it is loud and clear.

'I know an idiot when I hear an idiot.'

I shake my head and raise my voice. 'Is that because you *are* an idiot?'

There's a pause and I think I've gone too far. Mr Chavda always said I was too smart-mouthed, that I would never find a husband (as if I was looking), with a sharp tongue like mine.

I hear Jonathan shuffling on the other side of the wall.

'Very funny, Ravine,' he says.

I slide beneath the covers of my bed and, even though I know your brother can't see me, cover my mouth to hide my grin.

The
Constellation
of
Surprise

That winter, in the spirit of seasonal unity, we decided to have a joint Roy–Dickerson Christmas. Amma explained that, in England, you didn't have to believe in festivals to celebrate them. On Halloween people dressed as ghosts they didn't think existed; on Bonfire Night burnt effigies of a man they held no malice for; and on Shrove Tuesday stuffed their bellies full of pancakes and golden syrup without the slightest intention of fasting for Lent.

'This is the English culture,' she explained. 'It's how they *rejoice*.'

So that year we decided to rejoice in style. We decked your flat with enough tinsel and fairy lights to decorate a department store. The tree, a tall plastic number bought from Laser's car boot, stood at a wonky angle against the back wall, threatening to tip over and cover us all in a shower of glitter and baubles (even when we opened our presents,

Amma kept her hands hovering above us in anticipation). We wore our party dresses while Jonathan remained in the thunderstorm pyjamas he'd slept in, our busy hands ripping at the parcels as if afraid they'd run away. Colouring books, crazy markers, flimsy dolls and teddy bears – our presents were of the highest pound-shop quality. The more boxes we opened the louder we squealed. Even Jonathan seemed impressed with his building blocks, electronic thermometer and bargain-basement computer games.

'What's the weather forecast?' you asked him.

He froze mid-tear, a ball of holly-print wrapping paper clutched in his hand. When he spoke it was in a deep, serious voice.

'Sunny intervals followed by lightning storms throughout the region.'

We looked at each other.

'Coool.'

It was while we were playing a new game on Jonathan's Commodore 64 that Sandy Burke arrived. The Commodore 64 had been given to Jonathan as a birthday present by one of Mrs Dickerson's former boyfriends. He'd bought the out-of-date item to win him over but Jonathan wouldn't even open the box, demanding a Sega Mega Drive instead. It wasn't until they broke up that Jonathan's standards dropped. For hours we'd sit on his bed, watching acid-rainbow stripes flicker across the screen as the tape loaded. They have computer consoles now that are motion-sensitive; I've seen the adverts. You stand in front of them and pretend to play tennis without a tennis racket and go bowling without a bowling bowl. They take seconds to load and store more information than entire computer suites did when we were kids. The days of smacking arrow keys on the keyboard, watching the white oval of Dizzy the Egg spin round and round as the game crashed, are well and truly over.

Jonathan had detangled the mass of wires from his own television monitor to bring the Commodore into the living room. As Uncle Walter folded napkins and Amma came back and forth from our flat with tray upon tray of chilli-laced roast vegetables, we sat and yelled at the screen. We only realized Sandy Burke was in the room when she positioned her body in front of Dizzy as he was about to jump over a crocodile-infested river. Even then, she was so thin we could crane our necks sideways and still see the screen. She huffed loudly and clicked the power off.

'Oi!' Jonathan yelled. 'We were playing that!'

Sandy smiled, picking up the baby carriers she'd left on the floor.

'I've come to give you all your present,' she said, bobbing up and down.

Sandy hadn't been to the flat since the cat murder, and the sight of her candyfloss hair in front of us with the promise of presents was enough to make us forget the game. Amma and Uncle Walter looked up from Christmas crackers as though frozen in time.

Sandy became nervous. Her eyes darted from adults to children as she bobbed up and down like a boat lost at sea. This was unlike Sandy, who your mother once described as having 'more balls than a children's playpen'. Sandy eventually released a shaky chuckle.

'You'll be real happy when you see it,' she said, though the twitching in her left eye said otherwise. 'It's going to be such a surprise!'

You clambered on top of the sofa, peering over the edge.

'I can't see anything,' you said, turning back with a crumpled expression on your face.

Sandy gulped. Her throat was so thin back then that when she swallowed you could see the muscles move along it in a wave. Her eyes glanced sideways.

'It's at the door.'

We all turned our heads as though Santa Claus himself was about to step out from the shadows. Instead of a round-bellied man with a white beard, we saw a figure, tall and slim, moving towards us with exaggerated steps. The figure wobbled as it came closer, unsteady in six-inch stilettos and a tight denim mini-skirt.

'Surprise!' Mrs Dickerson screeched, fanning her hands out as though finishing a magic trick.

No one spoke. No one moved. I don't think anyone even breathed. Mrs Dickerson continued to hold her hands out until her grin began to falter.

'*Muuum!*' you screamed, jumping off the sofa and running into her arms.

The cry broke us out of our stupor. Mrs Dickerson's grin snapped back into place as she grabbed hold of your body, swinging you around at such a height we could see the pink soles of your trainers.

'That's right, darling,' she said as she slowed to a stop. 'I'm home.'

As she spoke, she looked over at Uncle Walter. He was standing with arms dropped by his sides and his mouth hanging open. Sweat was circling his armpits and his skin was as pale as the uncooked turkey in the fridge. When she caught his gaze, your uncle grinned an automatic grin. It was so forced it looked square on his round chubby face. In response, Mrs Dickerson lifted her chin and smiled back. Uncle Walter's expression crumbled. He hung his head and began fiddling with the napkins as your mother smacked a huge kiss upon your chin. You giggled manically and clung to her neck.

At the time I didn't understand why Uncle Walter looked away, but I've now watched enough wildlife programmes to have figured it out. When your mother grinned at her brother it was with the same menace as a tiger growling at its opponent. It wasn't a gesture of sibling affection or a symbol of joy at their reunion; that smile was a display of dominance. With a simple lifting of her chin, Mrs Dickerson had reclaimed her territory.

'It has taken you long enough!' Amma said.

She was standing with her hands folded over her midriff as her festively red and green sari hung down in pleats.

'We were thinking you would never come back.'

Your mother dropped your body to the floor.

'It was a holiday, Rekha. I was always coming back.'

'It might have been nice of you to tell your brother,' Amma muttered.

Mrs Dickerson's mouth twitched, but only for a second. She walked over to an armchair, falling down into it with an elaborate exhalation.

'Walt doesn't mind,' she said, as she produced a packet of cigarettes from her sleeve. 'He owes me one, don't you?'

She stared at Uncle Walter as she lit her cigarette. He dropped his gaze again and resumed folding napkins.

Jonathan had been watching the whole scene with eyes as wide as Dizzy the Egg's. His expression was the same as when he watched hurricanes on the television: mouth open, eyes afraid to blink. When your mother looked over at him he slammed his mouth shut.

'Come over here, little man.'

She leant forward in her seat, smoke trailing from her cigarette in spirals.

'Come and give your mum a hug.'

Jonathan spun his body away as though she hadn't said a word.

'Can we put the telly back on now or *what*?' he said.

Theirs was a battle that hadn't even begun.

When Amma leaves for her routine visit to the doctor's, I don't mention what Mr Chavda has said. When I see the kohl etched upon the rims of her lids, a new bindi placed artfully on the centre of her fore-head, when she bends down to kiss me and her usual rose scent is smothered by a sour new perfume that makes my eyes sting, I simply grin.

'Have a nice time,' I tell her.

'It is only the doctor's,' she says, before dashing out.

When she's gone I swing my feet over the side of the bed and begin my daily tests. I wiggle my toes, turn my ankles in circles and raise my legs at various angles. With every movement I feel my muscles growing taut then relaxed, the stretch and the strain as I flex and turn, but still no pain. After years of sitting in the shallow end of the pool I'm finally swimming in open water.

'Do you still carry that (*mumble*) everywhere?' your brother asks.

I glance over at the wall before dropping my legs. I ask him to repeat himself.

'DICTIONARY,' he says. 'Do you still carry that DICTIONARY everywhere?'

I sigh. 'I don't go anywhere, Jonathan.'

I push myself to my feet, turning Amma's chair to face the window as I sit by the wall with a glass pressed up against it.

'You don't go *anywhere*?' he asks.

I place my elbow on the flaking paint of the window sill. 'Just to the hospital. And I haven't been there for a while.'

There's a silence as I look out at the blocks of flats, the winding rib-bon of paths and roads. It's so vast, so wide; just looking at it makes me dizzy. I focus my gaze on the tree in front of me and ask Jonathan if he knows its name.

'Horse chestnut,' he says as I stare at the leaves.

I remember prickly green balls appearing on the branches each year. The brown orbs that emerge when they fall to the ground.

199

'Not conker?'

When we were younger Jonathan would have scoffed at me for saying that, rolling his eyes as far back in their sockets as humanly possible. I imagine him doing this on the opposite side of the wall, but when his reply comes back it's diplomatic, verging on sincere.

'They grow conkers,' he explains. 'But they're still called horse chestnut.'

'How do you know that?'

'I read a book on botany in the . . . library.'

The pause makes me wonder which word has been omitted. School library? University? Prison? I don't know which option is worst: that Jonathan has surpassed me in the world of education or that he's become a convicted criminal without my knowledge.

'Do you still have it?' Jonathan asks. 'The dictionary, I mean.'

I squeeze my eyes shut. 'Does it matter?'

There's a pause.

'I guess not.'

I look out at the horse chestnut that has loomed by my window my entire life. It's the same as me, that tree. Rooted here, stuck in this estate.

I press my cheek into the glass and look at the wall beside me. It's strange to think of your brother on the other side. Maybe it's because I can't see him. Maybe if I knew what he looked like things would be different.

I press my free hand against the wall, listening carefully through the glass.

'Why did you come back, Jonathan?'

The question pops from my mouth even though I've planned not to ask it. I don't want to ask because I don't want Jonathan to think I care. But maybe I do. Maybe I care more than I want to admit.

'Reginald's dying,' he says.

My hand drops off the wall.

'Who?'

I can hear his bed creaking as he sits up straight, the sound of his body shifting up against the wall.

'Mr Eccentric. He sent me a letter saying he wanted to see me before . . . Well, before it's too late.'

I scrunch the material of my robe in my hand. 'That's why you came back?'

'He's my grandfather. I thought I had to. But now—'

I sit up straight. 'I'm going to sleep now!'

It's still early morning but your brother doesn't question me as I climb back into bed. I coil my body and bury my head in my pillow. I'd scream if I knew no one would hear me. If he thinks he's upset me, he'll think he's won, and I won't let him win, not again.

'You all right, Ravine?' he says.

I can tell he has his face close to the wall because his voice is suddenly loud. Just the sound of it makes my stomach contort like small fists are punching me.

'Ravine?'

I lift my head up. 'Don't call me that!'

When he speaks again, he sounds confused. 'But it's your name.'

'*Don't call me that!*'

He's quiet after this and doesn't speak again.

I'm a fool, Marianne, a complete and ridiculous fool. For some ludicrous reason I thought your brother had come back to see me.

The Constellation of Yellow Eyes

Today is the general election and, although the polling stations will stay open until 10 p.m., Amma decides being ridiculously early will somehow help with the voting process.

'Women have died for this right,' she tells me, shaking me awake at 7.30 a.m.

I yawn. 'I thought the Suffragettes were trying to *stop* female suffering.'

Amma is too busy bustling around my room to appreciate the quip. She's excited, not just at the idea of voting but at me leaving the flat.

It's my own fault. When the poll card came I should have said the idea was ridiculous instead of letting Amma give me exercises and continually update me on political developments. On the day of the first TV debate we sat in my room with popcorn on our laps. Red, blue and yellow stripes adorned the television studio as party leaders made pleas towards the camera and rolled out names of 'ordinary people' they had spoken to, as though they were family members. They talked in long rambling monologues, gesturing with flat hands slicing through the air and forcing such insincere grins across their faces that Amma was afraid they would pull a muscle.

'So much grinning cannot be good for a person,' she told me.

'That explains why I'm so healthy,' I said.

Amma cleared up the popcorn without so much as a chuckle. She's so used to my sarcasm now that she doesn't even realize when it's in good humour. Perhaps I should try some straightforward jokes.

Man walks into a bar . . . Ouch!

That was one of your favourites.

When the debates had finished and Amma went downstairs, Jonathan began speaking to me through the wall.

'All sounds like bollocks to me,' he said.

I didn't gasp but chuckled at what he said.

Never again.

Since our conversation about Mr Eccentric I haven't spoken to your brother. I've decided to remain mute even when he knocks and calls for me through the wall. Yet still, for reasons I don't understand, I've carried on supplying him with midnight meals via his welcome mat. I'm not completely heartless after all. This surprises me more than anyone.

As I rub the sleep from my eyes and look over at the tray of matar paneer on the bedside table, Amma delves into my wardrobe with a frenzied grin. I watch as she pulls out saris and gowns more suitable for a royal wedding than a general election. Imitation silk and taffeta adorn the foot of my bed, low-cut dresses bought in the ghost of the January sales.

'I'll wear the red one,' I say, as the end of my bed is swamped in polyester. 'The one that goes in at the waist.'

Amma knows exactly which one I mean. She fails to hide her smugness at the fact I've looked through the outfits, grinning as she wiggles her head from side to side.

When I'm dressed I convince Amma that I've taken enough medication and painkillers to be able to walk down the stairs without her support. Each step is greeted with the same enthusiasm bestowed upon a baby learning to walk. Even though I know it's fraud, I feel pleased when Amma clasps her hands together, the joy welling on her face. As though it's deserved, as though I'm actually achieving something.

It's on the third step that I feel myself wobble. I glimpse the front door and remember the day I went out in this same red dress to meet Jonathan. I picture the world outside, the bright lights, the blank faces, the sea of the unknown. Fear crashes over me in waves, and at the crests of each I feel:

Shock   Panic   Dread

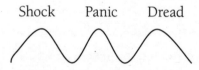

Like a child dropped into the deep end, I can feel my arms flailing, grappling for the water's surface as my lungs search for air.

Amma, witnessing none of this terror, only sees me freeze.

'I knew you should have taken more pills!' she cries.

I grab hold of the handrail, the flowers on the wallpaper blurring into a spiral of colour. I hold on tighter as I imagine all the things that lie outside. The metal railings where we saw your Uncle Walter for the first time. The winding path trailing down the hill, peeling paint on the rails, crisp packets blown across the ground. The polling station in the hall of our old primary school where you would do handstands in the dinner queue. The white-painted houses of other flats: Bonchurch House, Tewkesbury House, Battenberg House. Laser and his dodgy car boot. Old Mrs Simmons, even though she's now dead. Mr Eccentric in his room of ticking clocks. Jonathan.

It must be Amma's screeching that brings him out. Goodness knows how long he's been waiting or what he's been waiting for, but when he emerges from the living room, Amma's companion has a cup of tea balanced on the palm of his hand. As the spiralling of flowered wallpaper floats away I see him clearly for the first time.

The trench coat. The dark mottled skin. The yellow eyes.

Amma sees the change in my expression and begins to wave her hands in the air.

'Now let us not overreact!'

But I've already turned round, clambering up those three steps and into the bathroom.

'Ravine,' his voice calls out as I slam the door behind me. 'Please come back, Ravine. *Please come back.*'

When I woke up at the hospital the night after you disappeared, the Soul-drinker was sitting on a high-backed chair by my bed, hands balled up on his lap. If I hadn't been drugged up on medication, I would have thrown my head back and screamed. Instead, all I managed was enough squirming to hit the side table. The vase on top rocked for a moment and then settled back into place. I wanted it to tumble, to drop to the floor with a dramatic smash.

The wobbling of the vase was enough to catch the monster's attention and when he looked up at me I was confronted with the sickly yellow balls of his eyes. Under the brightness of the hospital lights I could see the visible bald spot on the top of his head, the thick-knit multi-coloured jumper that covered his pot belly. He had wrinkles across his forehead that vanished as he grinned. This creature could almost have been human.

'Rekha!' he cried, eyes fixed upon mine as he stood and waved his hands.

I tried to get away but when I turned my head the pain was excruciating. I'd never broken a bone, never had a tooth pulled out and though I easily bruised, my body was quick to recover. This pain was so intense that my muscles instantly clenched, my eyes streamed tears and, for a distinct period of time, the world disappeared.

When I opened my eyes again I found Amma hovering over my bed with two plastic cups in her hands, steam rising up from the rims. Her eyes were large; strip lighting was reflected in the darkness of her irises. Already I could see worry lines setting in the corners of her lids.

'Ravine Roy?' she said, as though checking I was the girl she'd given birth to in that same hospital.

I tried to blink the tears from my eyes as the left side of my body throbbed with pain. Each muscle was seizing up, my nerves prickling, my skin so tender that it felt like I was lying on a bed of broken glass. When my vision cleared I saw the blurry shadow of the Soul-drinker walking up behind her.

'Shona.' Amma was weeping as he stepped closer, moving a hand over her shoulder. 'My darling shona.'

Suddenly I found the power to scream.

It was a shrill, warbling cry and no matter how much Amma tried to calm me, I wouldn't stop until the monster was out of the room. Even once he was gone, I lay whimpering. It was only later, after a deep sleep and a hot bowl of vegetable soup, that Amma explained it all.

The Soul-drinker was not a Soul-drinker after all; he was my father.

*

I remain locked inside the bathroom. Amma tries to reason with me through the door. She tells me it's a simple misunderstanding, not the big conspiracy I think it is.

'Your father was simply having some chai,' she says. 'He was not expecting to see you.'

Your father, she says, after years of calling him nothing but a coward and a fool. I stroll up and down the bathroom, testing out the strength of my legs, wondering how far I could run on them, how fast I could get away.

Amma soon tires of her softly-softly approach and begins hammering at me.

'All he wants is to *see you*!' she says, even though she's just told me the opposite.

I've heard it all before. When my father tried to visit me in the hospital the day after I woke up, I refused to see him. Amma recounted his tales of criminal gangs and threats to his family as though they were proof of his sincerity. She told me about his years on the run, his attempts at tracking her down while remaining undercover. After seven years he opened the newspaper to see a picture of a small Asian girl under the headline 'CITY SCHOOL WINS VEGETABLE-GROWING CONTEST'. Even though I had no involvement in the gardening feat, I'd been shoved in front of the camera with a marrow in my arms, demonstrating to the rest of the country the diversity of Westhill Primary School. Behind me stood my undeservedly proud mother and at the sight of us, my father felt a swell of pride (he had a daughter!) and a reason to come out of hiding. So much melodrama and high jinks, it could have been in the DVD extras of *Amma's Soap Opera Life*.

When I came home and was put in bed for the rest of eternity, Amma decided it was time for me to see my no-good-disappearing father. She cuckooed the subject at me like a broken clock.

'Are you ready to see your father today, shona?' she asked, with enough sweetness to give a person toothache.

'No,' I said.

Another day, another tactic.

'Your father has brought you a present. Would you like him to come up and give it to you?'

'No.'

'Perhaps you would like to say Happy New Year to your father?'

'No.'

'Perhaps you would like to hear your father's good news?'

'No.'

Eventually she learnt that there was no way I'd respond with anything other than 'no' to a question that involved my father. She grew worn out, her smiles sandpapered to frowns and weary expressions that made me feel like a spoilt three-year-old refusing to get dressed. Eventually she stopped asking altogether. I thought he'd given up.

But no matter how hard I run from him, the Soul-drinker remains champion. This man who went *poof* out of the air is now worthy of our best crockery and is allowed to sit for hours in our living room, chanting numbers in Bengali through my floorboards. Amma's flimsy cover-up of their meetings is now exposed. Sneaking him in, ushering him out, coming upstairs afterwards with the high chin of innocence. Amma knows full well I can hear every tremor in this flat yet still she shoves the whole affair under my nose. She's daring me to call her out. To interrogate her and demand the truth.

But I don't want the truth. I want pretence. Pretence that he doesn't exist. Pretence that it never happened. But when I saw him in the hall all hope of that was shattered.

'He is your *father*,' Amma repeats through the door, as though the more she says it, the more it means something.

'He is your *abbah*,' she implores, as though stating the same thing in another language will somehow rewire my thinking.

I want to explain it all to her but there's too much to say and it's too hard to say it. She thinks I should see him, just once. That I have nothing to lose but everything to gain. Unlike you and Jonathan or even herself, I have a father who wants to know me, and for that reason I should give him a chance.

But I have tales looping round my head, the stories your brother told me as well as the image of the Soul-drinker coming after me in the woods. Childhood fears are the worst type of fears because they aren't based on logic but a reflex. A reflex so well worn in your brain that all you need is a smell or an image to trigger it; stomach twisting, tension shooting up your cowering shoulders, eyes wide and panicked. The only links I have with that man are based on fear. How can I look at his face without triggering that fear? Without remembering what happened to us? But Amma doesn't understand this because Amma doesn't know. She's never heard of the Soul-drinker, has no idea of the childhood terrors that plague me. She believes I'm being obstinate and that all I need is a bit of nagging to nudge me onto the right path.

'He is a nice man, Ravine,' she tells me through the bathroom door. 'You will like him. I know you will.'

When I was younger she told me he was a soppy fool no English woman would touch with a barge pole. Now he is *nice*. I put the lid down on the toilet seat and sit down on the chipped wood.

'I don't want to see him,' I say, curling my knees up to my chin.

'But *why*?'

'Because I don't.'

I hear my mother sigh and imagine the puffs of her sari sighing along with her.

209

'It's been *ten years*, Ravine.'

She says this as if ten years is enough time to get over your worst fears. As if ten years will banish the childhood reflex that has followed you into adulthood.

As I held on to my knees, I let my silence respond. I hear Amma begin to huff and mutter under her breath. I imagine her pulling her shoulders back, lifting her chin.

'Well, I don't know about you but *I* am going to vote,' she says.

She utters this like a threat, as if she's told me she's going to jump off a cliff. I can hear her marching down the stairs, mumbling to her companion and nearly knocking over the coat stand as she collects her belongings.

'Such a stubborn phagol betty!' she cries up the steps. 'I don't know where she gets this stubbornness from!'

'From you, *who else*?' I yell back.

My yelling is interrupted by the slamming of the front door, which is soon followed by another slam as my father chases after her.

As soon as I say the words I wince. Since my recovery I've made one promise to myself and one promise only: that as long as I'm keeping the truth from Amma I will at least try to be kind to her.

Promises, it appears, are as fickle as the truth.

The Constellation of Return

Your mother's return electric-shocked our world. It's not that we'd *forgotten* about her, but as the weeks turned into months her return seemed less and less likely. She was searching for her fortune, we'd decided, starring in Broadway musicals, trekking through Peruvian tombs in the style of Lara Croft. She'd come back one day, yes, but far in the future when she'd jet you off to whatever mansion she lived in and feed you cherry pop and triple chocolate ice-cream. This fantasy helped you to come to terms with your abandonment (there had been a *reason*, there would be a *reward*), so the shattering of this fantasy was hard to accept.

'Did you see any tigers?' you asked her. 'Did you go up mountains? Did you meet anyone *famous*?'

We both watched your mother's face as we waited for the fabulous tales that would tumble from her lips. She looked over at us with a sly grin.

'Don't you worry, girls. When you're older you can have your own adventures.'

Our expressions dropped. We already had our own adventures, what we wanted to know about was *hers*. We could still smell the change in her. Summer fruits, exotic flowers – somewhere along her travels she had collected the scents of the world.

After Mrs Dickerson's return your uncle became a timid creature. He dutifully cleaned the flat and made you meals every evening but he no longer invented elaborate names for the dishes, or chuckled to himself as he ate. He stopped playing the sleeping bear game with us and wouldn't show us any more strategies to cope with emergency situations. One time Mrs Dickerson caught him teaching us Italian. She stood beside him, watching with narrowed eyes.

'*Non preoccuparti, sii felice,*' you repeated. '*Non preoccuparti, sii felice.*'

'How do you say "mini dictionary" in Italian?' I asked.

Uncle Walter glanced over at your mother as she held her hands on her hips. Her eyes were fixed on him as he patted the sweat off his forehead with a handkerchief.

'I'll have to check that one for you,' he said.

Your mother chuckled.

'And how do I ask someone if they want to play emergency rooms?' you asked.

'I'd have to check that too.'

Mrs Dickerson looked over at your uncle and began to laugh so scornfully that he rose to his feet, telling us we'd carry on the lesson another time. We never did.

He slept on the sofa and although he still brushed your hair and washed your clothes, Mrs Dickerson was in charge. She organized your outings to the shops, dictated what you could and could not wear, and even gave me a curfew for when I should go home. This, from the same Mrs Dickerson who used to drink herself into such oblivion that you couldn't wake her for days. Who smashed up the flat whenever the whim took her, grabbing hold of your toys, plates and ornaments, leaving you and Jonathan to clear up the mess. You might have developed amnesia about these events, but I hadn't. I didn't trust her, I admit it, and neither did Amma.

'She'll be gone soon,' Amma told me as she was peeling onions one day.

Not one tear rolled down her cheek as she chopped.

'These people who disappear, they have no thoughts of others. They come and go *willy-nilly*, not thinking about the chaos they leave behind.'

She waved her knife in the air with such conviction I was scared into believing her. So I waited for your mother to leave. I admit this now because to admit it back then would have upset you. I watched and scrutinized her, searching for signs of potential abandonment. I *wanted* her to leave. She was bossy and mean, not just to us children (a curfew, for God's sake!) but to Uncle Walter too. She called him a slob, an idiot, a lard arse. She openly mocked him and, once, threw a dragon-shaped paperweight at his head while we were watching the National Lottery.

'Hey!' Jonathan cried. 'Are you trying to *kill* us?'

Your mother leant back on the sofa and began painting her nails.

'No,' she said with a chuckle, 'just your Uncle Walt.'

If she'd come back a few months earlier, your brother would have been in on the joke, laughing in the face of your stunned uncle as he clasped his lottery ticket tightly to his chest. But your brother wasn't at war with your uncle any more.

'If you do that again I'll knock your block off!' he said, pushing his chest out and balling his fists.

Your mother lowered her chin. The light of the television shone bright in the round globes of her pupils.

'Who do you think you're talking to?'

You made sure to interrupt before Jonathan gave her an answer. 'Jonathan's just saying it's not very nice to throw things.'

'Especially at Uncle Walter,' I added.

Your mother looked at us both as though we'd punched her in the stomach. The blood rushed up her neck like oil spurting up a rig.

'It's all right,' Uncle Walter said, sweat trickling over the mounds of his cheeks. 'It's a joke, isn't it? I don't mind.'

Mrs Dickerson began blowing at the varnish on her nails as everyone else turned their eyes to the spinning balls on the screen. As she whipped her breath back and forth, I could feel her gaze burning into the side of my face.

'Ravine,' she said, as the first number was called. 'It's past eight. You should go home.'

I tried to slam the door on the way out but the television muffled the noise. I went into my flat to find Amma had fallen asleep on the sofa with a bowl of unshelled peas on her lap. I cuddled my body up to hers, sinking into her familiar warmth.

Your love for your mother made you blind. You made excuses for her, told me everything was just *super-duper*! You thought the world had room for both your uncle and your mother, but I'd seen the look she'd given Uncle Walter on Christmas Day and knew better. All I hoped was that your mother would be the first to go.

I don't get up for my bath today. Amma doesn't pester me as she normally would, frightening me with stories of flesh-eating bacteria and gangrene, but instead allows the smell of vinegar and lemon to float to my door. When she comes up to my room, the toes of her trainers are poking out from a pair of purple jogging bottoms. She sticks her nose in the air.

'I'm going to Blackpool,' she says. 'And I won't be back until tomorrow.'

I hold the edge of the duvet up to my chin. 'Who are you going with?'

She narrows her eyes. 'Gordon Brown. I hear he has a lot of time on his hands now.'

Even when she's angry Amma can't resist giving me news updates. This morning she trotted around with the radio at full volume as she did the housework. I was repeatedly updated against my will. The election had received an unexpected turnout of voters, many being turned away from the polling stations because of the surge. The nation wanted change and so they got it in the fuzzy ambiguity of a coalition government. Gordon Brown was out and the Conservatives were aligned with the Liberal Democrats. The reporters were giving it a year.

I look at Amma standing in her purple jogging bottoms, a symbol that more change is on the horizon.

'What's happening with you two?' I ask.

She smooths down her dyed black hair. 'Between me and Gordon?'

I furrow my brow. 'You know who I mean.'

I say this as strictly as a school teacher and suddenly our roles are reversed. Amma's cheeks flush, a subtle blossoming of colour that would have gone unnoticed if it wasn't for her refusal to look away.

'We are becoming *reacquainted*.'

I sigh. 'You were barely *acquainted* the first time,' I say. 'He left you after a few months.'

Amma keeps her eyes narrow. 'You think you know everything, Little Miss Know-It-All?'

I don't answer but carry on clutching the duvet. She glares at me with beady eyes.

'I must leave,' she says. 'I have a train to catch.'

I feel my heart pounding as the front door slams. Silence leaks through the flat.

After years of hourly devotion, of pills and heartburn breakfasts, of routine trips to the cash-and-carry, doctor's surgery, park and *no further*, why has Amma decided to get on a train with the man who abandoned her nearly two decades ago and travel up to Blackpool with him? The answer is simple.

She knows.

The day of the election Amma couldn't find her poll card. She stormed back indoors as I remained locked in the bathroom, and began typhooning her way around the flat. As she marched up and down the stairs, she made sure to declare that as soon as she found the correct documentation she was going to go and carry out her right to vote. I heard her shuffling around in her room then in mine, but it wasn't until later that night that I discovered what she'd seen.

Amma came upstairs with her usual tray for dinner. Upon it was a bowl of tomato soup and a bread roll.

'What's this?' I said.

She looked at me with an upturned nose. 'What do you think it is?'

I looked at the pool of crimson. 'Soup?'

She nodded sharply. 'Correct.'

I frowned. 'No curry?'

'I was too busy to make curry.'

She sat down in her chair with her nose pointed to the ceiling.

To be honest, I didn't mind the absence of chilli, but the sudden change was disturbing. I slurped the soup up. A part of me knew she was testing me but I was so determined to enjoy this bending of the rules that I quickly finished the whole bowl. It was only when I put my spoon down that I realized something was missing. I looked along the top edge of my tray then down the bottom and along the sides.

'You forgot my pills,' I said.

Amma raised her brows in mock surprise. She opened her mouth ready to let the words overflow, then reconsidered and closed her lips tight. She bowed her head.

'So I did,' she said, getting to her feet and walking slowly out of the room.

If the heart flutters when in love, it also flutters when in panic. As I pushed the tray onto the bedside table and swung my head over the edge of the bed, I felt as though my chest was filled with butterflies. My heart continued to flutter with such a tickling velocity that I was afraid it would fly right out of my throat. I hung my head upside down and looked beneath the bed. The feeling stopped. The biscuit tin that housed three weeks of medication was still there but the lid that was usually pressed down tight had been lifted off and dropped to the side. There was no doubt in my mind what had happened. I'd been caught out.

When Amma came back upstairs I sat up straight in bed, placed the tray back on my knees and refused to look at her.

'Your pills,' she said, sticking her hand out.

I blindly took the pills from her grasp and placed them on the tray. 'Thank you.'

I could feel her looking down at the hard discs. It was clear that one of us would have to give in but I wasn't sure who. As Amma continued to wait, I took hold of the pills, stuffing their round bodies into my mouth and swallowing the whole lot down with a single gulp of mango juice. Amma said nothing, simply looking at my tray one last time before leaving the room.

So now we are both left tangled in the web of my lies. Amma won't admit that she knows my secret and I won't admit that I know that she knows. As I've come to realize, we're both stubborn mules and even though I know Amma will, as ever, emerge the victor, I keep digging my heels in the dirt. I'm not ready to give in, not yet. Secrets are destructive things and now the pin has been pulled out of the grenade, all I can do is wait for the explosion.

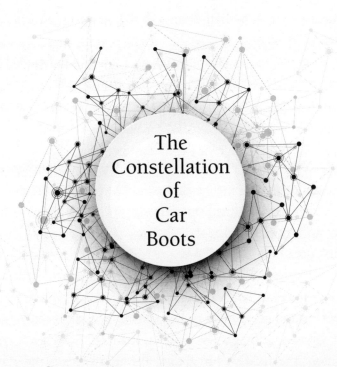

The
Constellation
of
Car
Boots

It happened at Laser's 'End-of-Century Car Boot Bonanza'. We'd all gone together, huddling around broken stalls in the chill of the morning, reading signs written with highlighters and taped to lollipop sticks. 'MILLENNIUM FIREWORX' I read, wondering how Laser had succeeded with 'millennium' while failing with 'fireworks'. We liked this stall best because it was covered in large boxes we weren't allowed to touch – stacks of Catherine wheels, rockets, fountains and sparklers; fireworks packed in gaudy boxes with names like 'Ice Fountain' and 'Emerald Nights' emblazoned across them in a fiery font. Your brother spent most of that morning trying to convince Laser to sell him a star-shaped set called 'The One-minute Spectacular'.

'Look, mate, I can't,' said Laser, pulling at the collar of his Tommy Hillfinger jumper. 'You won't believe the shit I'll get in if I sell to minors.'

'I'm not a miner,' Jonathan protested. 'I'm not even old enough to bloody work!'

Uncle Walter would usually have chuckled at this and guided Jonathan away but he was too busy mooching in his trench coat by the second-hand books. That morning, your mother had called him a fat lump when trying to pass him in the kitchen, and the taunt had made him retreat into a shell of silence.

If Uncle Walter hadn't been hiding that day, maybe things would have been different. But maybe they would have been the same. The dominoes were already lined up and once the slabs began to topple there was no way of stopping the results.

The first domino to (literally) be pushed was Mr Eccentric. He was standing behind your mother, rifling through a box of bric-a-brac, and she was showing Sandy Burke a faux-fur jacket. As she swung the fuzzy item around her shoulders, her arm clipped Mr Eccentric across the nose, knocking the glasses clear off his face. I can see it now in slow motion: the reddish fur gliding through the air, the clash of elbow against face, the ripple of disgust across Mr Eccentric's expression as thick glasses shot off his nose.

'I knew it!' he said, scrambling across the floor until he found his frames. 'I knew you'd have to start something!'

When he bounced up to his feet, berry-red suit scuffed at the knees, Mr Eccentric jutted a bony finger at your mother's face. Mrs Dickerson recoiled from it, the corner of her lip cobra-tailing into a snarl.

'Shut up, you old bastard,' she said, turning back to Sandy.

Amma gasped, covering my ears with her hands as if I hadn't already heard these words from Jonathan Dickerson's potty mouth. But it wasn't the words, it was the tone in which they were said and the person to whom they were said. Mr Eccentric might have been strange and mean but he was also old and unhappy.

'*Muuuuum* . . .' you said in one drawn-out syllable, the body of a second-hand Sindy doll hanging loosely in your hand.

'You've always been a foul-mouthed hag!' Mr Eccentric yelled. 'Rotten to the core!'

Your mother laughed, fiddling with the make-up pallettes on the stall in front of her. She was a wild animal, shoulders covered in faux fur, lip snarling. Nobody would be able to tame her.

'Bobby didn't seem to think so,' she said.

It was then that Uncle Walter emerged. He appeared out of nowhere, a giant stepping out of his cave.

'Don't you dare bring my Bobby into this!' Mr Eccentric cried. Uncle Walter's large bear hands were upon Mr Eccentric, pulling him back.

'Come on, Reggie,' he said in his ear.

Mr Eccentric didn't struggle, seemed placated in fact, then began yelling, 'She's a witch! A goddamn witch! She should never have come back!'

His kicking legs knocked one of the stalls, sending bumper packs of rockets and Catherine wheels tumbling to the floor. It was only then that I saw Jonathan standing behind the collapsed table. He wasn't looking at Mr Eccentric or Mrs Dickerson, but down at the pile of boxes.

'Let's calm down, shall we?' Laser said, panicking as his goods lay scattered across the floor.

He edged his way round the tables but Mrs Dickerson widened her stance and blocked his path. She placed her hands on her hips, furry shoulders shaking as she spoke.

'I've got as much right to be here as anyone else.'

Mr Eccentric lurched forward, his thin body held back by the giant weight of your uncle's bulk.

'You made a deal with me, you witch! You said you'd go!'

Your mother glanced at the faces surrounding her. 'I did go. Now I'm back.'

Mr Eccentric shook his head, flapping his hands as though flies were attacking him.

'Not now – *then*. If you'd gone when I told you to, my boy would be alive.'

My gaze became wild and darting. I looked up at Amma but she was as confused as me. I looked at you, your hand held in the air as if ready to ask a question. I looked at Jonathan, still standing by the firework stand, his eyes directed at your mother like pistols at a target. Behind him a crowd of Westhill residents had formed. They stood gawping as though watching a performance. Mrs Dickerson laughed.

'So it's my fault he's dead now?' she said.

Mr Eccentric stood still. You could see the crinkles in his berry suit slacken as he lifted his chin.

'I know you sent those men to finish him.'

Your mother's body reeled back.

'*Men?*' Mrs Dickerson said. 'What *men?*'

Mr Eccentric's glasses began to steam up. I could see the large panels of glass within the huge frames, his eyes filling behind them. Uncle Walter gently patted Mr Eccentric on the shoulder.

'Let's stop this, Reggie,' he said. 'Let's go back to your flat.'

Mr Eccentric held his head low, his suit hanging from his shoulders in a way that revealed his fragility, as he let your uncle guide him away. Uncle Walter glanced back at your mother.

That could have been the end of it. I wish that had been the end of it. But your mother wasn't finished.

'He did it to himself!' she cried. 'Bobby was never murdered, you stupid old git. He killed himself!'

Mr Eccentric turned back sharply.

'You're full of lies!' he said, jabbing his finger at her again. 'Wicked lies!'

I looked at Mrs Dickerson. Her eyes were darting between Walter and Mr Eccentric, the veins in her neck pulsing, the breath heaving through her nostrils. This was how your mother looked when she was about to attack.

'Ask your mate Walt if you don't believe me!' she said. 'He saw the whole bloody thing! Left him there bleeding to death, the stupid idiot.'

As soon as the words were out, your mother's expression crumpled. Her eyes blinked rapidly, arms hanging loosely by her side. She began to shake as the crowd whispered. You stood by her side, trying to take hold of her hand, but she shook you off without looking down. Her eyes flicked towards the crowd, her cheeks burning red. She straightened her back, collecting herself with a sharp intake of breath.

'What do you think to that, Reggie? Not so perfect now, is he, your mate? Nothing but a coward.'

She pulled a cigarette out of her bag, her hand struggling to hold it steady as she brought it to her lips.

'Playing around with knives the way they used to do. I kept telling them they'd have an accident someday. But I didn't send *anyone*! Call me anything, Reggie, but don't call me a liar.'

Nothing can demonstrate the gravity of a situation better than the reaction of a crowd. While some bystanders continued mumbling to each other, with hands held to chests, others quickly dissipated, realizing that they wanted no part of this particular drama. Behind Mrs Dickerson, Sandy Burke's face had twisted with confusion, her bony knees rattling against each other. Amma shook her head, grabbing my hand and pulling at me with a harsh yank.

But I was immovable, watching Mr Eccentric as he stood straight again, head held tall upon the tower of his wrinkled neck. He was furious, his glasses now shaking on the bridge of his nose. He looked at your mother with a glare that seemed strong enough to make her buckle. It was only when he looked at your uncle that the poison drained away.

Uncle Walter had taken a step back from the stick figure of Mr Eccentric. Standing by himself with nothing but the concrete of buildings around him, Uncle Walt looked as small as a beetle. He was shaking his head.

'I told him not to do it.' He glanced up at Mr Eccentric. 'I said, "No, Bobby, no!"'

Mr Eccentric's eyes widened. 'He wouldn't do that, not my Bobby,' he said.

'He had the knife,' Uncle Walter said, clutching his fist. 'But I don't think he meant to do it. Not really. And then . . . And then . . .'

'You left him there?' Sandy said. 'You ran away?'

Uncle Walter's eyes bulged. He looked as scared as a child waiting to be whipped. He blinked wildly as his whole body clenched tight, mouth muttering.

'I didn't mean . . . It happened so quick . . . I told him not to do it. There was so much blood! So much—'

Mr Eccentric was shaking his head so vigorously that his glasses fell to the floor again. He didn't bend down to collect them but covered his face with his hands.

'It's not true,' he said into his palms. 'It's not *true!*'

Uncle Walter stopped muttering and inhaled deeply. His shoulders dropped as he breathed out, a breath so long that I felt he could have blown us away. His eyes began to well up. We had never seen your uncle cry before.

'I was a coward, Reginald,' he said, voice cracking. 'And I'll never forgive myself.'

I don't know when he began walking but I do know that no one stopped your uncle that day on Westhill Estate. His slow, plodding footsteps were so resigned that there seemed no urgency. There was something in his walk that made it clear he wasn't coming back, that this was the last we would see of him, but still no one followed. As he made his way along the backbone of the steps that led down the hill, his outline grew fainter and fainter. The further he went, the more he disappeared, until soon he was nothing more than a ghost.

'Go on, *leave!*' Mrs Dickerson cried, long after he could have heard. 'Run away like you always bloody do! I'm not keeping your secrets *any more!*'

Mr Eccentric continued to mutter into his hands as his glasses lay by his feet. When I looked at you a stream of tears was covering your tan cheeks. I wanted to run over and hold you but every limb of my body felt as heavy as stone. I searched for your brother, afraid that he would be tearing one of the stalls to pieces in a fit of rage. Instead, I saw him marching back to Bosworth House, back bent over, jacket stuffed with boxes that poked out at the seams.

After Amma leaves I'm restless. I toss around in bed so recklessly I strain a muscle in my left shoulder. I curse the pain and it isn't even that bad. This is how quickly the mind forgets past traumas; there was a time when I would have longed for such a simple and short-lived sting. Still, I search beneath my bed, pulling the strongest painkillers from my tin. I swallow them dry, their hard bodies sticking in my throat until I gag to make them shift. It's then, as I lie head hanging over the side of the bed, that I see the corner of a book between the slats of the bed. It's covered with red-brick wrapping paper and as soon as I see it I remember what it is. Another part of the past, waiting to find me.

I sit up, trying to forget I've seen anything, and collect a crossword book from the bedside table. But the words swim before my eyes. So I move on to newspapers, making paper pellets out of them and throwing them at the dustbin. And then I lie. Looking up at the cracked paint on the ceiling, watching the white light fade to blue, then to black, then illuminate with orange as the streetlights click on. I try to think of crossword clues to keep my mind busy but keep coming back to the same one.

9 down: To be on one's own (5) = ALONE

I close my eyes but my mind won't sleep. I try to trick it with stories and lullabies yet it's inundated with the words of my mother, your brother and our past life. Eventually I fling the sheets off my body and stomp down the stairs to the kitchen. I search through the cupboards. I don't know what I'm looking for until I find it under the sink. Behind packets of sponge cloths and a randomly assembled first-aid kit (bandages, safety pins and a packet of hard-boiled sweets) I find a bottle of whiskey. As I draw it out from its hiding place it glimmers in the dusk; brown toffee liquid held behind a thick frosted wall. The foil-edged label is peeling back, the contents barely touched. I take four long glugs of the whiskey, choking with each swallow, before putting it back in its hiding place and returning to bed.

I giggle as the mix of alcohol and medication makes me drowsy. I feel myself sliding into sleep, a fuzzy haze of random images filling the darkness. I see the image of Pikachu, our favourite of all the Poké-mon, performing somersaults in the air. He twirls and whizzes, sparks trailing from his tail as he cries, 'Pika-pika . . . CHOO!' A My Little Pony flies off the curtains as if trying to compete, shaking its rainbow mane as fairy dust falls from its hoofs. Then I see you, or a version of you, lit up on the back wall. You're grown up, curly hair tied back from your face, a pair of red reading glasses perched on your nose as you sit on top of a mountain like the one in Bobby's postcard. Your hands are wrapped around your ankles as a ladybird umbrella hovers over your head, the mountain beginning to turn around, your figure turning away with it. The images continue to tumble as I fall into a disturbed sleep. Fluorescent strip lighting shaped like sheep, candy-floss horses strung up at a fair, the people standing waist-deep in the river Ganges as they wait for the eclipse.

It isn't long before the image of the Soul-drinker shocks me half-awake. Half-awake because even though my eyes are open I can't move my body. The room is filled with a green gas, dead cats lying across my bed. When I look at the walls, they're crawling with fat slugs that are being guzzled down by the birds in the wallpaper. Then, from the corner of the room, I can see his eyes, amber and as bright as traffic lights. They come closer and closer as I remain frozen in bed. My eyes run circles around my sockets, my heart pounds heavy blows against my ribcage, my brain demands that the rest of my body escape, yet still I can't move an inch. I don't know how long I remain in this half-sleep but time seems to stretch over hours. Then, quite unexpectedly, the image of a yellow ball comes whizzing across my vision. But it isn't Pikachu this time, it's a firework.

The whole room erupts in explosions. Rockets zoom to the ceiling, showering into chrysanthemum stars; Roman candles flare up from the floor, the noise of their sizzling fire filling my ears, making me dizzy. Sweat seeps through my shalwar kameez, my throat rattling as I try to scream through seized lips. The room fills with smoke as the explosions continue: first red, then purple, then green. All I can do is lie still, choking on fumes as the glare of multi-coloured fire dances before my face.

'RAVINE?'

The sound of his cry cuts through my sleep. When I blink sweat from my eyelids I can see the room is empty: no dead cats, no slugs on the walls, nothing but the orange glow of a streetlamp creeping through the gaps of the curtains. I have the free use of my limbs again and the hazy fug of the dream world lifts as I feel a thumping through my body. At first I think it's my heart but then I realize the noise is coming through the wall behind me.

'*RAVINE?*' Jonathan cries as he hits the wall. '*RAVINE!*'

'I'm fine!' I call back.

The sound of his thumping stops. My hands shake as I pinch myself on the arm. The sting is sharp, tangible.

There's still a faint ringing in my ears, a whiff of smoke in my nostrils. When I look to the corner of the room I expect to see two eyes staring back at me. Instead, I see Shiva, hands pressed at the palms.

'You sounded scared,' Jonathan says through the wall.

I roll over, tucking the duvet under my body, curling into a foetal position as I try to control the shuddering. I pray for sleep – pure oblivion, no dreams, no images, no sparks in the darkness.

As I squeeze my eyes shut I realize he's waiting for me to speak.

'Goodnight, Jonathan,' I say, because despite everything, I can't make myself thank him.

I can hear his body slacken, slump against the wall and slide down.

'Goodnight, Ravine.'

The tapping wakes me. At first I think it's accidental or a noise from my own mind, but after a while it begins to gain pace.

I sit up in bed and rub my eyes. In the broad light of day, the memories of the night seem distant. My temples are throbbing, limbs heavy. As I sink back into my mattress I can feel the thin fabric of my shalwar kameez drenched with sweat.

The tapping continues. To drown it out I switch on the television where a line of 'experts' in suits are standing in front of the Houses of Parliament. I turn the sound up.

'Well, the result is quite startling,' says a short blonde woman, a diamond-studded brooch clipped to her lapel, 'but there's no question in my mind that this is a viable union.'

The man next to her snorts. 'Of course you'd expect that statement from a party who was basically runner-up. You've hit the bloody jackpot!'

The debate is interesting for approximately thirty seconds but as the bickering continues I soon grow bored. I flick through the channels until the flashing images hurt my eyes. Eventually I turn it off.

Your brother continues to tap. In fact, throughout the whole debate he hasn't stopped. There's such a rhythm to this drumming that I imagine he's created some elaborate device from the leftover pieces of the Ahmeds' former life. A device full of cogs and pulleys, elastic bands and nails, constructed with no other purpose than to irritate me.

I search the side table for my stereo remote and begin to blast out Stevie Wonder tunes through the speakers. I skip through 'We Can Work It Out' and 'He's Misstra Know-It-All' until I get to 'I Ain't Gonna Stand For It'. I put the volume up to its highest setting and programme the song to repeat.

I bury my head beneath my pillow but still I hear the tapping. I block my ears with my fingers but still the hammering leaks in. *Tip-tip-tip-tip-tip*, like a woodpecker trying to enter my skull. My head still hurts from the exploits of the night before and the tighter I squeeze the pillow, the more I hear the thudding of my own migraine. As Stevie sings, '*Oh no . . . OH NO!*' I tear the pillow off my head and sit up straight.

'Give it a rest!' I yell.

Yet still the noise continues. *Tip-tip-tip-tip-tip*.

'Jonathan Dickerson, stop that noise *now*!'

There's a pause long enough to indicate that there's no great machine behind the noise, that it's your brother himself who's enacting the torture. Within seconds he starts up again, *tip-tip-tipping* until I fling my pillow across the room and swing my feet over the edge of my bed.

'If you don't stop that bloody noise I will come and *make you stop it myself*!'

The noise stops. It takes a second for me to register its absence but when I turn the CD player off it's no longer there. I sigh with the joy of my victory and breathe in the silence.

BANG-BANG-BANG-BANG!

He's hitting the wall this time and at a far greater speed. With each strike my body jolts and my shoulders tense. Not used to this form of abuse, the partition wall between our rooms begins to shake, making Shiva wobble in his cosmic dance.

If there was ever one thing your brother was good at it was rattling me, and within seconds I'm marching down the stairs. I have nothing on but a damp shalwar kameez, pillow clutched in my hand with my hair ruffled into a bird's nest of bed hair. I mutter to myself as I pull the key from beneath the WELCOME mat, an incoherent gaggle of words. I rattle the key in the lock as if noise will strike fear into Jonathan's heart. When the door swings open I storm through the empty flat and straight up to your old room, throwing the pillow directly at your brother's head. He holds his arms up against his face and it's only then, as I stand in front of his curled-up body, that I realize I've given Jonathan exactly what he wants.

Me.

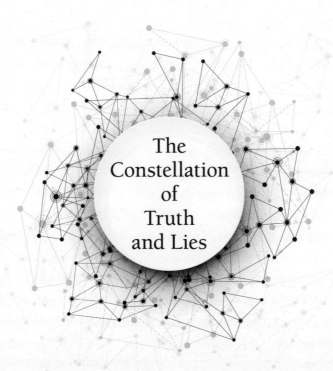

The Constellation of Truth and Lies

When your uncle left, a gloom hovered over Bosworth House and despite all her efforts, Mrs Dickerson couldn't waft it away.

'Let's all go to the zoo,' she said one Saturday.

The sound of heels arrived long before her voice as we sat watching the morning cartoons. We both glanced over to her as she stood by the front door. She was wearing a baggy black blouse, red leggings and zebra-print boots.

'I've even asked Rekha so Ravine can come too,' she said.

With reluctance, Amma had left me under your mother's supervision. She was so worried about calling in sick and being fired from her minimum-wage cleaning job that she overlooked her previous opinion that Mrs Dickerson would abandon us *willy-nilly*. In truth, I think Amma felt sorry for her. The other residents had been avoiding her ever since the incident at the stalls, whispering behind her back and steering clear of her on the streets. Even Sandy Burke was too heartbroken to talk to her. Mr Eccentric had been spotted visiting the police station, and rumours had spread that the investigation into his son's death was about to be reopened. He was convinced Uncle Walter had played a bigger part in Bobby's death than he'd let on. He'd sit behind his desk, scrutinizing the rest of the estate, then shout through the window as your mother walked past.

'They'll find him soon! Any day now!'

The strain was starting to show on Mrs Dickerson. Where once she spent hours applying coats of make-up to her face, she now managed nothing more than a quick circle of colour to her lips. Her pouffed-up hair was considerably deflated, her clothes worn for comfort instead of style, and the sweet scent she'd brought with her from her travels was replaced with the stale stench of cigarettes.

The zebra boots had been a good sign and as she smiled at you from her position at the door, I could see the flutter of false lashes on her eyelids. You sat up straight on your seat and pursed your lips.

'Maybe another time,' you said, pulling your biggest smile as a form of compensation.

You were never the type to hold grudges but if you were one thing you were loyal. The zoo was the place Uncle Walter took you. It was the place where he taught you about sucking out snake venom and scaring mountain lions. It was your uncle's place, not your mother's.

'Jonathan?' Mrs Dickerson said, moving her gaze with a distinct lack of optimism.

Your brother, slumped belly-up on the sofa, produced a gorilla-style snarl before storming up to his bedroom and slamming the door. He hadn't spoken to your mother since the car boot, had hardly spoken to anyone. He spent the majority of his days in an all-consuming sulk, lying back on chairs and sofas, shoulders rolled forward, chin on his collarbone. He spent most of his time in his room and, as a result, we were never allowed to leave the flat. It was late December, frost settling on the pavements outside, and, according to Mrs Dickerson, only your brother could keep us safe. The rules of the pre-Walter days had returned, but even though your brother was technically in charge he never took on the role. He'd sneak off out the flat, then, when he came back, refuse to tell us where he'd been, marching off to his room without so much as a jibe or insult. I preferred the original Jonathan, full of egotism and cruelty, to this moping Jonathan that hung back in the shadows.

Mrs Dickerson was no fan of knockbacks and, having received a double whammy from both you and Jonathan, she decided to deal with the snub the best way she knew how. She went out to the shops and returned with two carrier bags full of alcohol. She placed each bottle on the dining-room table; long thin ones next to short squat ones, bright blues next to raspberry reds that glimmered in the light.

We knelt on the sofa, watching with our noses propped over the backrest. After Mrs Dickerson had slammed the bottles down, she marched into the kitchen, returning with a large tumbler. With all this clatter, even Jonathan emerged to see what was happening.

'If you don't want to go out, I might as well have my own fun!' she cried.

She filled the glass with a drink so green it looked toxic. The liquid sloshed against the sides and had barely settled before she put the tumbler to her lips.

'Bloody *typical*!' Jonathan cried, before running back upstairs.

Mrs Dickerson began to splutter. She looked at our eyes peering over the edge of the sofa and held up the empty vessel.

'Happy New Millennium!' she cried, even though there was still another day until New Year's Eve.

It was nice to see your mother smiling again but we knew that it wouldn't last for long. One minute she would be dancing around the living room singing 'Ding Dong, The Witch Is Dead', the next she would be blubbering into a pillow, complaining about how much she hated 'this hellhole estate'. As the hours passed and your mother grew more and more inebriated, I looked at the clock and prayed for Amma's quick return. She was never late and as the minute-hand clicked past five o'clock I started to fear that she'd been killed in a bus crash. Waves of panic hit me at the thought of a) Amma being dead and b) being left in your mother's care for the rest of my life.

We carried on playing the game we didn't know how to play, hoping that the busier we looked, the less attention your mother would give us. It seemed to work and, when she began singing a high-tempo version of 'Over The Rainbow', we decided to go and put our party dresses on. We lay on our bellies as we moved pawns and kings randomly around the chessboard, safe in the knowledge that no one would lecture us about getting our dresses dirty or crinkling them up.

'Rekha!'

We looked up from our game to see your mother propped up unsteadily on a wall as she spoke down the phone receiver. With the mention of my mother, I rose to an upright position. My relief at her being alive was dulled by the fact she was calling instead of knocking at the door.

I watched as your mother took a deep breath, coughing into her hand as she tried to convince herself sober.

'What can I do for you?' she asked.

As my mother spoke, Mrs Dickerson nodded her head, her expression revealing nothing. She looked over at us once, giving me an exaggerated wink as though I was in on some secret.

'*Marvellous*,' she said. 'Don't worry about it, hon. See you later. B-bye.'

The words 'see you later' didn't fill me with the greatest confidence and, as Mrs Dickerson put the phone down and began wobbling over to us, I knew I was on my own.

'Someone'sss mother'sss gone on a date,' she said, wiggling her finger towards my face.

At first I was confused by who this 'someone' was, but as the finger continued to wiggle at me, all doubt disappeared.

'*Date?*' I said.

'You know,' Mrs Dickerson said, 'with a man.'

I knew the meaning of the word. I'd looked it up in my mini dictionary and had watched *Blind Date* enough times to get the idea. What I couldn't understand was what Amma was doing on one.

'She had an admirer turn up at her work today,' Mrs Dickerson said, taking hold of a square bottle filled with orange liqueur. 'He was waiting for her with a bunch of red tulips. Complete surprise, she tells me. Isn't it *romantic*?'

Mrs Dickerson slumped down on the sofa, the orange liquid splashing on the armrest. Red tulips. I should have known then, but my mind was too busy computing the words 'date' and 'admirer' to see the clues. If I hadn't been so busy coming to terms with the love life of a woman whose only purpose was to be *my mother*, I might have connected the dots. The way Amma could often be found huddled in the corner of the kitchen with a telephone in her hand. The way I heard her giggle, then saw her blush as she realized I was standing in the doorway, mumbling some Bengali before slamming the receiver down and offering me a samosa. It was all there for me to see, but I was blinded by my own egotism. I didn't notice the things that didn't directly involve me and it was only later that I realized that, just like the constellations, everything was connected. You just needed to find the right patterns.

Mrs Dickerson began to take swigs from the bottle in her hand. Her eyes were dopey, blinking in slow repetitive beats, her lipstick smeared over her cheek. When she spoke, her speech was slurred and heavy, each word dragged through tar.

'I never even wanted to come back here,' she said. 'I could have been a model back in the day. I could have been anything. But this place, it drags you *dowwwn*.'

She looked around the flat as though she was sick of the sight of it, then took a swig from the bottle.

'Men used to love me,' she said.

You sat up straight. '*I* love you.'

She didn't seem to hear.

'Bobby loved me,' she said.

We looked at each other with wide eyes, remembering what Jonathan had told us in Mr Eccentric's gallery of clocks.

'If it hadn't been for Reggie and Walt, we might have been happy,' she said.

She gazed straight ahead at the television, though she wasn't looking at the screen. The flash of colours reflected back on her clammy skin, making her eyes shine in the glare.

'Wait a minute,' she said, suddenly excited. 'I've got something to show you.'

She pulled herself up clumsily from her seat, bottle still in hand, went over to the cupboard and rifled through a box of papers. When she came back, she was clutching a photograph.

'Look at thissss,' she said, passing it to you before flopping back onto the sofa.

I leant over your shoulder to see the image. It was of three teenagers huddled together. It was grainy and crinkled at the edges but it was clear to see Mrs Dickerson stood on one side, plaits trailing down either side of her head; Uncle Walter, with chubby cheeks and fingers in a V peace sign, on the other alongside a tall, pale boy in the middle. Bobby; the boy was Bobby.

'It was daft, really, what happened,' Mrs Dickerson said, as she sunk back. 'Bobby getting all upset like that. I mean, I took the stupid money but I was never actually going to *leave*. And those two, playing with knives in that stupid shed of theirs.'

You opened your mouth to speak but I squeezed your wrist, afraid you'd interrupt your mother's flow.

'They think Walt went crazy after it happened,' Mrs Dickerson said. 'But he was never right in the head. He'd been bullied all his life, see? Had to develop strategies. You know, to cope.'

Your brows rose high on your head.

'Survival strategies,' you said. 'Like he learnt at the camp.'

Your mother giggled, taking another swig from the bottle. I tightened my grip on your wrist again as you brushed the curls away from your cheek.

'He was an expert, you know?' you said. 'Trained in the army. That's where he learnt Italian and how to scare off bears. They were going to publish a book by him. He told me the title: *Dickerson's Endurance Guide*. There's too many survival guides already, so he had to put "endurance" in the title. The market's *flooded* with survival guides, you know?'

It was hard for you to stop speaking once you'd started and, even as I kept on squeezing and Mrs Dickerson chuckled quietly to herself, you still didn't stop.

'He's probably out in the woods right now,' you said. 'He's probably made himself a shelter from branches and having Penguin Stew.'

Your mother stopped laughing and instantly you realized your mistake. In the old days she would have duct-taped your mouth shut, but that night she simply ran her finger over the lip of her whiskey bottle.

'You really loved your uncle, didn't you?' she said.

You nodded so rapidly that curls fell over your face. I admit my part didn't help matters, but once the words came out I couldn't stop them.

'We all loved him,' I said.

Mrs Dickerson looked at me with an icicle stare. She leant forward, the stench of alcohol flowing from her lips. She'd thought Uncle Walter's cowardice would have weakened our love for him but it only made it stronger. She couldn't stand it. She couldn't stand being second place in your life.

'He was a liar,' she said. 'That fat waste of space you love so much was an out-and-out *liar*.'

She took another swig from her bottle.

'He wasn't even in the bloody army,' she said, wiping her mouth with the back of her hand.

Your face was full of crinkles. 'That doesn't make sense.'

Your mother kept her eyes fixed forward.

'He's been in and out of the nut house for the last six years. Went completely loopy after the whole Bobby incident . . . And the Italian? He learnt that from tapes. Planned to move to Italy with Bobby and live in the mountains. What a laugh! He couldn't bear it when we got together. Thought I was taking his best friend away. Then, when I got pregnant, he knew it was over. I'd won, you see? Bobby was *mine*. If it hadn't been for Reggie, buying me off like that, and your stupid uncle trying to get Bobby to leave with him . . . But Bobby wouldn't leave me, not my Bobby. He'd rather—'

She stopped talking, looked down at her bottle and took another swig. She carried on running her finger around the rim as she looked over at us.

'He came crying to me, you know, your uncle? Crying like a big stupid baby. "*I didn't mean to leave him*," he kept saying, sobbing and wailing. "There was so much blood . . ." It took all my strength not to wallop him.'

She picked up the remote and began to flick through the channels.

'Course that's when he started with the panic attacks,' she said, still flicking. 'And mummy dearest decided to have him sectioned. The stupid cow said it was my fault. *My* fault! Said I should never have started anything with Bobby . . . Then she went and popped her clogs and poor little Walt had nowhere to go. He wrote to me asking for help. *Begged* me to let him stay so that he wouldn't have to go back to the ward.'

She looked you straight in the eyes, as though accusing you of something terrible.

'You think your uncle came to look after you? It was *me* who was helping *him* out.'

Mrs Dickerson looked back at the television until she found a makeover programme and instantly lost interest in her own conversation. When I looked over at you there were tears in your eyes.

'Bitch!'

We looked behind us to see Jonathan standing in the doorway. He was wearing the same jeans and jumper he'd worn for the last week, his hands curled up in fists as his face turned devil red.

'Bloody stupid bitch!' he cried again, storming back up to his room, slamming the door shut and kicking it so hard it sounded like thunder above our heads.

*

It shocks me to see the grown-up Jonathan in your room, even though I've known he's been there all along. It isn't his presence that surprises me but the size of him. Even as he lies curled on the bed, wide hands raised up to protect himself from the pillow I've thrown, I can see his arms are long and gangly, the length of his legs immense. Did I expect him to never grow? Perhaps. It was always easier to imagine him as a boy with too-big glasses than as a fully fledged adult.

He lowers his arms, a hesitant move as though he's expecting more missiles at his head. A familiar nest of brown hair emerges. It's thinner, less glossy than when he was a child. His skin is familiar, that pallid grey colour that would never catch the sun, but there are no longer any glasses propped upon his nose and, for the first time in my life, I can clearly see the olive green of his eyes.

He's a handsome man, I won't deny it. Handsome, that is, in that scruffy, homeless fashion. But I'm not the best person to judge. The last man I talked to was Mr Chavda and anyone a few decades closer to my age would probably seem attractive.

'Ravine,' Jonathan says, as I stand before him in clammy paisley swirls.

I whip the pillow off the floor and use it to cover my torso.

'Jonathan,' I say, aware that I haven't yet brushed my hair or teeth today.

Jonathan opens his mouth, then swallows, opens his mouth, then swallows. As he lies on the bed, he looks like a trout gasping for air on a riverbank.

'I didn't think you'd come,' he says.

I look at the walls, a brown smudge on the blue paint from where he's been tapping.

'You didn't give me a choice,' I say.

I flop down in defeat, sitting cross-legged on the worn-out carpet.

240

It's the same carpet as when you were here, that pale-lilac colour your mother got cheap in the bank holiday sale. Apart from the bunk bed Jonathan is lying on, the room is empty. Clearly left behind by the Ahmeds, the bed frame is covered in football stickers and graffiti. MAN U IS RUBBISH. FAIZAL LIKES GIRLS. The sight of these things makes me feel hollow. It's as if they've erased your existence.

The mattress squeaks as Jonathan pulls himself to a sitting position. He has to bend down to avoid hitting his head on the frame. He's wearing a moss-green hoodie and navy-blue jeans. His cheeks are smooth and flawless like just-bought soap.

'You didn't sound well last night,' he says.

His voice is deep, far more authoritative than the muffled sounds I've heard through the walls.

'I had a nightmare,' I tell him. 'I don't want to talk about it.'

Your brother nods as though this is a perfectly reasonable response, then purses his lips. He looks around the flat as if searching for something, then slaps his hands together.

'Looks like it's going to rain,' he says. 'Or at least that's my forecast.'

He grins, neat square teeth revealing themselves as the muscles flex around his stubbly chin. I'm not used to seeing your brother smile, even when he was a child, so his smile, along with the stubble, bamboozles me.

'What do you want, Jonathan?' I ask.

His smile drops and the frown I remember rises up on his forehead. It's strange the memories that can be triggered by one expression. Suddenly I see your brother standing in his thunderstorm pyjamas, dancing his fairy dance and singing 'Ravine Ravine Dictionary Queen', before slamming a door in my face.

'I just want to talk to you, Ravine,' he says.

I hug the pillow as I sit on the floor. He lowers his face, raises an eyebrow.

'Do you think we could talk?'

I look down at the lilac carpet, trying to remember what the white stain by my foot was caused by. Mayonnaise from egg and cress sandwiches? Slug slime from when Stanley escaped his jar? I curl my bare toes as I consider Jonathan's question and think of how lonely I feel in the flat next door, how I don't know what time Amma will be returning. I think of her with my father, sitting in a café in Blackpool, drinking tea and discussing their new life in Bangladesh together. I imagine them holding hands over a wipe-clean tablecloth, smiling at each other and singing the Bengali national anthem as the sea hits the pebbled beach in the distance.

As I contemplate this I realize your brother hasn't questioned me about the speed at which I'd come dashing to this room, the perfect health I seemed to be in. In all the years I've been stuck in my lifebed I haven't had anyone to confide in. No one real. Amma was always too close, Sandy too distant, Mr Chavda light years away. I look at Jonathan with his long grown-up body and scruffy brown mane.

I shake my head. 'We've got nothing to talk about,' I say, pushing myself to my feet.

He calls after me but I have no intention of listening. I've lived for all these years without Jonathan Dickerson. I've slept day after day in that bed without so much as a postcard from him. I didn't need him; not then, not now, not ever. I take my pillow and march down the stairs and through the living room, having decided that I will never see your scruffy-haired brother again.

If it hadn't been for the umbrella I would have been back in my flat, up those stairs and lying beneath the warmth of my duvet within seconds.

The umbrella propped up against the wall is short and crayon red. I gaze down at it, drop my pillow and pick up the umbrella by its U-shaped handle. As I push it open, large goggling eyes pop out, black spots revealing themselves on the round red body.

'They were going to throw it away,' Jonathan says.

I turn around to see him standing behind me.

'I couldn't let them throw it away,' he says.

The light from the window behind him turns his body into a towering silhouette. For a moment I can't see his face, just the dark hollow where it belongs. When my sight readjusts, he's staring straight at me.

'Look,' he says, stuffing his hands in his pockets. 'I know you're mad about Reginald. But there's a reason I came back to see him.'

I close the umbrella and shrug my shoulders.

'He's dying,' I say. 'You already told me.'

He shakes his head. 'Not just that.'

'Because he's your grandfather,' I offer.

He carries on shaking his head. 'Not that either.'

I try to appear aloof, twirling the handle of the umbrella around my finger. The twirling is so vigorous I almost poke myself in the eye and have to slow down the pace. Your brother presses his hands together in prayer, thrusting them forward to punctuate each word.

'I want to find Uncle Walter,' he says. 'And I think Reggie might know where he is.'

I almost laugh. 'Why?' I ask.

He thinks for a second.

'Because I know Walter sent him letters. He wanted Reginald to pass them on to me, though of course he never—'

I stop twirling the umbrella.

'No,' I say, shaking my head. 'Why would you want to find Walter?'

He looks confused, then places his hands over his lips. The flat is so still and quiet, it makes me feel nervous. I don't know what I expect Jonathan to say but I know I need to hear him say it. Eventually he sighs and drops his hands.

'I want to say sorry,' he says.

I look into Jonathan's green eyes.

'Oh,' I say.

The
Constellation
of
Fireworks

Your mother was unconscious. It was late evening by then and she'd drunk so much that even when you shook her, she wouldn't wake up. We stepped back from the sofa to look at her slumped body, a trail of drool falling down her chin.

'Maybe we should do CPR,' you suggested.

'What's CPR?'

You closed your eyes as you tried to remember. '*Cardio Resurrection.*'

I pulled my mini dictionary out of my bag, flipping the pages to the letter *R*.

> **resurrection** *n.* rising from the dead

I looked back at Mrs Dickerson's face. A bubble of spit had formed in the corner of her mouth and her body was jolting from a series of hiccups.

'She looks pretty alive to me,' I said.

You picked up her hand by the wrist, then let it drop. It fell on her lap with a loud smack. You sat beside your mother, the peach skirt of your dress making a crinkling noise as you sighed. Your mother hadn't got this drunk since she'd returned.

Some things never change, I wanted to say in that serious grown-up way. I'm glad I didn't because it's not true. Everything changes, whether you want it to or not.

'Do you think what she said is true?' you said, looking up at me. 'You know, about Uncle Walter?'

I opened my mouth to speak but, as usual, your brother got there before me.

'Of course it is.'

He had a bin bag in his hand, pulling it down the stairs behind him. When he dragged it into the living room I could see the jagged corners of boxes pushing against the black plastic.

'They're liars,' he said. 'The whole lot of them are liars.'

'Mum doesn't lie,' you said, as she lay inebriated beside you.

'Ha!' Jonathan cried. 'She's the worst one of them! Her whole life's a big shitty lie.'

You told him not to be rude; he told you not to be stupid. You told him to be respectful; he told you to show him something to be respectful *of*. This back and forth went on for some time until eventually I butted in.

'What's in the bag?' I asked.

Jonathan looked back at the bin bag as though he'd forgotten it was there.

'None of your beeswax,' he said, dragging it to the door.

We went to the hallway to watch him. It was only as he reached for the keys on the coat rack that I realized your brother had wellies on.

'Where are you going?' I asked him.

He didn't reply.

'Where are you going?' you echoed, but louder, as though he hadn't heard.

He tried to ignore you as he opened the door. You asked him over and over again, your voice getting shriller each time.

'Where are you going? Where are you going? Where are you going?'

'For shit's sake, Marianne, I heard you,' he said. 'I'm going to Bobby's Hideout, *OK*?'

We both blinked at each other.

'What for?' I asked.

Jonathan sighed dramatically. 'Because I don't want to live with Reginald Blake,' he said.

We both blinked again.

'*Who?*' we said.

He sighed again, rolling his eyes. '*Mr Eccentric.*'

We watched as he pulled a woolly hat over his head.

'He eats sardines all day,' he told us. 'I don't even *like* sardines.'

This fact didn't aid our comprehension.

'But we're not going to live with Mr Eccentric,' you told your brother. 'Mum's back now.' She nodded towards the heap on the sofa.

'Yes,' he mumbled, 'but for how bloody long?'

He was out of the door before you could answer. We ran out after him in our party dresses, standing at the top of the staircase as we watched him hauling the bin bag down each step. You looked behind you, as though considering the state of your comatose mother, then back down at your brother.

'Wait!' you cried. 'I've got to get my wellingtons.'

You dashed back into the flat as I stood dumbstruck. Even Jonathan seemed shocked, eyes darting from side to side behind the thick lenses of his glasses, skin paler than ever. I looked out at the dark night, feeling the frosty chill against my bare legs as droplets of rain pitter-pattered against the edge of the stairwell.

'What's the weather forecast?' I asked.

Jonathan pulled his serious weatherman face, gesturing his hand out to the side as though a map of the British Isles was right beside him.

'Temperatures will be reaching an all-time low. Expect rain, thunder and snowstorms.'

'Rain, thunder *and* snowstorms?' I said.

He lowered his arm. 'Don't shoot the messenger.'

I looked back into the flat. You had your buttercup raincoat on, sitting on the floor as you pulled a wellington boot on your foot. I thought of Amma out on her *date*. I thought of the Soul-drinker coming to get me in your flat with no one conscious enough to help. Then I thought of you out in the dark and my promise to protect you, and with that, all my fear drained away. I looked down at your brother as he wiped the condensation off his glasses.

'I'm coming too,' I said.

I pulled the spare key out of my bag and ran next door.

'For shit's sake!' I heard him cry.

But when I came back with my coat, gloves and wellingtons, he was still waiting for us. Then, when we followed him down the stairs on tiptoes I saw a small smile creep across his face. Your brother didn't want to be alone any more than the rest of us did.

*

I follow grown-up Jonathan as he gives me a tour of the flat. He's so tall he has to duck beneath door frames as he shows me the great bounty of goods he's discovered.

'They just left this stuff,' he says, holding up a rusty kettle with loose cords wiggling out the back.

As well as this treasure, the Ahmeds have left a sofa covered in repeat-leaf patterns in the living room and an old wardrobe they'd managed to get down the stairs but had obviously abandoned in the hallway at the last minute. There are computer cables tied into a figure of eight, a wooden step-stool painted ultramarine, a deflated football that Mr Ahmed had probably punctured the day the boys refused to come up the hill. I try to look for signs of your previous life. Things left behind. I find dead flies along the window sill, dust on the staircase banister, but nothing that was part of you.

Jonathan decides to make me a cup of tea from the more than dubious kettle. I follow him through the hallway and watch as he fills it up in the kitchen. Stacks of Pot Noodles are arranged in a pyramid across the kitchen work surface and empty boxes of Tupperware are piled up in the sink. If it hadn't been for Amma's excessive cooking the man could have died from malnutrition.

'No milk, I'm afraid,' he tells me. He passes me a chipped mug filled to the rim with black tea and shrugs his shoulders. 'It goes off too quickly.'

I sit down on the stool that's been left by the oven and wrap my palms around the cup. Looking down at the chip, I remember the crash of china I heard when I bailed out of visiting him. It reminds me of his hot temper. The way he used to be.

'When we were younger, Reginald made a deal with me,' Jonathan says as he leans against the sink.

He takes a sip from his cup and I, trying to mimic him, take a sip from my own. My face twists as the bitterness hits the sides of my tongue.

'No sugar either,' he says.

I place the mug on the floor. 'What type of deal?' I ask.

He breaks away from my gaze and looks down at his mug. He continues staring into it as though the answer is sitting on the surface of his tea. After a while, the cup begins to shake. He brings his other hand around it to keep it steady. He's nervous. Jonathan Dickerson is nervous of *me*.

'It was the day he caught me with the marbles,' he says. 'He dragged me back to his flat and made me eat pâté sandwiches with him.'

'Sardines,' I interrupt. 'You mean sardines.'

'No,' he says, his body retching with the memory, 'definitely pâté.'

He places his mug on the kitchen work surface as I sit questioning my memory. Jonathan tells me about his conversation with Reginald Blake. He tells me in such an elaborate yet detailed way that I realize he's been planning this speech since we stopped speaking a few days ago. I let him tell me because I want to know, but as he speaks I can't help but examine his gestures and mannerisms that not only belonged to his younger self but also belonged to you.

That day in the flat, Reginald had told your brother about Mrs Dickerson and Bobby. How they'd started a relationship behind his back, how she'd come to Tewkesbury House to declare she was pregnant and how Reginald had paid her to go away. He'd never liked the woman and wasn't going to let her ruin Bobby's future. She didn't need much persuading. Your mother took the money and even though she went back on her word and never left, the damage was done. Bobby didn't want anything to do with her and Reginald was convinced he'd won.

'But I think Bobby got depressed,' Jonathan says. 'Maybe there was something in him that made him spiral down.'

He looks wistful as he says this. I roll my eyes.

'You're not the same as Bobby,' I say.

Jonathan looks at me and blinks. Then he smiles. After the initial shock it doesn't take me long to get used to his smile. It's more genuine than the sneers and pouting lips of his youth and far more pleasant to look at.

'You could always read my mind, Ravine,' he says.

I don't like him saying that. I don't like him even saying my name. I fold my arms.

'You said you made a deal.'

Jonathan closes his eyes and nods.

'Reginald said if I told him what Mum was up to he'd find a way of getting rid of her. Then me and Marianne could go and live with him in his flat.'

It's the first time he's said your name but he's gazing at his mug so doesn't see me jump.

Marianne. It's been so long since I've heard it spoken.

'I was angry with her for running away so I agreed,' he says. 'I never thought that Uncle Walter would leave. I never thought that I might have to *go through with it.*'

Jonathan throws a hand up in the air and, along with it, the burden of his secrets. I watch them fly into the air like doves. But he doesn't look any lighter afterwards; if anything, his shoulders are weighed down. He lowers his head, picking at the loose skin on his fingers.

'It didn't even happen,' he says. 'In the end they just took me away.'

I remember the image of him standing in the hospital. How he'd stared at my hospital chart as the social worker pushed him towards the bed. The skin beneath his eyes was loose and baggy, the flesh around his nostrils sore and red. Despite everything, I'd been pleased to see him. In that world where the Soul-drinker was giving Amma shoulder rubs and the pain was shooting through every ligament of my body, he was something familiar, something I understood. But he wouldn't look at me. Not once. I've replayed the scene over and over in my mind with the vague hope that if he'd looked up, connected his gaze with mine for just one second, things would have been different.

'He wrote to me, though,' Jonathan says. 'When I was in care he'd send me letters, and it was in the letters he said Uncle Walter had been in touch. That he was living somewhere up north. That's why I came back, Ravine. Not for Reginald—' He stops, swallows deeply and clears his throat. 'For Uncle Walter.'

He looks at me. I pick up the mug from the floor, look down at the broken film floating on the surface of the liquid, then back at your brother.

'Are you sure it wasn't sardines?'

Jonathan lifts his gaze and rolls his eyes.

'Yes, Ravine, I'm sure.'

When we got to the entrance of Bosworth House, the rain had turned to snow. Tiny white flecks spun in the lamplight, swirling down to the pavement and melting into the concrete. Making our way down the spine-steps of Westhill, I realized party dresses were not the most suitable outdoor wear. Even with wellington boots, my legs were so numb I could barely bend my knees, and you were shivering so badly it looked like you were performing an interpretive dance with each step.

When I looked up, patches of the night sky revealed themselves amongst the clouds. I saw a cluster of stars and stuck my tongue out, imagining the snow was stardust, twinkling and crackling as it fell on my tongue. When I lowered my head your brother had his hood up. He'd pulled the toggles so the fabric scrunched around his face.

'Rain . . . snow . . .' I said, counting the words off my fingers. 'What else did you say?'

He narrowed his eyes, looked up at the sky. 'Thunder.'

You quickly put your umbrella up.

We took turns dragging the bag to Bobby's Hideout, asking Jonathan repeatedly what was inside. His final response came in the form of a growl so low and deep that we didn't ask again.

'Top secret,' you said, tapping the side of your nose.

When we reached the main road, my teeth were chattering, the feeling in my fingers lost. I looked back at the estate in search of an orange sari, the flash of white trainers, hoping that Amma had finished this so-called 'date' and was arriving home. She'd somehow figure out our plan (as adults always did), march us back home and save us from Jonathan's bitter expedition. But no matter how I searched, I couldn't see her and soon we were walking through the thin line of trees and into the darkness.

'We're here,' your brother announced.

He took the bin bag from your hands as we stood before the hideout, and immediately dumped the contents on the floor.

Fireworks. Large boxes, sealed-up bags and loose rockets; the quantity of explosives your brother had gathered was staggering. He dropped down on his knees, ripping the boxes open and making a pile of their contents.

'*Errrr*,' was all you could say.

Jonathan carried on in a blind fury, his fingertips turning white as he tore at the cardboard. I placed my hands on my hips and tried to scowl.

'You're not supposed to play with fireworks.'

He didn't flinch.

'Jonathan, *you're not supposed to play with fireworks!*'

He glanced up at me with an apathetic shrug. 'I'm not supposed to do a lot of things.'

I blinked, unsure how to respond. The more fireworks emerged, the more I panicked. Eventually I threw my hands in the air.

'Stop being such a *philistine*!' I cried.

Jonathan paused, lifting his hands to wave from side to side.

'*Ravine Ravine Dictionary Queen*,' he sang, but distinctly less passionately than usual.

'Shut up, *Weatherboy*.'

'Now, fellas,' you said, holding your hands up in Police Officer Mode. 'Let's calm down before someone gets hurt.'

Jonathan's face wrinkled with resentment. He flung his head back, shouting up to the trees. 'For shit's sake! I never even asked you to come! Why don't you just fuck off back home?'

You dropped your umbrella in the snow.

'Jonathan Dickerson!' you said. 'Take that back *now*.'

Jonathan's cheeks turned tomato red. He clenched his fists and pounded one on the floor.

'You're not my mother!' he cried. 'You're *barely* even my sister!'

We both stood baffled as Jonathan shook his head. He got to his feet and began marching in and out of the hideout, placing fireworks in whatever nooks and crannies he could find. You followed him, pulling out each one systematically while I stayed outside, attempting to put all the unopened boxes back in the bag.

As I crawled across the thin layer of snow, a blinding light shone in my eyes. I looked up as the rumble of a car engine followed. As Jonathan shouted at you to stop touching his property, I looked through the black body of tree trunks to see a taxi pulling up on the road ahead. My eyes widened as the door opened and a flash of white trainers stepped into view.

'*Am*—' I began until I saw who was following behind.

I know now that the figure with slicked-back hair and a bunch of red tulips in his hands was not only human but my father, but at the time I could only recognize him as the Soul-drinker. A monster, come to take possession of souls so as to feed his own; a vicious beast who now had my mother literally in his clasp, holding her hands by the roadside, looking straight into her eyes with the power of his yellow gaze. He'd tricked her soul from her. Next, he'd be coming for us.

I took the whistle out of my bag and began to blow, a foolish move as the Soul-drinker's eyes immediately darted over to the trees as he heard the trill.

My eyes widened. I got to my feet and pushed past your brother as he lined the doorway of the hideout with explosives.

'Hey!' he cried, as I took refuge in the corner, sitting with arms wrapped around my bare legs, the whistle between my lips.

He stepped inside and from behind him I saw your figure, rockets filling your arms, as you followed him. It was dark in the hideout but there was enough moonlight coming through the doorway to illuminate the fury on Jonathan's face.

'Stop being stupid and get out of here!' he cried.

I let the whistle drop from my lips. 'I'm not going anywhere. He'll find us,' I said.

Jonathan shook his head then looked at you. 'What's she talking about?'

You, just as confused as your brother, looked down at the fireworks in your arms and quickly dropped them on the floor.

'We need to get out pronto, Ravine.'

I continued shaking my head, looking towards the entrance as I waited for the Soul-drinker's eyes to appear. You didn't understand my fear, nobody did, but a monster was coming to get us, a monster that already had hold of my mother.

I buried my head in my knees as your brother began to curse. He only stopped when he realized I was crying.

'What's wrong with her, for shit's sake?' he asked.

I didn't hear your reply but the next time I looked up you were knelt down beside me. Your round tanned face was right up next to mine, the curls of your hair lit up in a halo around your head. I tried to gulp back the tears, wiping my face with the sleeve of my coat as you gently tapped the bag hanging loose over my body.

'Look up the meaning of *brave*,' you said.

My breath was erratic, my knees shaking, yet still I pulled out the mini dictionary from my bag. It took me a while to find the right entry, and when I began to read I had to force the words out of my rubbery lips.

'*"Brave: able to face or endure danger or pain. Splendid. Spectacular."*'

You smiled, prodding a finger into my chest. 'That's you it's talking about.'

I looked back at the book and reread the explanation. 'No, it's not,' I said. 'It's *you.*'

You looked at me confused, as I wiped the wetness from my cheeks.

'*C'est la vie,*' I said with a shrug.

You began to chuckle. '*Non preoccuparti, sii felice,*' you whispered.

'Enough already!' your brother screeched.

He was standing in the same spot with his glasses steamed up. Behind him were the postcards Bobby had dotted along the wall: mountains, waterfalls and deserts. Jonathan balled up his fists.

'Now get the bloody hell out of here or I'll blow up this place with the two of you in it!'

The roof of the hideout was barely higher than Jonathan's head, the small stretch of floor covered with fireworks. He could do it if he wanted to; he could blow it all up.

I put my dictionary back in its bag and wrapped my arms round my legs.

'You wouldn't do that,' I said.

Jonathan's jaw tightened. 'Yes, I bloody would!'

I looked at him as he drew a box from his pocket. I recognized it because it was the same box of matches my mother had in her kitchen drawer.

'I'm going to do it!' he cried.

Your eyes grew round but there was no reason to panic. The only danger I knew lay outside the hideout with a bunch of tulips in his hands. I shook my head.

'You wouldn't dare.'

You looked at me with alarm and right then I knew I'd gone too far. Jonathan pulled the box open and withdrew a match, striking it against the side of the box and holding the lit match in the air.

'Wanna bet?' he said.

You got to your feet and held out your hand. 'Ravine, for Cod's sake, get up.'

I took hold of your hand and squeezed.

'Shit.'

When we looked over at Jonathan, the match was no longer in his hand. He was looking frantically around him but it wasn't until we saw the glow of the fireworks piled up on the floor that we knew what had happened.

The sizzle came first, then the bang. Sparks. A speeding body of light hit the roof with a clang and then fell straight back down. For a moment there was silence, but it only lasted a second.

The explosions were quick and fast. The whistle of another rocket, the sudden spinning of a Catherine wheel. By the time we'd fallen to our knees, we didn't even have time to shriek. The noise was so loud we held our hands over our ears, jumping at every new explosion, pushing our heads low as we tried to keep watching. Multi-coloured fire blazed so brightly it left streaks across my vision. I squeezed my eyes shut, trying to remember our survival strategies. When I looked up again, I saw Jonathan looking back, his mouth screaming as my ears rang. It was my job to protect you. I had to think quickly, before it was too late. You began to crawl forward.

'Lie down and be still!' I cried. *'Lie down and be still!'*

It was as I reached out for your arm that the rocket hit me.

At first it felt like nothing more than a kick to the calf. But then came the pain. It didn't feel like I was on fire, or like knives stabbing into my leg. It didn't feel like anything you'd expect, though in truth I was never told what to expect when a firework incinerates your leg. It was like melting, my whole leg curling in on itself as my body seized into shock.

What happened next is a blur. I remember screaming. I remember you crying out to your brother ('Get Ravine! *Get Ravine!*'). I remember my eyes drooping so heavily that I didn't feel as if I would ever be able to open them again. It wasn't until Jonathan dragged me out of the hideout and the cold fresh air hit me that I began to see clearly again. The blades of grass across the floor, the cloudiness of smoke. When I looked over at your brother I could see the criss-crossing fibres on the toggles hanging from his hood. He was holding me tightly, as if the world would crumble if he let me go. Then, after a few more steps, he laid me down gently on my back, raising my leg as he placed it on a rock.

'I've got to get Marianne,' he said.

It was only when he ran away that I realized what he'd meant. You were still in there; you were still in the hideout.

A faint ringing vibrated in my ears. I tried to lift my head, only to see the hazy image of the building, concrete bricks cracking, gaps illuminated in flashes of colour.

'Non preoccuparti, sii felice. Non preoccuparti, sii felice,' I repeated over and over, hoping the words would wind back time.

The pain increased and soon I lost the energy to hold my head up. As I lay flat on the grass, I looked up at the patches of night sky: stars shining brightly against the indigo canvas, renegade fireworks exploding in fiery blooms, a rocket streaming across the sky like a shooting star. I began to choke on the smoke surrounding me and only dimly heard the crash of bricks and corrugated iron as the hideout collapsed.

You disappeared that night, Marianne. Your body lost in the rubble of a makeshift home. My life changed for ever.

Non preoccuparti, sii felice.

In Italian it means *don't worry, be happy.*

As the hours tick towards midday, your brother guides me to the living room. He shows me a hacksaw he's found in the abandoned wardrobe in the hall. The D-shaped body is rusty along the blade and looks more like a hazard than a treasure.

'I'm thinking of chopping wood with it,' he says.

He begins to saw imaginary logs in front of him. The gesture reminds me of how he used to build animal traps in the woods, never managing to catch anything bigger than a frog.

'What do you need to chop wood for?' I ask.

He sticks out his bottom lip, mumbling vaguely before placing his saw alongside a pile of similar goods lined up across the carpet. A ball of string, a 2004 telephone directory, a rolled-up prayer mat. He sits down on the autumnal-patterned sofa, his head lowered, his fingers scratching the back of his neck. The cushions are so soft that his body sinks down into their fatness, his legs angled out like fishing poles. He looks up at me.

'I still haven't seen him, you know?' he says. 'Reginald, I mean.'

I blink.

'Right,' I say.

Jonathan flops back in his seat, his chin resting on his chest the way it used to when he was sulking. Except he isn't sulking this time, but deliberating as though my reply is a valid comment. Maybe he'd never been sulking. Maybe all that time after Uncle Walter left he'd simply been thinking. Planning, concocting.

'Why did you go to Bobby's Hideout that night?'

I'm as surprised by the question as he is. We haven't ever mentioned that night until now, simply skirting over the issue as though it never happened. I'm glad I've mentioned it. I'm glad because it makes it real. I'm tired of pretending.

Jonathan lifts his eyes, yet his chin remains on his chest. He examines me for a few seconds then stares straight ahead.

'I was angry.'

At first I think that this is the totality of his response. I feel a prickle of irritation.

He rubs his palms against each other. 'I thought if I destroyed the hideout it would make everything better. I thought that Uncle Walter would . . . you know, *come back.*' He glances up at me then shakes his head with annoyance. 'It made sense at the time.'

I kneel down on the floor. Even though the sun is streaming through the bare window, I feel cold and push my fingers between the warmth of my thighs.

'You wanted him to come back even after what he did?' I ask.

His jaw clenches, hands clasping each other. 'I missed him.'

His voice is quiet and, as he avoids my gaze, I realize he's admitted this truth to no one else. I've not been the only one without a confidant. All this time, we've both been trying to forget.

But you can't forget the things that make you. I think of Uncle Walter's ghost body walking down the Westhill Estate. Getting smaller and smaller, fading into obscurity. The memory makes my throat tighten, my eyes begin to glaze. I have to perform a small cough to shake off the feeling.

'Do you think you'll find him?' I ask.

Jonathan shrugs and suddenly I'm angry again because, even if he never finds Walter, I want to hear him say he will.

'You look different,' he says. 'I mean, *nice*.'

My heart begins pumping quickly. When I look at Jonathan, his olive eyes are so dark and vivid that I can't fathom how I'd forgotten their colour.

'I'm wearing a nightie, Jonathan,' I say.

He smiles that neat tidy smile of his. 'I know, but you still look nice.'

He holds my gaze and I realize your brother has grown up in more ways than one. As he pushes himself to his feet he waves for me to stand.

'Now come to the hall,' he says. 'You won't believe what I found in the airing cupboard.'

He moves to the doorway but freezes when he realizes I'm not following. I look down at a loose fibre on the hem of my shalwar kameez. I begin pulling at the thread.

'I can't do it, Jonathan.'

The fabric starts to unravel, the paisley pattern disappearing before my eyes.

'It'll only take a minute,' he says.

I keep on pulling.

'I'm sorry about Mr Ecc— I mean, *Reginald*. But it doesn't change what happened.'

There is silence. A stream of light shining down on me makes my vision sparkle.

'It was an accident, Ravine.'

I stop pulling at the thread. 'No, it wasn't.'

The sun slips behind a cloud as it begins to rain outside. When your brother speaks, his voice is strained.

'You think I *meant* to do it?' he says.

I remember the match in his hand as he stood in the hideout; the way he struck it with such venom.

'No.'

The carpet feels rough beneath my palms as I push myself to my feet. I want to leave but your messy-haired brother is blocking the doorway to the hall. I try not to look at him, because of fear perhaps, but also because I don't want to say anything I'll regret. But he reads my mind and opens the floodgates.

'You think it's my fault she's dead,' he says. 'Don't you?'

Dead. The word shocks me more than the mention of your name. I've tried not to think of you as dead before. Just vanished, the same as my father. It made it easier to think that one day you might come back. That you'd run into my bedroom, hair springing up and down, and scream, 'Look, it was just a trick! I'm back in one whole piece!' But you never did. You never came back.

I quickly scratch a tear from my cheek as though it's nothing but an itch. When I look at your brother I lift my chin. I'm still afraid of looking weak in front of him, even after all these years.

'Yes, Jonathan,' I say. 'I think it's your fault.'

The answer doesn't break your brother the way I think it will. He doesn't begin to rage, marching over to his pile of treasures to stamp them into the ground. He doesn't swear or tell me I'm crazy as he should do. He barely even flinches. It's as though, all the time we've been talking, he's been delaying this moment and now, like the end of a beautiful holiday, he's resigned to the fact it's time to go home.

'That's OK,' he says. 'So do I.'

He leaves the room and I, like the coward I am, run back to my flat and hide.

The Constellation of Regret

The millennium came and went as I lay unconscious in my hospital bed. Parades were marched, trumpets blasted, fireworks launched into star-spangled skies. City streets were filled with smiling drunken faces staring up at giant big screens of other drunken faces staring up at giant big screens all over the world. The Millennium Dome was opened, millennium babies were born, millennium dolls were pressed on the belly to squeal 'Three, two, one, Happy New Millennium!' before shaking in convulsive glee. Planes did not fall out of the sky, computer systems did not combust and the world did not come to an end. And I, in my bottomless sleep, was oblivious to it all.

Amma remained glued to my bedside as the year 2000 was welcomed into the world. She'd been praying to various gods she didn't believe in and ignoring the watchful eyes of her returning husband as he sat on the chair opposite. She allowed this man she once called a fool to sit in this seat because now he was no longer a mere 'date', he was a hero.

This is the great irony of what happened to us. The Soul-drinker – the man I thought *took* souls – was the one who came running to save us. He'd spotted the first explosion of fireworks in the night sky and had sprinted to the hideout. He'd found me unconscious on the grass, foot propped up on a stone, and ordered Amma, as she ran up behind him, to call the emergency services. She later told me that she'd watched her once cowardly husband scanning the surrounding area and running over to wrestle with Jonathan's thrashing body. He was trying to tunnel through the rubble of Bobby's Hideout, tossing broken bricks to the side as smoke clouds quadrupled in size above him.

'She's inside, you idiot!' Jonathan cried, kicking and screaming as he was pulled away. 'My bloody sister's *inside*!'

My father tried to go in for you himself, but there was too much fire and smoke. By the time the sirens came it was too late.

They recovered your body at 2.45 a.m. on the morning of New Year's Eve 1999. Your legs and arms had been battered and bruised by falling bricks but the cause of death was smoke inhalation. Mrs Dickerson wasn't to find this out until an hour later when a police unit smashed down her door. She'd been so intoxicated that she hadn't heard the bangs and could barely speak when the policemen came charging in.

'What the hell ya talking 'bout?' she'd said through the fuzzy blur of alcohol.

It was only when they brought out the ladybird umbrella that she began to scream.

There was an investigation soon after. Details of Mrs Dickerson's drinking and recent desertion led to national news coverage and Jonathan was transferred into foster care. Your mother's favourite picture, eighties hair and pink lipstick, was splashed across tabloids with the headline 'MOTHER'S PARTY LIFESTYLE LED TO TRAGIC DEATH OF EIGHT-YEAR-OLD GIRL'. After it was all over – years of court cases, television debates and hate campaigns – your mother went into hiding. I found out from Sandy that she now lives in Spain under the name of 'Trixie'.

'She's thinking of opening a bar,' Sandy told me once.

She seemed baffled when my jaw tightened, hands ripping the crossword book on my lap. She stubbed out her cigarette on the wall outside my window before making a flimsy excuse to leave.

I've been angry for a long time, but more than this I've been confused. From the moment I woke up in the hospital and found you weren't beside me the confusion grew. Why did I survive when you didn't? You were the one with the potential (so illuminous, so charming). You were the one who had prize-winning racing slugs and possessed an ever-growing grasp of the Italian language. You saved worms from being trodden on, followed rules as if they were laws, and even shared your bounty of sweets when you won first prize on the behaviour chart at school. You didn't light up the room when you entered it, you made it erupt. You never grumbled or griped or allowed yourself a grain of self-pity. Your father was in prison, your mother an alcoholic who abandoned you and your brother alone in a flat without so much as a note of explanation. The uncle you idolized had not only left his best friend to die but had then left you to deal with your alcoholic mother all over again. You should have been angry, you should have been livid. But you were happy, always so happy, and because of that I was too.

You saved me that night when it was me who was supposed to

save you. I had failed in the one job that had given me meaning. The pain stabbing through my body was a punishment for that failure. The imprisonment in my room the penalty for my crimes against friendship.

Even at this I'm a failure. If it had been you that had survived that night and been left bedridden, you would have done nothing but blazed forward in a cartwheel of undiluted zeal. You would have battled through the illness, run marathons, set up charity events, taken extra GCSEs and excelled in all of them just to *spite* the damn thing. And even though you would have felt every inch of agony I felt, you wouldn't have let it show. You, Marianne Dickerson, would have grinned your gap-toothed grin and uttered those illustrious words to the world. *C'est la vie*, you would have said, *c'est la vie*.

You didn't deserve to die and nothing in the world will convince me otherwise. You should, to this very day, be climbing up trees and speaking so rapidly that your mouth needs to be taped up. You should be travelling the world, leading your trapeze-artist-veterinarian dream and spreading joy to every person that comes across your path. But you left, and not only that, you left *me*. Even as a child I knew that my life was rooted in yours. How am I meant to carry on when the roots have been pulled out?

ravine *n.* a deep, narrow, steep-sided valley
ravine *adj.* undistinguished, uninteresting, useless and meaningless

The Constellation of Goodbyes

I don't know how to stop writing to you. Even in death you're more of a friend to me than I am to myself. Without you I can't write a single line without striking it out. Words seem futile, self-centred, banal. But I need to write this down, I need to tell you.

Jonathan has gone.

When I get back to the flat I pace around my room, unsure of what to do. I listen for noises with a glass pressed against the wall but can't hear anything. It's then that I lift the mattress of my lifebed and pull out the small brick-print book I pushed underneath when I tried to get rid of memories of you. It's a squishy wedge of a book, worn and battered at the corners but the writing across it, painted with correction fluid, is still bright white.

Marianne + Ravine = Best Friends 4ever

It looks like chalk scrawled against a wall; a graffiti effect of our friendship. This is The Book of You.

A scuttling noise comes through the wall, followed by the clanging of objects. I hold the book close to my chest, not quite ready to open it up and see all the memories. As the noises get louder I think Jonathan's trying to show me he doesn't care about what I've said, but when I hear the slam of the front door and the silence that follows, I realize it hasn't been a tantrum, it's an invitation. Through the bang and clatter of his limited possessions Jonathan is telling me he's leaving. He's giving me the chance to make amends. When I go downstairs to check if this is true, I open the front door to find a stack of washed-up Tupperware at my feet.

I pace the hallway. After a good ten minutes I hear a coughing from below and realize my steps are infuriating the people beneath. An MP once said our flats were like 'rabbit warrens'. I remember seeing this on the news and wondering what everyone was looking so angry about. A rabbit warren seemed like a perfectly nice place to live (this was before I'd watched *Watership Down*). Now I can see the truth. We live so close to each other that you can hear a sneeze through three floors. We have our systems, our Westhill rules, and sometimes we even think ourselves free. But even though we soar high in our battle-blocks, we are cornered off from the rest of society like patients in a hospital ward for contagious diseases. The only people who want us are each other and sometimes we're not even wanted then.

As soon as I hear the cough I stop pacing. I look at the hallway table and see the answerphone flashing a red '0'. I don't know when Amma's coming back (for all I know she could be walking up the stairs this minute, a bagful of Blackpool rock clutched in hand), but I feel a strange tingling in my feet and know that I need to do something. I run up to my room, making sure to look away from Shiva as

I open the wardrobe, blocking out the sound of squawking birds on the walls and the frolicking of My Little Ponies on the curtains. I pull out the first outfit that comes to hand and get dressed.

When I leave the flat I have no time to panic. Dressed in a turquoise knee-length prom dress, I cover my elaborate clothing with one of Amma's old cardigans and rush down the stairs. I don't know where I think I'm going but I know that I have to find Jonathan. I have to say it, to tell him what I can't tell myself.

When I reach the bottom of the steps, I smell the mustiness of damp pavement. It's still raining and there are only a few people scurrying along the paths. They're too busy covering their own heads to take much notice of me, barely glancing up as they run. I stand at the entrance of Bosworth House and feel my muscles deaden. Instead of pain there's a numb, weighted feeling, as though my body is full of sand. I know it might happen, that the pain might return, but I also know that I can't let that hold me back. Not now.

So I step out in the rain, letting it soak me for the first time in years. A few weeks back, the hard beads would have sent a thousand pain signals along my body, the pound of each drop stinging against my skin like a bolt of electricity. But instead, the rain seems to wake up my deadened nerves as it trickles cold down my face, making my hair flat, dripping down my collar. As I reach the side of the hill my fluffy slippers are so waterlogged they nearly fall off my feet. I scan the paths and road around Westhill but still can't see him. The tall lanky body, the scruffy hair that would be matted like wet dog fur. The olive eyes. The tidy smile.

'Brad*leey*!'

I look up to see Mrs Patterson sticking her head out of the top-floor window of Bosworth House. Her hair is wrapped in a towel, shrewd eyes skimming the landscape in search of prey. At the same time two men are running to the entrance of our building, hands held together. They're both laughing as they find shelter, sneaking a kiss before the taller man glances around to see if there have been any witnesses. He locks eyes with mine and it's only when he shifts his shoulders back that I realize who he is.

'Bradley Patterson, get your backside up here *now*!' his mother screams.

Bradley looks up the side of the building then back at me, but I've already ducked behind a bush. He gives his boyfriend one last stroke along the arm before marching his way up the stairs. I don't know what surprises me more: that Bradley Patterson's gay or that Bradley Patterson has a black boyfriend.

Things change in the most unexpected ways.

As the shower grows heavier I try to decide whether I should make my way back home. I glance at the squares of shiny glass towering up into the sky, before looking over at the pebble-dashed walls of the building ahead. I know where I need to go. I run along the criss-crossing paths to Tewkesbury House, repeating the name *Reginald* in my head. Not because I've forgotten it, but because I've called him Mr Eccentric for so long I'm afraid I'll say it by mistake.

He leads me through the hallway in unsteady steps, taking me to his gallery of clocks. I'm soaked, Amma's cardigan weighing heavy on my shoulders. Before I sit down, Reginald holds a hand up, placing a tea towel across the crushed-velvet seat. He hobbles over to his oak desk and sits down on the other side, interlocking his fingers as though conducting an interview. If it wasn't for the bathrobe tied loosely around his skeletal body I could almost take him seriously.

As I look at him sitting opposite me, I realize how ill Reginald is. Blue-tinged bags hang beneath his drooping eyes, his hair feathery and white as opposed to the dusty grey it was when we were kids. A yellow tone sits upon his skin. The more I look, the yellower he seems to become.

Clocks tick as I wrap the sodden folds of my cardigan around my body.

'Have you seen Jonathan?'

The question seems to stun the old man. His eyes blink behind the lenses of his glasses. He pushes them to the bridge of his nose before readjusting his expression.

'Should I have?'

His voice is exactly as I remember, each word long and drawn out.

'He came to see you,' I say, louder than necessary. 'He's been squatting in the flat next door to mine.'

He seems surprised, eyebrows rising above his thick frames. He presses the tips of his fingers together and narrows his eyes.

'Are you his *girlfriend*?'

He says this with such disdain, as though asking if I'm his drug dealer. I shake my head quickly. 'God, no!'

His shoulders drop with relief, though his eyes remain narrow. The sound of the rain against the window competes with the ticking of clocks. I brace my body against the cacophony.

'I'm Ravine Roy,' I say. 'I used to live next to Jonathan and Mari– Marianne.'

Your name trips from my lips like an unsteady song but he doesn't twitch. Instead, he leans back in his seat with a nod. On his bathrobe collar, flakes of dried-up cereal are embedded in the fabric.

'I haven't seen him,' he says.

I sigh.

'Don't be disappointed,' he says. 'There's no point.'

There's no comfort in his voice and when I look up at Reginald

Blake I see something close to satisfaction in his expression. He folds his hands over his stomach.

'You can't trust anyone, you know?' he says. 'They make deals, promise you things, but they never follow through. No morals, that's the problem with the youth of today.'

He begins to tut as he gazes out of the window. I shuffle forward on my seat.

'Jonathan said Walter sent you letters,' I say.

He snaps his eyes open, lips squeezed tight. 'I threw them away. I want nothing to do with the man.'

He gazes back out of the window.

'Why didn't you give them to the police? Tell them where he was?'

He lets out a snort. 'The police couldn't catch a cold if you sneezed on them. Besides, that man is doing his time. Every day he has to live with the death of my son. Every day he has to listen out for the knock on the door, petrified that they've finally got him. They say it was a suicide, but I know the truth.'

He nods at me knowingly.

I clench my fists. Uncle Walter was many things but he was not a murderer.

Reginald leans back in his seat as though this is the end of the matter. In the reflection of his glasses I see the second hand of the grand-father clock moving in stilted steps. We once thought that he had the ability to turn people into clocks but it's him who's a machine. Alone in this flat. The days ticking by with nothing but his misery to keep him company. I don't feel sorry for him. It's hard to feel pity for some-one when you're so alike.

'I should go,' I say.

He takes hold of his walking stick and follows me out to the hall. When I open the front door, I stop and turn back.

'I told Jonathan it was his fault, what happened to Marianne.'

The old man releases a sardonic laugh, his jaundiced face taking on a new colour. The laugh takes me by surprise. It rattles in his dry throat and echoes down the hall.

'From what I hear, it was.'

I shake my head, thinking he's misunderstood. 'It was an accident.'

Reginald leans the weight of his body onto his walking stick. His face seems heavy, every muscle pulled down like dripping paint on a wall.

'That doesn't mean it wasn't his fault.'

I look at him bent over like that and remember the way he used to take steps two at a time and scream at us to 'get gone!' when he caught us in Bobby's Hideout. All the energy has seeped out of him. It's as though he's been drained of life.

'You know my advice?' he says as I hover at the door. 'Don't trust anyone.'

I look at him and blink.

'I don't,' I say.

He seems disappointed by this response, as though he's set up a trap and I've skipped right over it. He stands up again, pointing his finger at me.

'Don't love anyone either.'

My expression falters and suddenly he's smiling, a row of black stained teeth on show. But the grin is only short-lived. He looks up at me through thick lenses.

'Close the door behind you.'

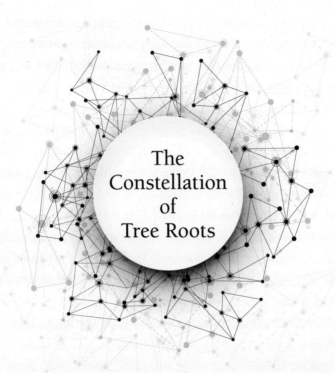

The Constellation of Tree Roots

When I step out of Tewkesbury House my foot sinks into a puddle. The rain has stopped, leaving the pavement as shiny as fish scales, the grass as soggy as seaweed washed up on a beach. My clothes drip as I shake my foot and make my way back to Bosworth House. By the time I get home, my mind is full of us. Us skipping along the same paths, us finishing off each other's sentences as we spoke to passers-by, us playing games along the very same steps I'm walking up. When I shut the front door the memories keep coming. Our games in the woods, running from Mr Eccentric, being grabbed by Uncle Walter as he growled like a bear. Italian lessons. Slug races. Marbles and mini dictionaries. As I stand in the hallway, trying to forget all the memories, I see a flashing '1' on the answerphone. I push wet strands of hair behind my ears. When I press 'play' a short beep comes out of the machine, followed by the familiar rhythm of Amma's voice.

'Ravine, come pick up the phone. I know you can pick up the phone! Look, we have missed our train. We will have to get the next one. I know what you think. You think I did this on purpose. Not true! I didn't mean to leave you this long. I will see you soon, shona . . . There is dahl in the fridge.'

I play the message over and over. I wrap Amma's damp cardigan tight around my body, smell the old scent of rose perfume upon the fabric. I consider going back upstairs. I glance at the banister next to me, think of my friend Shiva on the dresser, the crossword books, my lifebed with a Ravine-shaped groove in the mattress. But the steps seem too steep, the climb too far. That room is something different to me now, a prison cell I've only just been released from. The objects within it aren't my friends, they're just objects. I look along the hall-way and find my feet moving towards the living-room door.

I haven't sat in the living room since the day I received my GCSE results. The living room was my mother and father's room. It held their secrets and I didn't want to know their secrets. I didn't want to know any of it.

I've never considered that Amma might have changed the décor. So when I enter the room to find pale green painted over bird-print wall-paper I release a dramatic gasp. You'd think Amma could have done the same for my room. Wiping out that menagerie of flapping birds and beady eyes with a few tins of paint.

I glance around, trying to grasp the familiar. The floral netting and clashing curtains, the cross-hatched sketches of Bangladeshi paddy fields with the price labels still stuck on the corners. The coffee table that's far too fancy for us. On top of the table is the same metal fruit bowl that has always been there, with the same plastic fruit it was sold with.

In an attempt to marry up the elegance of the coffee table with the tacki-ness of the bowl, Amma has placed paper doilies along the edges of it.

I sit down on the sofa and as I do so, feel something hard against my foot. A handle is protruding from beneath the table. When I tug at it, I find it's attached to an old leather suitcase. The buckle's broken on one side and when I lift it out I can feel it's empty. Placing the case on my knees, I consider a plan.

Life is suffering. Life is struggle. But, more than this, life is *choice*.

I look down at the doilies, put the suitcase to one side and pull out a pen from the coffee-table drawer. I begin writing across the clean sheets, using four of them before getting to the final draft. The first one was too detailed, the second had no conceivable end and the third was so messy I could barely read the words myself. For my final attempt I keep the message brief, writing in my best handwriting.

Dear Amma,
   I'm better now and have decided to go away. I hope you and ~~your companion~~ my father have a happy life in Bangladesh. Please don't worry about me.
   Ravine xx

When I get to the bottom of Bosworth House, I do up the buttons on the raincoat Amma bought me last year. It's a clear plastic thing and the turquoise ruffles of my dress are visible through it. As I begin to walk down the steps of the hill, I look like I've been caught in an earthquake during a debutante ball.

It doesn't matter what I look like, I decide, not where I'm going. But then I realize I don't know where I'm going. I thought that writing the note, packing the suitcase and leaving the flat was all I needed to begin a new life. But I have decisions to make. Where? How? *What?* I've never

left Leicester before, have barely left Westhill Estate. I have no qualifica-
tions save two paltry GCSEs and there's only so far £480 will get me.

It begins to rain again. I put my hood up. Back at the flat I exchanged
soaked slippers for a pair of dusty but unused lace-up boots sitting at
the back of the wardrobe. Even though they're so tight they squish my
bones, they're sturdy and warm. Walking boots, I think, imagining
myself marching over hills of heather, along jagged cliff faces and up
rocky mountains like the ones in Bobby's postcards. But as the flesh
on my legs turns to goose-pimples I look down at my outfit. Boots and
a party dress. I'm wearing an almost identical outfit to the one I wore
the night of the fireworks. Nothing has changed. I'm as prepared for
the world as I was back then.

As I get to the bottom of the steps I take one last look at the
white-bricked walls of Bosworth House. I think I see a pair of legs
sticking out of the railings on the top floor, but the image is only an
illusion. I imagine the three of us sitting on the balcony, my brown
legs, your tan legs and Jonathan's pale legs all dangling in a row. I felt
a hardness in my throat as my eyes began to tear up.

We were born with no choice, raised in the middle of other people's
tragedies and swept along in the riptide of life. It's this that makes me
cry; this sadness, this inevitability. We were too young to know how
to free ourselves and too weak to fight back. Our lives were a series of
crossword clues and none of us knew the answers.

I turn around, ready to walk down to the bottom of the hill and
away from this place. Away from the past. Away from my life.

Then I see the taxi.

As soon as I see it, I know Amma is inside. I run back to the
entrance of Bosworth House and hide behind the main doors. I crane
my neck to look through the gap, searching for dyed black hair tied into
a bun, the flash of polished white trainers. The taxi pulls up. Seeing

it reminds me of the day we watched Uncle Walter stepping out of a taxi but this time, when the door opens, the pot belly of an Asian man with a suitcase in his hand emerges. My father puts out his hand and I see Amma reaching out to take it as she bows her head and steps out.

I run up the steps, my boots pounding against the concrete. I'm going in the exact opposite direction I need to go but I can't let Amma see me. As I glance over the staircase balcony I see her and my father climbing up the steps to the entrance. I carry on running, my chest heaving with the effort. When I reach the flat my hands are shaking so badly that I drop my keys on the floor. It's as I'm squatting down that I see the postcard sticking out from beneath the WELCOME mat at the front of your door. I stare at the corner where a swirl of purples and greens makes up one part of an image.

'Of course there is reason to worry!' Amma cries. 'It has been *two days*.'

I pick up the keys and open the door, running up the stairs and into my bedroom. I whip off my coat, pull off my boots, shove my suitcase under the bed then jump straight in with the party dress still on.

Then I remember the doily.

I leap out of bed, scramble down the stairs, grab the thin paper sheet and run back up on the balls of my feet. A key turns in the lock. I hold on to the doorframe of my room, swinging my body in, pushing the door shut, then grabbing the handle so it won't slam. I stand still, body bent low as I continue to hold on. The loudness of Amma's voice sails up the stairs.

'Fool!' she cries. 'You understand nothing!'

I climb back into the bed, pushing the doily under my pillow. As I hear the thud of Amma's feet coming up the stairs, I lie flat on the mattress, smoothing the sheets across my body and pushing the wet ends of hair behind my shoulders.

The bedroom door opens. Amma steps through. I look down at the side of my bed and see the corner of my suitcase sticking out.

'Shona, did I wake you?' Amma says.

I look up at her with blinking eyes.

'No, no,' I say, trying to calm the panting of my breath. 'How was your trip?'

She's visibly surprised at this upbeat reaction and, for a moment, doesn't know how to respond.

'It was so-so,' she says, flicking her hand in the air as though shooing off the matter. 'Have you eaten?'

I nod, even though it isn't true. Amma steps forward, pointing her finger at me.

'I shall never leave you again,' she says. 'I told your father this. He says you are grown up but you are not, Ravine. You are my baby.'

I frown when she says this but Amma just sits on the bed, feeling my forehead with the back of her hand. 'You're hot.'

I pull my frown into a wide smile, hoping that the less I say the less I'll incriminate myself. She nods her head.

'You are still unwell.'

I blink and begin to open my mouth but Amma quickly seals my lips by pushing her forefinger over them.

'No, no, Ravine. You say nothing. You are not ready and I cannot *make* you ready. I told your father this too. He has all these plans. Telling me we can fly away together like one big happy family and make everything better. He was always too ambitious, you know? Him and his Roobix Blocks, him and his Bangladesh. He thought he had found someone to cure you. I almost believed it, all this nonsense about *healers*. I was ready to fly us over there. Such a fool I am!'

She tuts loudly at herself, finger still pressed over my lips.

'But I realized it yesterday. I told him you are not ready for all these plans. When you are ready you will tell me. I know this now. So you don't have to say anything. Not a word.'

I try to compute everything she's told me. The tickets, the plans; they'd all been for me.

'You go to sleep now,' she says, patting my cheek. 'You need your rest.'

She's up and gone before I can protest, leaving the door open behind her.

I listen to Amma's steps as they fade away and bring myself up to a sitting position. I look around the room. It's dead to me: the wallpaper birds no longer flapping their wings, Shiva standing perfectly neutral on the dresser.

A part of me knows that I've got away with it and everything can stay the same. Amma will stop forcing me to leave the flat. The ghost in the room next door has left. But still all I can think about is the corner of the postcard I saw beneath the WELCOME mat. All I can think about is Jonathan.

I swing my feet over the side of the bed. Light filters through the dark clouds outside, making the leaves of the horse-chestnut tree glow. I've been stuck in this room like that tree is stuck in this estate. Even if it were chopped down to a stump, the roots that bind it to the ground would remain, lacing down in an underground network, keeping it fixed where it is. The tree is the same as Mrs Dickerson, always pulled back by her roots. It's the same as Uncle Walter, trapped by his memories of what happened here. It's Amma, Mr Eccentric, old Mrs Simmons, Sandy Burke, Mrs Patterson, Bradley Patterson, and all the people with their feet stuck in the concrete.

When I walk over to the window, the light dances across my face. I place my hand on the glass and feel the coolness of it on my palm.

Condensation begins to circle my hand as it lies against the glass. I curl my fingers into a fist.

'I am not a tree,' I say.

I look down the long trunk of the horse chestnut to the ground beneath. Children cycling by, people walking their dogs and carrying their shopping. I hit the window so it shakes in the frame.

'I am not a tree!'

I grit my teeth and collect my boots.

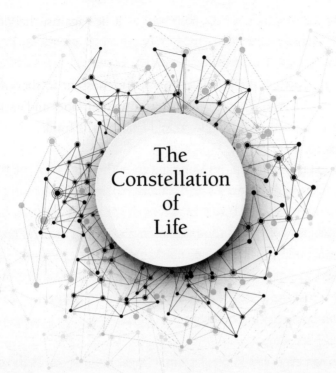

The Constellation of Life

I stand across the road from the woods. In one hand I hold my suitcase, in the other the postcard. On the front of the postcard is the thin silhouette of mountains with streaks of colour sailing across a starry sky. On the back of the postcard is a message.

MEET ME AT THE HIDEOUT.
J

It's been hours since I heard Jonathan leave the flat, so the likelihood of him still waiting for me is slim. But there's a part of me that needs to go back to the woods whether Jonathan is there or not. Bobby's Hideout is where everything ended. Not only your life, but the life I'd taken for granted.

The path to the hideout is a thin trail of stones we laid to signpost the way. They're covered in moss now, strange plants curling up around the edges. The trees seem smaller; I have to turn sideways to stop myself from getting tangled in the branches. The smell of damp wood, the colour of lime-green leaves, the mud beneath my boots make me feel a rush of nostalgia. When I arrive at the hideout my face is actually smiling.

The smile is short-lived. As I step out from the trees I see the rubble where Bobby's Hideout once stood. Breeze blocks are broken in pieces while faded remnants of boxes lie across the ground. The front half of the hideout has collapsed, the back corner standing like the remains of a historic building. Black singe marks pepper the grey stone, yellow tape is tied to posts around the wreckage with 'DO NOT ENTER' stamped across the plastic. I look at the rubble, half expecting to see a wellington boot sticking out from the debris.

Instead I see slugs.

They cover every brick. Big, fat slimy slugs crawling across the damp stone, glistening wet with rain. They've formed a colony upon the debris; black slugs, orange slugs, small and giant together in union. So magnificent is this gathering that it feels like they've come in pilgrimage for you. It's as though they know you were one of them and, in the fashion of Reginald Blake, want to pay homage to your memory.

I watch the slugs wiggling in the rain. Their bodies cover the grey brick like buttons sewn randomly over a cardigan. I think of you. I think of Stanley. I think of all the things we thought we knew.

'Hello, Ravine.'

The voice is deep and cold. When I look back I see a figure sitting on a log, head hung low with a bin liner by his feet. When he looks up, his eyes are as green as olives, a ladybird umbrella held over his head.

The
Constellation
of
Us

When I was younger, I couldn't decide what to be. A Hindu, a Muslim, a Christian or a dentist, the choices were too many. You always seemed to know what you were. You always seemed to know how to be. Maybe that's what made you brave.

I want to run away from him. I want to run away from your brother and back to my room, to my stack of crosswords and Stevie Wonder CDs.

7 across: To be frightened or in fear (6)

Scared.

There, I admit it. I'm scared of the world and that's why I've been hiding from it for so long. This fear is the same fear I felt about the universe as a child; overwhelmed by its enormity and our minuteness within it. Remember that time, in the middle of the night, you dragged

285

me and Jonathan to the top floor of Bosworth House and made us look up at the sky. It was so vast, filled with an abundance of dazzling gems that covered us like a diamond-encrusted sari. Just looking at that sky made us wheezy yet still we continued naming the stars.

'The Constellation of Cartwheels . . .' you said.

'The Constellation of Thunderstorms . . .'

'The Constellation of Mini Dictionaries . . .'

After we brought our eyes back down to the estate I remember feeling giddy from glimpsing something so magnificent. Something so immensely wider than our imaginations could comprehend. Something we were part of, without even meaning to be. We were the universe, Marianne. We were everything.

I want to feel that feeling again. I want to be part of it all. And that's why I don't run.

I want to be brave, just like you had been.

The rain continues to fall at a slant. My mouth splutters droplets as I speak.

'I didn't think you'd still be here.'

Jonathan shrugs, the bug eyes of the ladybird umbrella bouncing up with the movement of his shoulders.

'Sorry to disappoint you.'

He drops his gaze in his old sulky manner. It looks ridiculous, a man as big as him being so petulant. But I don't get annoyed because I can see the act for what it is now. A shield to protect him from pain, a cloak to cover up his wounds.

Jonathan kicks the dirt on the floor. 'I'll go if you want.'

I sit down next to him on the log, placing the suitcase beside me. He shifts the umbrella towards me, still not looking at me but creating enough of a shelter for me to put down my hood. I pat my hair flat.

'I don't want you to go.'

He glances over at me before kicking the ground again. I'm glad to see him, even in this grumpy state, and know that I've been handed my last chance. I pull the suitcase to my knees and open the one working buckle.

I haven't filled the case with many items. A few pieces of clothing, the statue of Shiva and a tub full of lentils. I've left behind any pills I might need in case of a relapse, have even forgotten to bring a fork, but I made sure to pack one more thing. I pull out the book carefully, as though it's an old relic, brushing spots of rain from the cover. I thought the water might smudge the correction fluid written across the brick print, but it stays thick and solid.

Marianne + Ravine = Best Friends 4ever

Jonathan looks over at me with raised brows, letting me take the umbrella from him so I can pass him The Book of You. He doesn't say anything but accepts the book with the uncertainty of someone taking a gift that could well be a bomb. He opens the cover to the first page with the words '*Marianne Dickerson*' written across the white sheet. When he turns the page I lean in close to have a look myself. Ten years and I haven't opened that cover and even now I need someone else to do it for me.

We stuck parts of you in the book. The wrappers of your favourite sweets: lemon sherbets, Black Jacks and toffee creams. There was the winning raffle ticket for the incomplete chessboard you'd won and a curly lock of your hair stuck on with tape. I watch as Jonathan runs his finger over the strands and remember how you chopped several pieces from your mane until we found a lock representative enough of all its colours. Afterwards, you had to wear your hair up in a ponytail for a month, just so Mrs Dickerson wouldn't notice the hack job you'd made.

On the next page of the book is a school photograph of you and Jonathan. You sat with shoulders angled to the camera in your matching school uniforms, the only day you ever wore them. You were smiling your rugby-ball smile with your cheeks glowing bright, while Jonathan's bottom lip stuck out in a scowl. I remember the day you had that picture taken because the photographer, no matter how she joked, couldn't make him smile.

Jonathan brings the picture close to his face.

'I look bloody awful.'

I frown. 'You always looked like that.'

He sits up straight as if offended and I try not to smirk. We both look down at the photograph again, the tan of your skin, the hazel of your eyes. Although neither of us says it, we're both thinking the same thing. You were beautiful, Marianne. Not in a Hollywood-actress type way, not like a model stuck up on a billboard, pert bum on view. You shone a beauty as warm as the sun; everything around you glowed.

When Jonathan turns to the next page he begins prodding it with his finger.

'What was this for?' he asks.

I look at the object, a lanyard made out of red shoelaces attached to a gold chocolate-coin wrapper. It took me a whole afternoon and seven attempts to make that medal. When you saw it, you suggested I make a silver one for Jonathan as well as a miniature one for Stanley. I almost threw the thing at your head.

'The slug races,' I say. 'She kept winning them and we kept losing our marbles. In the end it seemed easier to just make a medal.'

For the first time since I've sat down, the wrinkles on Jonathan's forehead lifted.

'Jesus!' he says. 'I remember that. We had a ceremony for it in the woods.'

It takes a moment for me to remember. It was autumn and we'd found a tree stump circled by red and yellow leaves. We'd lifted you up on it and passed you the jar that housed Stanley. To compensate for no silver, Jonathan elected himself Prime Minister of the Woods and draped the medal over your head before firmly shaking your hand. I handed you a bouquet of dandelions and daisies, and then you kissed the jar and lifted the slug's fat body high above your head. I remember how Jonathan looked over at me and rolled his eyes and I, in a brief moment of solidarity, had rolled mine too. We both clapped politely afterwards.

My mouth widens into a grin. Jonathan looks at me, lifting his brows in a 'well I never' expression. I look down at the medal and see the holes I punctured into the disc in an attempt to make a slug-shaped outline. My grin slips away.

'I killed Stanley,' I say.

Jonathan frowns as the gravity of my confession hits him. 'Who?'

I fidget on my seat. 'Marianne's slug.'

Again he frowns. 'The *slug*?' he asks. 'How?'

I push my knees together, curl my shoulders over the body of my suitcase. 'Salt.'

The light glows red on his face as it shines through the umbrella. His eyes widen. '*Salt?*'

He gawps at me as though he's looking at a new person. No, worse, he gawps at me as though he's *impressed*. I fiddle with the buckle on my suitcase.

'I've never told anyone that.'

There's a silence as I continue to fiddle. I feel his body relax, his arm brushing against mine.

'It's not raining any more,' he says.

When I look up, Jonathan nods out to the woods and I realize he's right. The slugs are still squirming over the rubble but the puddles

289

surrounding them are still. I put down the umbrella as Jonathan continues to turn the pages of The Book of You. He passes the survival tips you scrawled in felt tip, the Italian phrases you wrote. I try not to look, too distracted by the next confession I'm about to make. From all my years confined in a bed I've learnt one thing. It's the things you never do that haunt you the most.

'*Ravine Roy*,' Jonathan says, but it isn't until I look at him that I realize he isn't calling my name but reading it.

I look down at the book and see my name written in your uneven script. I'd forgotten about this, how the book had not only kept the fragments of your life but mine as well. On the next page are the wrappers of my favourite sweets – Cherry Drops, Fruit Salads and Space Dust – with a lock of my straight black hair taped in the corner. There is a page with a list of my favourite words (*hybrid, philistine, shenanigans, hussy*) as well as their dictionary definition. Next to them is the newspaper cutting with a picture of me holding a marrow.

'You can give me that back now,' I say, reaching out.

Jonathan yanks the book away. He begins reading the article in a loud, newsreader voice.

'*Above picture: Ravine Roy with proud mother, Rekha Roy, holding the winning vegetable for Westhill Primary School.*'

He starts chuckling as he looks at the picture of my disgruntled face. You insisted on putting that article in our book and I remember protesting, knowing full well that it would come back to haunt me one day. This is the day and as Jonathan continues to chuckle at my humiliation I realize it's time.

'It wasn't your fault, Jonathan,' I say.

When he looks at me his grin falters. I can see him opening his mouth, ready to make a wisecrack about the article as a distraction. But I have to say it. I have to say it all.

'If I hadn't been so scared, if I hadn't gone in there, it wouldn't have happened. I was supposed to protect her. If it was anyone's fault, it was mine.'

It's a relief to see the shock on his face. He pushes his finger into his chest. '*I'm* the one who took you there.'

'It's not like you could have stopped her following you, Jonathan,' I say. 'She wouldn't have left you, and I wouldn't have left her.'

'But—'

I lift my hand. 'You were just a kid.'

He looks at me and shakes his head. 'So were you.'

I blink, my throat swallowing hard.

'So whose fault was it?' he asks.

I think carefully about his question. I see the image of Mrs Dickerson unconscious on your sofa, Uncle Walter disappearing down the side of the hill, Amma standing with the Soul-drinker by the taxi that night.

'Everyone we knew,' I say.

We both sit on the damp wood with the cloud of this statement hanging between us. I let my hand drop to my calf, feeling the waxy scars embedded on the skin.

'But that's true of the good stuff,' I say, 'as well as the bad.'

I lift my hand and push the hair off my face, feeling no aches, no stings, no jolts of agony. Without meaning to, I smile.

Jonathan drops his head with something close to a nod. He closes the book on his lap and, as he does so, the corner of a photograph sticks out from the back. We both look at each other before I pull it out, feeling my cheeks flush as I see the image. It's the three of us: you, me and Jonathan. We're on the steps that lead to Bosworth House, me standing with mini dictionary clasped to my chest, Jonathan with his hands shaped into claws as he growls at the camera and you in the middle, arms wrapped around our shoulders with your head tilted, eyes closed and grinning. I feel myself squirm on the log. There's something so familiar about that photograph. It's just like the shot of Mrs Dickerson, Bobby and Uncle Walter.

I push the photo into the back of the book. We both sit, trying not to look at each other.

'Are you still going to find Uncle Walter?' I ask.

From the corner of my eye, I can see him shaking his head.

'I wouldn't know where to start.'

I bite my lip. 'I could help you.'

He laughs then looks at me, expression dropping. I shrug and look down at my boots.

'Or whatever.'

When I look back up, Jonathan is looking ahead at the slugs squirming over the debris. I follow his gaze before turning my face to the sky, remembering how it had exploded with fireworks that night and how your brother carried me so tightly, placed me down on the floor and propped my leg up on a rock. He saved my life and I know I should thank him but already it feels that enough has passed between us. We're frail creatures; to say any more might break us.

I look down at the suitcase on my knees and think of Amma coming up to my room to check on me. She'll see that I've gone, find the message I've written and stuck under my pillow and screech loudly as though she's found a corpse. She'll dial 999 only to be told that an eighteen-year-old girl deciding to leave home is not considered to be a missing person. She'll search my room for any evidence of where I might have gone before collapsing upon my bed. She'll weep so many tears that the covers will become soaked, thinking about how she hadn't seen what I was about to do, how she hadn't stopped it from happening.

She'll blame herself. I can't let her do that.

I fasten the one working buckle on my suitcase and hold on tightly to the handle.

'I've got to go back,' I say, standing up.

Jonathan opens his mouth to protest but I'm already running over to the stone trail leading back to the road.

'Ravine!' he cries.

My feet jam in the mud as I stop and look back. He's standing, with his hands dropped to his side, your umbrella leaning up against the log beside him.

'Yes?' I say.

He takes a deep breath. 'I'm glad you're better.'

I smile. 'Thanks.'

I turn and run.

'Ravine!'

I turn around again. His body is a blur between the tree trunks and I have to run back to see him.

'*Yes?*'

He looks at me and blinks. Then he holds up The Book of You. No. The Book of Us.

'Your book!' he cries.

I look at the brick-print cover and almost step forward to claim it. Then I look at your brother, remembering what the professor taught me about the amazing coincidence of a solar eclipse. For a brief period in our childhood the three bodies of Marianne, Jonathan and Ravine aligned and, like the fine glow cast over the river Ganges, our friendship became a sight of wonder.

The things that happened to us were the things that made us. You helped me become who I am, Marianne. Life is not struggle. Life is not suffering. Life is being.

'Bring it to me,' I say, stepping backwards. 'Tomorrow?'

Jonathan holds the book up for a few seconds. He lowers his arm.

'See you then, Dictionary Queen,' he says.

I smile.

'See you then, Weatherboy.'

Acknowledgements

This book is dedicated to everyone who made me, and to be more specific . . .

Family Shah and family Snaith: I will be eternally grateful for the lessons you've taught me. You guide me in ways you'll never know. Particular thanks to Judith, Ian and Katie Snaith, whose generous baby watching helped me complete the edits of this novel.

Tasha-Marie-Branston-Pickled-Onion-Flavoured-Crisp, my fellow fraggle and Best Friend Forever. This novel is a celebration of our childhood.

All the Knitter Knatter girls. We may not knit much but we sure can knatter. Thanks for all the gruesome stories that could fill a book by themselves and, of course, for your friendship.

Leicester Writers' Club (and in particular Kate Ruse and Margaret Penfold), through which I have been given brilliant advice and support over the years, including: 'The beginning only began for me when . . .,' and 'There's just one little nit-pick . . .' Your voices are now my inner critic.

Dave Martin, Maxine Linnel, Judith Snaith, Leonie Ross, Laura Wilkinson, Jeanette Bird-Bradley and Kerry Young, who read the manuscript in its entirety and whose advice made me cringe at my blunders but also made me a far better writer. Also Kadija George and

Dorothea Smartt at Inscribe who have been a bedrock of support over the past few years, and Nikesh Shukla who has been a brilliant champion of my work as well as being a generally cool dude. The people at SI Leeds Prize, Bristol Short Story Prize and Mslexia, whose support for my writing spurred me on through the bleak times. And, of course, Farhana Shaikh, editor of *The Asian Writer* and a truly valued friend.

My agent James Wills, editor Lizzy Goudsmit, publicist Becky Hunter and all the great people at Transworld. Your belief in this novel has turned childhood dreams into reality.

All the many books on my shelves. You have been my writing courses, my mentors and my guiding lights in the wilderness. Without you I could never have dreamt of a life so rich. A special nod to the songs of Tori Amos, which have become the soundtrack of my life as well as of this novel.

And John, always John, who has helped me become the best person I can be. Thanks for all the washing up, visits to the shops and general level-headed advice. You're awesome.

Mahsuda Snaith is the winner of the SI Leeds Literary Prize 2014 and Bristol Short Story Prize 2014, and a finalist in the Mslexia Novel Writing Competition 2013. She lives in Leicester where she leads writing workshops and teaches part-time in primary schools. Mahsuda is a fan of reading (obviously) and crochet (not so obviously). This is her first novel.